Cold Boy's Wood

CAROL BIRCH is the award-winning writer of
twelve novels, including *Jamrach's Menagerie*,
which was shortlisted for the Man Booker
Prize in 2011. Her first novel, *Life in the
Palace*, won the David Higham Award for
Fiction (Best First Novel of the Year), and her
second novel, *The Fog Line*, won the Geoffrey
Faber Memorial Prize. Born in Manchester,
she now lives in Lancaster.

Cold Boy's Wood

CAROL BIRCH

HEAD
of ZEUS

First published in the UK in 2021 by Head of Zeus Ltd

9 7 5 3 1 2 4 6 8

A catalogue record for this book is available from
the British Library.

ISBN (HB): 9781838939410
ISBN (XTPB): 9781838939427
ISBN (E): 9781838939403

Typeset by Divaddict Publishing Solutions Ltd

Printed and bound in Great Britain by
CPI Group (UK) Ltd, Croydon CR0 4YY

Head of Zeus Ltd
5–8 Hardwick Street
London EC1R 4RG
WWW.HEADOFZEUS.COM

Cold
Boy's
Wood

1

We'd been driving across England, west to east, somewhere in the middle, hours it seemed in our old red and white Ford Anglia. Everything had gone on for so long and so boringly that it felt as if we'd been driving for a million miles, and I'd fallen asleep and woken up feeling sick over and over again in the back seat. I was fourteen with greasy hair and slouchy shoulders. It was a lip-chewing, knicker-wetting time of crying secretly in closed rooms, and it seemed, like the journey, to have been going on forever. There were vans along the sides of the road selling stewed tea and oily hotdogs and hamburgers.

I woke: hedges, fields and such, the car tootling along, my dad saying, 'This is no good, we'll have to stop somewhere.'

I can't remember what it was for. Maybe they needed a chemist. It doesn't matter. 'Over there,' my mum said.

There was a spire a long way off, across fields. Woods running over hills. A turning and a signpost. Andwiston 2, Copcollar 4, Beggar's Ercol 9.

The lane was long and twisty. There were cornfields with rolls of corn in neat symmetry. The windows were wound down for air, but the car still smelt strongly of petrol and heat, and more faintly of cleaned-up sick from me and my brother. And in spite of the heat there was rain on the heavy air and the clouds were bruising, and in the village there was a haywain in an open shed and all the shops were closed. Not a soul was in sight.

It was a strung-up Adlestrop kind of a moment. Andwiston.

It was not like seeing it for the first time. Thunder murmured far away. My brother Tommy said he wanted a wee.

'There in that grid over there,' said my mum. 'Go with him, Lor.'

'So where is everyone?' shouted my dad, at us, as if everything was all our fault.

'Maybe it's early closing,' said my mum in a tight strained voice.

'He can't wee in a grid,' I said. 'What if someone comes?'

'He's only five!' My mother pulled off her glasses and started polishing them furiously.

'Let him go in the woods,' I said.

'*What* woods?'

'What woods? The woods all around.'

'I know what you mean, Lorna,' my mum said. 'But in case you haven't noticed, we're not *in* the woods, are we, we're in the village.'

'So drive out a bit. There's nothing here.'

'Bloody ridiculous,' my dad rumbled, 'village of the dead.'

My mother started putting her glasses back on, but just at that moment my father yanked his jumper up over his sweating face and tossed it into the back. His hand knocked her glasses.

She went 'Uh!' and grabbed at them as they fell. The jumper, warm nylon, sweat-smelling, landed on my knee and I flicked it away as if it was a snake. It started to rain. My mother caught the glasses and put them back on her face. Through the open window I saw across the rough triangle of the village green a small row of shops: a butcher's, a co-op, a ladies' hairdressers with a window full of faded blue-tinged images of smiling girls with meticulously regimented flick-ups and ruler-straight fringes. The rain sloped across it all, bright and clean and steely. I felt funny. Why don't people like rain, I thought. And the feeling grew that I'd seen it all before.

'You've just knocked my glasses off, Ray,' my mum said in a martyred voice.

He ignored her, turning his beet-red face to the back seat. 'Well, are you getting out or what?'

I felt as if I'd been much older a long time ago, not just old but ancient, and we'd just dropped out of somewhere else into here.

'I *said*, are you—'

'No,' I said. 'Go to the woods, I'll take him there. We can keep dry under the trees.'

So we did. Just outside Andwiston I took my little brother Tommy for a wee in the woods. If I looked one way I could see our car through the leaves, if I looked the other I saw the back of Tommy's head, his fragile neck and jug ears, and I could hear him singing to himself, '*a pig is an animal with dirt on its face,*' and all around us was the whisper of rain on leaves and the smell of wet forest. I sent him back to the car when he'd finished.

'*I'm* going to have one now,' I said, 'won't be a min,' and sent him scooting off while I went in deeper, further and further from the track. I stood still in a tiny space among dark green holly and ivy. The trees stretched far away above my head, and I was almost completely shielded by wet leaves. If I could write music, it deserves music, it deserves music, I thought, something sharp and ripe and rich. But I couldn't write music so I just stood there getting softly wet from the filtered rain, and thinking, if only I could not go back.

Then things tilted again, and I went back to the car.

That was my first time in these woods. A strange thing happened as we drove away. A sudden wind whipped itself up and the rain got heavier. I was rolling up the window and for – oh I don't know – maybe three seconds, I saw a boy in one of those big fields that come after the woods. Two fields over. Naked in the pouring rain, thin and white, arms round himself. His face looked towards me but he was too far away to make out any features. The hedge hid him, and then I saw him again for maybe another second or two, from a different angle. There he was, just standing still for no reason in the middle of a field in the middle of the day.

'Stop the car!' I said.

'What's the matter?'

'I can't stop here,' said my dad.

'Stop the car!'

'Why?'

I was opening the door.

My father shouted, 'You bloody fool!'

The car stopped and I jumped out and ran back.

He was still there.

Don't misunderstand. I haven't got a clue about anything but I'm not a fool. I'm not talking about fakes and frauds, videos on YouTube, screamers, all that. I'm talking about things that happen in a breath in the middle of an ordinary day. I know the explanations. A hallucination is something physical in your ridiculous clown of a brain, not uncommon, all quite normal, but when it comes, the creature is as real as anything ever was. Not the same real, a different real. Still, it can touch you and stop your breath and look you in the eye, shake your mind out of your head. A hallucination can sometimes swing upon the air as it comes into focus, a shimmering appearance. And sometimes, like the cold boy, it's solid, sharp as a fox or a hare. Until it isn't.

Gone while you blinked.

Which is what happened.

My father was furious. My heart beat twice as fast all the way to Hothemby by the Long Wights where they'd booked a holiday cottage. I never said another word, but when we got home a week later my mum took me to the doctor's because she thought I was depressed and he suggested I start reading the *Guardian*. 'That's a very lively paper!' he said kindly. 'It'll give you a lot to think about. What newspaper do you get?' He addressed this to my mother, who had insisted on accompanying me into the consulting room and had been sitting looking at me with a mild worried smile while I didn't know what to say or do.

'The *Daily Express*,' she said.

'Oh, well, that's very good too,' said the doctor.

'She sometimes says she's seen something,' my mother said nervously.

'Something?'

And I had to tell him about the boy in the field.

'Mm,' he said, 'has anything like this ever happened before, Lorna?'

It had, but not so startlingly, and I'd learned to keep my mouth shut about such things. I shook my head. Then I told him I'd read in a book how there was a poor boy killed and thrown out naked in those woods, and the doctor asked where I'd heard about that.

'It was in a book,' I said, 'in the cottage where we were staying.'

'Ah!' he said, looking relieved. 'You know what's happened.'

He gave my mum a big smile. 'You know what's happened,' he repeated, 'her memory's playing tricks.' And explained that what had really happened was that I'd actually read the story in the book before I saw the boy, and that because I had such an impressionable mind and such a highly developed imagination I had manufactured a kind of – he paused, looking up and sideways to his left as if a small helper was holding a prompt board over his head – a kind of projected thought-picture. It was actually not all that unusual. He gave me some pills anyway. He was the first of all my doctors, and I've forgotten his name. I forget most of their names and some of their faces but a few stand out: old Dr Walse with the bottle-top glasses and elaborate jowls (he used to pull them out to a distance with his fingers and let them slap back, he didn't know he was doing it) and the one called Muriel whose eyelids rippled. This one was a nice young man, enthusiastic and kind. He talked about the tricks the mind could play, the illusions, the reasons for déjà vu, crackling synapses, short circuits, nothing to worry about unless of course it becomes a problem. It's just a dream, he said. Only it happens when you're awake.

'But we didn't go back to Andwiston,' I said.

'You probably did but you don't remember.' He smiled, drawing his prescription pad across the blotter. 'I'm always getting mixed up myself. I get the days wrong all the time.'

'Oh, so do I!' said my mum reassuringly. 'It's awful, isn't it? I forget people's names, it's terrible.'

I can't remember what the pills were called. They worked. I didn't see anything else for years and I no longer had those disturbing frissons, as if someone came and stood in my space, invisible.

2

Waking Monday morning in his stale bed, Dan thought first of the three ravens that had landed on the lean-to roof last night and jabbed the bathroom window with their sharp beaks. Later, a fallow doe, heavily pregnant, had walked out of the wood behind his walled garden and stood in the deepening dusk watching through the slats of the high gate while he pulled some mint and a few leaves of cabbage. He was a superstitious man and these things bothered him.

He'd dreamed that the cats were all gone, but the rough orange tom with scruffy ears stood by his bare feet, addressing them with a monotonous, persistent harangue as if they were the seat of his intelligence. Another cat, skinny and black with an expression of fixed amazement, glared from the windowsill.

Growling, he withdrew his feet under the duvet. None of them was his. They just lived here. His mouth was sour, his head thick. He kicked the cat off the bed and turned over, but it came back again and again, wouldn't stop, and in the end, scratching his belly in its dirty vest, grunting and sighing, he got up, went downstairs in his underpants and rattled some biscuits into a couple of dishes on the steps outside the back door.

The house, slightly grand a long time ago, was old and square and too big now. In the rains the water dripped downstairs through the night, gurgling peacefully like a mountain stream. After the terrible storms of last week the woods were still, though it had rained hard all night and soft mist blunted the outlines of things. It was his birthday. Sixty-eight, -nine, maybe more, he hadn't kept track. Also – his mother's deathday, the day he was supposed to take a bunch of flowers to her grave. He went in and made instant black coffee in his cowboy mug. The tremble in his hands was noticeable when he stirred the grains and it got on his nerves. A swig of Laphroaig quelled it a little. Kicking the back door open again he walked out into the middle of the yard and stood there yawning, looking at Pete Wheeler's kid's Venza that he should have had fixed by today. The morning brightened as the whisky warmth settled. A black cat washed itself on the roof, not the one that had sat on his windowsill, another, serene with the morning and the world.

Someone had been at his garden. Something to do with the way the rope on the gate had been looped, too sloppy, not how he did it. Probably kids. Once last week, twice since Sunday. He walked round the side and checked the hives. OK. Mess with them, he muttered, see what you get, you fuckers, tightening the rope on the gate one-handed, coffee in the other. Draining it, he gagged and spat and decided not to go to work yet on the car. He went in and cleaned his teeth, swigging lukewarm water round his bleeding gums.

In the mirror, big greasy pores. Sore red eyes. The veins, vermilion worms.

Two paracetamol, two ibuprofen. Another coffee. Put Al Green on the Bose and turn it up really loud.

Around twelve Pete Wheeler came by. Dan had got the bonnet up and was just getting started on the engine.

'How's it going?' Pete asked.

'Nearly there.'

'Did you hear?'

'What?'

'Big landslip over by Ercol. Last night. The road into Gully's closed off.'

Dan raised his eyebrows and went on working.

Pete took a squashed roll-up out of his pocket and shoved it in his mouth. 'They found a body,' he said, bobbing around on his trainers as if he was a jumpy kid rather than a grandad.

'Kidding,' said Dan.

'Got police tape.' Pete flicked his lighter with a long double-jointed thumb. 'All that stuff. They only do that for murder, don't they?' Pocketing the lighter, he sucked hard. 'Murder! Fuck's sake!'

Dan said nothing.

'It's these rains,' Pete said. 'It's all buggered up there. Terrible mess. You know what it's like, it's all holes. Doesn't take much.'

Then he laughed. His forehead turned into wavy ridges. 'Racking my brains,' he said, 'thinking back. Did anyone go missing round here? Back when – when – it's an old one. The body. Just bones, I suppose. Been there a long time.'

'Yeah?'

'Well – so they say.'

'Old how?' asked Dan, looking up from the Venza's engine. 'Old like medieval or old like ten years?'

Pete bent down to stroke a cat but it scooted away. 'Not medieval like historical medieval,' he said, rising, fiddling with his stubbly chin. 'They wouldn't put up a tape for that, would they?'

'Might do,' said Dan, straightening and stretching. Upright he was at least six inches taller than Pete. 'Keep people off.'

'Well anyhow,' said Pete, spitting tobacco off the end of his tongue, 'it's a right bloody mess. Bloody mud everywhere. Not surprised. Half them storm drains up there are useless.'

He waited a while, making little blowing sounds through his lips.

Dan didn't respond.

Like talking to a brick wall, thought Pete.

'Big mess to clean up,' he pushed on. 'All across the road. Gone on the graveyard. Awful.'

He waited a minute or two more, pulsing up and down on his toes, looking towards the edge of the woods that crowded up against the back wall, then he said, 'Getting foggy.'

When still no response came, he ruffled a hand through his short pale hair and said, 'So what time shall I pick this up then?'

'Five,' said Dan. 'Ish.'

'Well then,' Pete said. 'Adios, amigo,' and headed off.

What a terrible thing. As if a faint bad smell was drifting

from over there. Made you wonder what else was lying around under your feet. Mud on the graveyard. Well. He was going up there anyway.

He felt like walking in this nice spooky mist, so he threw everything down just as it was and walked off. No dog no more to call, no dog at his heels. An absence. Long time since. Just the cats, and they were indifferent, watching him go. He couldn't look after things. The cats hunted. He gave them water and cat biscuits from the market, and they came and went through a hole in the wall where a pipe used to be in the side of his house, God knows how many, it changed all the time. They hung about the yard and the field and the woods beyond, and they got in his garden and he chased them out with hoses and shouts, and filled clear plastic bottles half full of water and laid them about the place, and kept the doors closed and the walls protected by cat repellent, and still they got in.

It was cold for April. He walked along the lane, skirting the lower edge of the woods and cutting across the fields, thinking about the body, someone lying dead and unknown near here all those years. Man or woman? Did he say? Poor sod anyway, laying in the ground all alone and no one knowing you're there. Except for the murderer, of course, if it *was* a murder. Poor sod.

Ravens. The wet nose of the pregnant doe. A body returned to light. Things falling in sequence. All these things seemed significant.

It wasn't as bad as Pete said. The mess was mostly down at the far end, low by the trees; the really old stuff where time had rubbed out all the names and all the dates, all the things recorded in memory of; smoothed down into ripples on stone.

Three men in yellow coats were cleaning up with shovels. A lorry was backed in at the gate.

His mum's grave was well out of the danger zone. Yes, there she was, poor old Mum. Audrey Jane Broom, safe and sound. OK for now, not too much overgrown, but the jam jar was empty and he'd forgotten to bring flowers. Should have picked her some bluebells on the way. Oh well. Next time. And there was his gran, Ocella Mary Morse. He remembered her well, lying on her old green chaise longue when he took her a cup of tea in her upstairs room that smelt faintly of pee. The two of them, his mum and his gran, going like hell at one another, Grandma's tone lower and scarier, his mum's shrieky. And he under the bedclothes with his ear to the radio listening to the music.

He left the graveyard and climbed to the top of the Edge, walked a little way and sat down on a hillock looking towards the woods. There was activity on the road below, figures moving about, cars. Towards the heights, the Long Wights hid behind an outcrop of rock. The land up there, beyond the old stones, was potholed and full of shafts from the long-disused mines.

Not too long ago they were open. Maybe someone fell in.

He'd gone to school in Ercol. His mum made him walk over there because she said it was a better school than the one in Andwiston.

And don't you ever, ever, *ever* go anywhere near those shafts, never ever *ever*.

So of course he hung around them all the time like all the

other kids. Peering into them. Utter blackness. That swift shudder, and the recoil. Now they were all fenced off for health and safety.

The climb had set his back off. The sun shone silky through a milky sky. He lit up. Smoke on the air, into the fog. The wood's edge was fuzzy. Or was it his eyes? His sight was getting pretty fucked these days. He remembered him and Eric Munsy and a big daft boy called Frankie, daring each other to jump across the smaller shafts, idiots, going to the edge of the big one, lying down. Your head hanging over, someone holding your feet. Then running down through the woods to play in the ruins.

When we were thirteen.

'See, what I think,' said Frankie, 'is it's like we're all just ghosts. Only we don't know it.'

Frankie's theory was that we're all actually dead. All this is the afterlife, only we can't tell. Dan imagined all the dead people crawling about in the earth like worms. 'That's shite,' he said, because he thought it sounded tough.

They ran whooping through the trees, and he went home past the field with the horses, Little Sid and Lady and the big bay called Pepper. He stood for a while with his arms hooked over the gate. His mother wouldn't let him ride. She wouldn't let him do anything. Every time he stepped out of the door she foresaw terrible disasters, cars smashing into him, cows trampling him, slates flying off roofs in breezy weather and decapitating him. There she'd be at the gate when he got home, peering mournfully down the lane with her long white face.

The fog was clearing, just a little. He went down, walking

heavily, keeping his back consciously straight against the niggling pain. Along the edge of the wood he imagined how he'd look to someone on the far side of the field: like a ghost coming out of the fog, emerging like a developing photograph.

3

The forest is ancient, beech and ash and oak. There are wild strawberries, and tiny purple-pink flowers found shining at the side of the track like stars in the crisp dark green. People don't come in this far, only the deer, the creatures, and the strangeness comes and goes, like weather. I write by the light of my Tilley lamp at night. In the daytime, the constant shimmering leaf light is enough. I'm drawn, of necessity, to the theory that half-light's good for the eyes. I've stocked up on reading glasses from the Pound Shop. I have a den against a rock face, a perch on the side of the hill looking out on the glade. I've loved these old woods ever since that first time, when I saw the cold boy. They've kept bringing me back. I've loved them in memory, seen from afar, dancing merrily over three hills, and I've loved the rocky ups and downs of them, the silence in the centre, and the birds' far-away murmur, full and soft. When I am an old woman I shall wear purple, says the poem, but purple's not my colour so I came to the woods instead. First there was childhood, then here then Carmody Square then here then Childhallows then Crawley then here. Always back to here.

I had a job for the past few years, but it came to an end.

I was working in a place that closed down. It was called Childhallows Farm, but it wasn't really a farm, it was in the middle of town and attached to a big building that had once been a school but was now what they called a Welcome Centre, because it was for inadequate people like me.

An odd little family we made. When it was gone, I saw them about: Henry whose head was too full, Jane who loved dogs, Hilary who looked like the Duchess in *Alice in Wonderland* and scared people in the street by roaring Hallelujah.

When Childhallows closed they gave me a place in Crawley. That was weird, I mean *really* weird. My room smelt like the elephant house at the zoo, circa 1956. One morning there I was in the bathroom brushing my teeth, face in the mirror, then suddenly the horror, the horror. Those deep hollowed bird's eyes, bare and strange, looking back at me, but it wasn't me, I had eczema round my eyes, the horror, the horror.

It's a damn thing to be old and not know what any of it was for.

One night I nearly smoked my contact lens and put my dope to soak in saline for the night. And in the mirror there was me – behold the crone, the ancient of days. I was pretty once. A man stopped in the street and looked at me and sighed as if I was a sunset. But it happened, that thing that was always so far away, the place you were never going to get to. Others aged, your father and mother, their faces changed and then they died. You were never going to change. Then you did. Your face looked back at you from mirrors and dark windows, different, and you saw that only Death awaited, sweet and savage. And I got that deep humming noise in my head, the way it came before. Here we go again, just like before. I knew it was coming. I sluiced out my mouth, rinsed my face, went into the kitchen, poured out last night's heated-up coffee and stood at the window. I looked at my fingers wrapped round the nice warm mug and they were peculiar to me. Then I looked out of the window and I was dizzy and there were people walking up and down, and they were remarkable. Truly do they not know fear? These people walking about and talking on buses and sitting in pubs as if nothing's wrong. *I* have fear. It never goes away. It underlies my existence. Things block it out. I've taken meds. They slow me down. Fog the mind. Dry mouth. Dizzy. Speed I gave up. Dope I like, and booze. Just those really. Without them life's just so dull, so boring. Oh, and anti-depressants; I had to take those because if I didn't I lay in a coma forever. It's a matter of survival.

There was a knock on the door, and I froze.

Who? My head ran through the possibilities. Oh I don't know. Quickly – pull yourself together.

I opened the door and it was this woman called Sue who lives downstairs.

'Hi, Lorna,' she said. She has a nice face, her eyes are soft and kind. She's round and red and so eager to be good.

'Hello.'

Click. I'm on. Pretend to be OK.

'I've brought you the paper,' she said. 'I've finished with it.' She has a high little-girl voice.

'Oh, that's great. Thanks.'

Monday morning, of course. Yesterday's *Sunday Mirror* with all its bits.

'You know that funny woman,' Sue said, timid and earnest, 'that walks up and down with a cat in her pocket?'

'Yeah.'

'Have you seen her about recently?'

I thought. Poor old mad thing. Poor old cat.

'Er – I'm not sure. I haven't really been looking out for her.'

'No,' she said. 'I'm just feeling a bit worried. I haven't seen her in a while.'

'Oh,' I said. 'Well. Do you think something's wrong?'

'I don't know.' She looked away, folding her arms in her big fluffy jumper. Her skirt was long and huge. 'I don't want to seem nosy,' she said, looking back at me with small dark eyes full of hurt, as if at some stage, someone had badly upset her feelings, 'but you know, you never know…'

'No,' I said. 'Where does she live?'

'I've no idea. But she's usually on the benches near Sainsbury's. I think I should take a walk down there.'

'Yeah,' I said. 'That's probably a good idea. She is a bit – I don't know.'

'She is, isn't she?'

'Yeah.'

There was an awkward silence. I didn't want to get involved in any way.

'It's just that she goes right past my window,' she said, 'just about every day. Two or three times usually. And that little cat's face peeping out of her pocket, poor little thing.'

'I know.' The little cat's face came accusingly into my head. 'Have you ever tried to talk to her?'

'I used to,' she said. 'There's not much point really, is there?'

'No,' I said, pushing the cat away, 'not really.'

'Oh well.' She smiled and set her shoulders. 'I'll take a dander down there. I've got to get some bits and bobs anyway.'

'OK,' I said. 'Let me know, will you?'

'I will, yes.'

'It's probably nothing,' I said and closed the door.

'Oh, I'm sure!'

When she'd gone, I sat down on the blue wicker chair. The room was not yet mine. It had nothing much of me, and I thought, I have become like those boys when I was young, those boys with their sad little pads they couldn't make nice. You'd go round and they'd try and get you to stay and sleep with them. The humming was loud in both my ears. I looked at the newspaper. There was a picture of a gorgeous little boy crying his heart out. The headline said: Thousands flee fighting. But it was blurry and I had to keep blinking, and my heart started: Boom! Boom! Boom!

Breathe, dear. Go on.

The coffee wouldn't go down, it just wouldn't. I couldn't make it to the bathroom so I pushed up the window and spat it out onto the sill. It left a foul taste in my mouth. I thought I might be sick so I left the window open and lay down on the floor, and stayed there till the sick feeling passed and my heart slowed. I had no idea how long I'd lain on the floor. The little boy was still crying and I cried along with him. I thought how useless I was, when all I did was lie here on the floor; and how even poor Sue who many a time had got on my nerves, her with her mimsy little voice and do-goodish verve, was better than me because she actually helped people, while I didn't even notice they needed it. Then I thought about Johnny and how affronted he was by life. Couldn't watch a sad film without tearing up, couldn't cope with the daily horrors, the murdered babes and cruelly dispossessed, the staring starving toddlers, the suffering, like Prince Siddhartha, only Johnny didn't become the Buddha, he became a morass, a porridge of love and fury. I've seen him smash his fist through a wall after watching the news.

My chest ached. The world's cruel. Not a thing you can do to make things not have happened. I got up and looked out of the window. There was a carpet shop across the road, a taxi place, a sad Christian bookshop and a BetFred, and a little further along, a triple-layered concrete car park where pale youths drove cars too fast round and round and round in the evening. I didn't want to grow older looking at that. I closed the window.

That's why I came here: tent, sleeping bag, Tilley lamp, camping stove, stewpot, frying pan. Knives. Spoons, forks. A bowl. Plates, of course. Mug. Long life milk. Soap – toothpaste, matches… I've always lived by lists. The practicalities. Who cares? It can be done. And as nothing matters, why should I worry? I was never any good at living with people anyway. There was a quiet babble in my head and I didn't know what to do with it. If I go to the woods I'll be better able to pay it attention, I thought, I'll go there, I'll find out. I got a bus. It took three or four trips with my stuff, and after the last I threw my mobile over the bridge into the little stream that runs through Andwiston. I was alive again, on an adventure one more time. Hallelujah! I got out of it. I'd never really thought about what I'd do with my time. Just live and listen from day to day and think about things, something like that. Of course it would be strange in the depths, but it seemed very necessary for me to do this, and it was so much better to be homeless in the country than in the town. Much more dangerous in town. Here, all you've got to worry about is being scared of the dark, and that's just the same as being scared of yourself. If I stayed in town, I'd end up like old Norm and those people under the bridge, and that old woman who scared me shouting in the street near the tube station once when I was walking home very late. Johnny came back one night with old Norm, in the early days before Carmody Square and Harriet: this is Norm, he's staying the night, it's freezing out there. Looked a hundred years old and smelt like a hundred jars of pickles. Oh! Hello. Swaying about with his red eyes and red face, saying nothing. Well. What do you do? We only had one room. Me and him and Lily and a sink and draining board, the cooker behind a partition. Lily woke up and was scowling out at us from her bed in the corner. I made a cup of tea and Norm nodded off on our sofa. It was hard sleeping with him in the room. He snored and grumbled in his sleep and his smell pervaded the air. In the morning his bare knobbly feet, all brown and dried up, hung over the end of the sofa. Me and Lily went over to Talgarth Road and stayed at Wilf's for a couple of days. 'Dad!' she said, running in. 'There's an old man moved into our house!' We had a good laugh about it, me and Wilf and Jananda. When I first met Wilf I thought he said his name was Wolf and I thought, Wow, what a cool name. But it wasn't, it was Wilf. I mean. Wilfred. What were they thinking of? The only Wilfreds I could think of were Wilfred Pickles, Wilfred Owen and Wilfred Hyde-White. That was it. Wilfred never made a comeback like some of those other old names. It was never cool. That night we put her to bed with the cousins and Jananda's Jeannie, so it was a huge treat for her. They didn't quieten down till after eleven. When we got back Norm was still there and he'd been joined by a couple of his mates. Johnny was making chips. It took him three more days to get them out.

He was like that in those days. Soft.

There's this nice old bloke lives on the edge of the wood. Well, he's not nice really, in fact he's a bit scary, but he plays good music.

Trouble in mind, oh, I'm blue, oh but I won't be blue always.

Those old days, in the Music Exchange, sifting through albums. I'd been for coffee with Fiona. The shine on the cover of *Blonde on Blonde*, the music playing. This man, immediately striking and attractive, there on the other side of the sloping boxes of records. Your eyes skim off each other's glance. I didn't look at him so much, he was just a huge presence, very dark, eyes, hair, eyebrows, the rough hair around his sweet mouth. He followed me outside. Asked me where I was going. Said, 'Want to come for a coffee with me?' He was well spoken.

'OK,' I said.

So we walked down Ladbroke Grove.

'I'm Johnny,' he said.

'I'm Lorna.'

A big old coat, a guitar on his back. Said he played at the Cellar Upstairs sometimes and would I like to come? And we went in that old co-op place that used to be there, plain board tables, good coffee and soup, freaks and junkies and ska. I've got to go for my little girl, I said, and he came with me. She came running out from school, her first year and she loved it, her smile, two big front teeth, the gap between. 'What a lovely little girl,' he said.

God, wasn't he lovely then though! I'd watch him sleep and refuse to believe that the soul that made that face could be anything but beautiful.

I've nicked a few cabbage leaves from his garden, just the outer ones. I sing, to the tune of 'Autumn Leaves' and a silent Miles Davis accompaniment:

The outer leaves are in my stew pot

The outer leaves that I have stole

The words are a kind of blur until: *But I miss you most of all, my darling, when the outer leaves start to boil.*

Nothing fits, nothing rhymes.

I've forgotten things. Quite a lot, I'd say. It's raining. It's so cosy in here. I don't know why I didn't do this years ago. The rain runs down the rock face at my back, but it's OK because I put a big tarpaulin between the tent and the rock, and there's another overhead, and I have branches all over the top of that. I love the sound of heavy rain on woodland, a roaring. Silver. Kind. I fish out the big strong cabbage leaves, fill them up with rice and herbs and wild garlic from my pot. Then I eat them. After a while, I get up in a dreamy state and walk through the wood. The rain's stopped. I live close to the ruins. I'm so hidden, there's no chance that anyone visiting the ruins (that's if they're lucky enough to find them) would ever get to me. But no one ever comes, and so it should be. Me and the ruins, we go back a long way. There used to be a path and a clearing but they're long gone, and there's not much left now but three blackened walls higher than your head, and some old lichened grave stumps. The ruins straggle on, stumps and bumps and hidden things to scrape your shin on. Me and Lily came looking for them when we stayed in that cottage by the bridge where the water runs under the road and you hear it all night. The ruin was hard to find, all buried away under ivy, and we'd searched twice before and not found it, then suddenly, when we weren't really thinking about it any more, there it was, walls, things to fall over, stumps. My God, she said, this is like the setting for a horror film. Now how'm I s'posed to sleep tonight? I was telling her the old story, about the stable boy murdered by his master, and about the boy I'd seen in Gallinger's field all those years before. I used to sit up on the hillside looking over the fields but I never saw him. Poor boy, I'd think, still shivering and hurt after all these strange centuries, whoever he is, whatever he's done. And she said, Bloody hell, Mum, don't creep me out. She was fourteen, the same age I was when I read the story in the book I stole from the holiday cottage. A murder hiding here and there in folk tales, cross-bred with elf and boggart and fairy lore, a branched story. Poor boy courts the baron's daughter. Or sleeps in too long, or skimps on his work, pulls one mocking face too many. The cruel baron beats him, puts him out naked in deepest winter. Cuts off his head, strikes a fell blow, feeds him poison, stabs him with a pitchfork. Tosses him from a high high crag, hurls him in a reedy pond or a midnight tarn, or down down down in a deep dark well full fifty fathoms deep.

The boy of Ercol woods hasn't walked in years and no one remembers him now.

Still he sings, along with his fellows:

Wae's me, wae's me,
the acorn's not yet fallen from the tree,
that's to grow the wood
that's to make the cradle
that's to rock the bairn
that's to grow to the man
that's to lay me!

Fourteen, so a couple of years before everything went crazy, before horrible Phoebe Twist and poor thick Terry and all that stuff. Lily was a lovely kid. She thought she was fat. I used to point out pictures of Marilyn Monroe and Jane Russell and say, they'd be thought fat these days you know, just goes to show how ridiculous it all is, but of course she never believed me. She, in jeans and a butterfly-patterned top, picking little pink flowers among the ruins; then she got nettle-stung and started whining, sat down on a stump to poke at a blister that was coming up nicely on the back of her heel.

There's a bright moon rising tonight. I walk all the way up past the Long Wights till I'm rambling in small boggy fields not much used, and there's a wide rusted-up farm gate hanging askew at the end of an overgrown track. If you stand still, you can hear the water running off these high fields through the maws of storm drains that hide under hedges. Through that broken-down gate, across the field, if I look to the left I can follow with my eyes the dim up-and-down line of the hedge against the sky and I think I know the exact spot where one old drain I used to walk by in the old days gapes like a mouth widened in a grimace. I walked up here with my little brother once and he shouted down it. 'Something's crawling up!' I said, and we ran away giggling.

If someone saw me here now they'd probably think I was a ghost. Standing like this, so still in the muddy entrance to the field. In a way I do feel like a ghost, haunting this place where so much happened.

It was early morning by the time I'd come down and drifted along through the wood till I found myself again at that place where the track comes out by a cottage with a small garden and a corrugated roof. Typical holiday cottage. Bigger than the one I stayed in with my mum and dad and my little brother. It had been full of dopey little signs and wooden plaques on the wall. A Dream Is A Wish Your Heart Makes. Don't Fear The Storm, Learn To Dance In The Rain. The one in the toilet said Flush Your Cares Away. Anyway, it's not a holiday cottage any more. The garden's too much of a mess for that, full of tortured bicycles and scooters, a sand pit, a trampoline. They've had the roof done and put in white uPVC windows upstairs. Doesn't look anywhere near as nice as it used to.

The people are still in bed. I don't go into the garden and up to the windows to peep inside. I stay near the trees. We came out of the wood and there they all were in the garden, Johnny talking political philosophy with Maurice Albin, Harriet, missing her two front teeth, running towards us with her worried forehead and a tortoise in her hands, held up as if an offering to the gods.

'Oh no,' said Lily, 'what's *he* doing here? This is our holiday.'

There's the old bench still. She's sitting on the back of it licking her pink ice cream.

'Look!' croaked Harriet. She always croaked.

Eternity in a second. The day of the tortoise and the bees. I see them. Oh God, the pair of them, Maurice in a denim jacket, wholesome and clean, Johnny a limp blue t-shirt, a handsome satyr with brown corkscrew curls hanging into his dark eyes. The noble warrior, the beautiful rebel, sun on his brow, deep in some high-level intellectual conversation in that garden. It is the cause, it is the cause, my soul. Johnny was a Knight of the Round Table. He loved humanity, justice, the downpressed, gave his time to the poor and needy, fed soup to the cardboard box people, the huddlers in doorways.

'What are *you* doing here?' I said to Maurice. 'Were you pining?'

Couldn't keep away. The two of them were so bloody boring. Yak yak yak all the time. The low wall, the small round table with garden chairs, the ropey deckchair. Johnny said he'd told me and I'd forgotten. Maurice had come down from Blackpool and was picking Johnny up, the two of them were off to London on some urgent Hatchet business. Should only be a couple of days though, Johnny said. Hatchet (Small Axe originally, after the Bob Marley song, but the name was already taken) was the small bookshop and press in Shepherd's Bush run by Maurice (logo: a tree, an axe) and it was always demanding last-minute, drop-everything attention. They had a high-brow bi-monthly journal (reviews, agitprop) that did OK in students' unions, alternative bookshops and little co-ops, but really the whole thing was only ever hanging on by its fingernails. Johnny never had anything that lasted till he met me, not even a father or mother; he'd dropped out and in and out and in and read everything he could get his hands on, sang and played his guitar for money not beer, did this and that of nothing much and really couldn't stand any of it. He'd left jobs in the middle of afternoons, of shifts, of tea breaks and sentences, just walked out. 'I thought I was going to burst,' he'd say. And he never kept a job till he went to Hatchet and met Maurice and found his place in life, and the job that became more than a job. First he was just sorting out and shelving books: *The Squatters' Handbook*, Marx, Mao, *A Critique of Pure Tolerance*, Marighella. Soon, though, he was up and about early with the others, dedicated, out restoring the plumbing in smashed-up two-years-empty council flats.

I was glad he was going because I was sick to death of Lily and him always going at it hammer and tongs, driving me mad. Things were souring with me and Johnny by now. Lily grabbed the tortoise off Harriet and kissed the top of its head. 'I wouldn't kiss it,' I said. I thought she might catch something from it. Its mouth was a placid drooping slit, its legs scrambled against open air. Maurice had rescued it from a house in Blackpool, some people he'd been seeing, sweet but dim beings, he said, think they're being radical by living in shit, and I don't mean that metaphorically. Some clown going on about the Lords of Misrule. This child, I kid you not, walking around like some kind of deformed beast with a horrible growth, this nappy that looked as if it carried a ton of bricks like a builder's load, and the fragrance – and this poor thing underfoot with all the other mini-beasts, you name it, getting kicked around, tripping up over, just a toe-stubber really, pets, can't see the attraction. So I thought of your little one here.

That was nice. Maurice had no one else to give it to, no wife, no kids, no ties. He used to boast that he could vanish, just like that, and it was rumoured that his name was just one alias among many. Never believed it, myself. He'd brought ice cream too, a big tub of strawberry, there we are, all of us eating our pink ice cream out of plastic bowls, Lily perched on the wooden bench, long brown toes curled round the edge. Harriet, pushing her way backwards onto Johnny's lap with her spoon dripping onto his jeans. Maurice supine in the deckchair, one arm behind his head of close-cropped colourless hair, holding forth vertically in his sing-song Cockney voice about Americanisation and advertising and media collusion, how there was nothing to choose between the two main parties now, Tory and Tory.

We told them about the ruins and Maurice said he wouldn't mind seeing the Long Wights some day. Johnny and Lily had a big row, stupid and pointless as ever, just before he left. She threw his books on the floor. *The Society of the Spectacle*, its pages bent. Adorno, Deleuze. Weird afternoon: it can't have happened this way but it's how I remember it. I was standing near the back door. Johnny set down the spoon, bent down and tickled the back of the tortoise's neck and its head started to rise. He chuckled. 'Look at this!' he said. It was standing perfectly still, its claws splayed out on the grass. The more he tickled, the higher the head rose and the longer grew the neck, longer and thinner, up and up, one inch, two, three, still going up. The creature's face was outraged. Still Johnny chuckled and tickled. Longer and thinner, longer and thinner, and the face hideous, agonised.

It made me feel sick.

'Stop! Stop!' I said. 'It's horrible! Stop it!'

But it went on rising till it was level with the lower edge of the table top. Then – and I remember this in slow motion – its mouth opened very wide but no sound came out.

Johnny stopped tickling. Slowly the head went down.

'Yes,' said Maurice, 'amazing creatures, aren't they?' His blue eyes, guarded and steady, looking out on the world with vague distaste, crooked-teeth smile. His teeth were disgusting. You could always see the whitish-yellow crud building up between them. It toddled away towards the hedge, slowly, pointlessly, pushing its way through the grass, the pink-tipped daisies and the clover.

'Are you all right, Mum?' asked Lily. 'You look funny.'

'I'm fine,' I said. I felt hot and had to sit down.

And then the bees came; Maurice yelling, 'Woah! Woah! Fuck me!' and ran in shouting, 'Close the windows! Quick! Close everything! A big swarm of bees!' And we ran about wildly, closing windows and doors, and stood in the kitchen and watched as the swarm came down, magnificent, coming down over what remained of our strawberry ice cream and our coffee, and over the tortoise still crawling somewhere in the overgrown lawn. I never saw a tornado or a waterspout but I'm sure the swarm had something of that quality. It was wild and dark and deafening and overcame the walls and fixtures of the small garden.

'Toby!' screamed Harriet.

'It's all right,' I said, 'he'll go in under his shell.'

A thick black cloud whirling madly on the other side of the glass.

'Can they get in?' Lily, soft-voiced, materialising at my shoulder.

'No!'

But none of us were sure.

Johnny stood behind me with his arms round me. You could cuddle for England, I used to say. You should be one of those people that charges money for hugs. We'd be rich. When the swarm cloud lifted and whirled away, the farm where we went for our eggs and milk was once more visible, its red roof above the hedges where bats would soon be flitting, and the tortoise was gone. It was as if the bees had carried it away with them, though none of us could recall seeing it go. Toby the tortoise was never seen again. We looked everywhere for him. Lily and Harriet cried. I had a little cry too. It had been such a nice day, and then it hadn't.

After a while we gave up and came back in, and Lily flung herself down on the sofa and turned on the TV, and sat there with swollen eyes. A crier from the day she was born. Anger, joy, sadness, whatever, she cried. She produced a bar of chocolate from somewhere and took a big bite.

'You'll get fat,' Maurice said. Johnny picked up her red-yellow-I-am-crap-screaming shiny magazine from the ugly retro coffee table and showed it to Maurice. 'The girl that taste forgot,' he said.

'Fuck off,' she said, baring her big teeth.

I saw them off.

'The Wights,' I said. 'They're worth seeing.'

After they'd gone I smoked a joint all to myself as the bats began to swoop and the girls went searching for poor Toby once more, calling his name as if he'd recognise it and think: Oh! Must go home! But soon the dark came down for real and the search had to be abandoned.

I was awake most of the night worrying about that poor tortoise. Those things are supposed to be slow, but he must have shifted. I fell asleep and had a dream that the tree tops outside were moving in a strange slow deliberate way that made me scared, and when I woke up I lay staring at the dark and listening to the small stream that ran by the side of the house, on across the field and off under the road to dissipate who knows where.

Fuckers are in my head, arguing –

You're nothing if not consistent, love.

She hated the way he called her love in just that tone.

And you, in her best bored voice, are such a patronising shit.

I'd never have said a thing like that to my dad in a million years. He'd have walloped the shit out of me.

... these magazines she gets, seven million adverts to every fatuous article.

So?

I'm not being horrible, Lily, I would just love to see you read something decent, for your own sake, not mine.

Maurice butting his big nose in: What are you reading, Lily?

None of your business. I'm not reading all that boring crap if that's what you mean.

Pet Sematary, Johnny says.

What's wrong with that?

Read what you want. I'm only trying to help you.

Fuck off.

And Maurice, who'd read everything of literary, philosophical and intellectual importance and probably nothing at all of pulp or anything approaching it, just sniggered.

'I'm going to make soup,' I said. 'You come and help me.'

So fucking up themselves! Peeling carrots.

And then one day while I was rambling around down here in the woods (after the bees this would have been) I turned into a mole and tunnelled. I was just thinking, what if you just go deeper and deeper in, under the bushes, under where the swathes of ivy and curtains of moss fall, if you cross the forest in its least accessible places, burrowing – as a mountaineer fathoms height or a spelunker depth. And I just went off the path to a track, off the track to a smaller one and then one smaller still; till I was off into the deepest parts of the wood where no one else goes. I lay down and tunnelled, and I was fourteen again, standing in the rain in the woods that first time. Exactly the same. Deeper and deeper I moved into the beautiful depths, darker and more pure, and the depths said, well, my little dear, come in and play with us. We're all here and we know all about you. I sat in the green darkness and thought, I can always come here. It stayed with me like a comfort blanket.

4

O n the way home Dan detoured into the village to get a paper. Madeleine was in Ollerenshaw's, and by the time he saw her she'd noticed him and it was too late to get out.

'Hello, Dan.' She smiled fondly.

'Hi.'

Must have been about five years, he thought. She wore a green floaty thing and a pink cardigan and her chest was freckled. She'd caught the sun. The lines on her forehead were deep and amiable, and her hair, long and loose round her shoulders, was no longer red but light brown and fuzzy at the ends. Human Remains Found In Mudslide Chaos, said the headline on the front of the *Examiner*. Outside, a truck started reversing. 'Danger!' it said in a loud irritating voice, then a load of jumbly stuff meaning get out of the way. Something had gone wrong with the sound system so it sounded like Donald Duck.

'And how are *you*?'

Years of running around sorting out other people's problems had given her the capable, approachable air of a popular teacher. When she bundled up against him to let someone get to the door, a mutual shrinking of the flesh occurred.

'Fine,' he said, turning away to read the paper. Male, cause of death unknown. Identity unknown.

'Now *that* is really quite creepy,' she said, putting a packet of cherry flapjacks and a carton of eggs down on the counter. He should ask how she was but the words didn't make it as far as his mouth.

'It'll be some idiot potholer,' said the small grey man behind the counter.

'Could well be,' said the woman in the purple coat.

'I was over seeing someone at Hothemby,' said Madeleine, getting her purse out of a shoulder bag with a bright tropical forest pattern. 'And I saw all these cars.' Her face was large and sensible and big-nosed with high wide rosy cheekbones and a Slavic cast. The creases at the outer corners of her eyes were symmetrical and intricate like tiger markings. 'You know,' she said, 'the word on the street says it's foul play.'

The word on the street. Something about that really irritated him, as if she thinks she's a fucking Brooklyn gumshoe or something.

'Danger!' quacked the truck.

'God knows how they know these things.' Madeleine paid for her stuff. 'I mean, there can't be much left.'

He wished she'd go, but she hung about while he bought his paper and then walked out with him. 'It's a terrible thing to say,' she said as they walked towards the green, 'but there's a kind of horrible excitement about it. This body. You know, like something's actually happening round here for once.'

She was all excited about it, wanted to talk about it, wanted him to see how savvy she was, her phone bingbonging some stupid tune, and yap, yap, sure will, be in touch, sorry, I'm on a job, can't speak to you now. Later. Bye!

They reached her car and stood for an awkward moment looking at one another. Oh look at him, God bless, she thought. Poor old Dan. The idea of people knowing she'd ever been involved with him in any way was now terrible. Simply awful. And the physical thing, oh God, what the hell was I thinking? And his horrible mother! When you think of how he was, though. Poor Dan! What an embarrassment he was, she thought, and always had been. She'd thought he was sweet. Well, he was in a way in those days. She'd had a lucky escape. Thank God she got away.

Ach, too horrible to think of.

We all make terrible mistakes when we're young.

'Well, Madeleine,' he said.

She remembered how irritating he could be.

And how he could turn, the temper on him.

Her eyes were noticeably narrower. They'd been pale blue and very wide. Still nice though.

He turned to go and realised he was blushing. It had been ridiculous when he was sixteen but now it was just pathetic.

Half-way home he realised he hadn't got milk for the morning, swore, plodded back, and returned by the track along the back of Gallinger's field. On the dark stretch where the trees joined arms above, and along this lonely track he realised someone was on the other side of the hedge.

He stopped. Stared at the bushes with his big fierce look.

Don't you mess with me, I'll split your fucking skull. But it was nothing.

Pete Wheeler's kid, Sam, an affable lad with spiky yellow hair and a pierced lower lip, picked up the car, and after that Dan put his boots over his trousers and went to check on the bees. He never bothered with all the gear, the smoke, all that, never had. It was OK as long as you kept it all slow and steady. They never troubled him. The two hives were up against the garden wall, the land in front of them, covered with white and purple clover and thyme and spotted with dandelions, sloping gently down to another arm of the wood. Cautiously he lifted the cover and began chivvying out the first frame, removed it and let it rest against the side of the hive. Now the next one. The bees crowded, crawling. There she is, the queen. Everything looked fine. Put the new super in tomorrow. He still glanced sideways and up before he left, to the far end of the wall – always would, even though it was, Christ, nearly twenty-six years since his mother hanged herself there. There'd been spikes all along the top then, put there by the fabled Grandad Jack to keep kids from climbing over, and she'd tied the belt of her dressing gown to one. The spikes had been removed after that. He'd been somewhere between Shetland and Faroe when the word came, and by the time he got home it was all over, someone had cleaned the house and she was in the chapel of rest in Gulliford. He didn't go to see her. No point, poor silly soul. It was a terrible thing. Terrible.

Time for a drink. Three or four straight whiskies fast, then toast. He fried a few eggs, shoved them down while watching the news. Bloody depressing crap. The body was on the local. A man, they said. Blow to the head with a heavy object. Dan walked out the back with his bottle and stood swigging. His yard was a tip. A heap of broken bricks was piled up against the hedge, and tyres lay about near a half-dismantled wreck. The fog had gone completely. Wild kittens skittered by the gate leading into the wood. He went round the front for no reason, just walking aimlessly with his bottle. The swish of the tail of something whisked itself away between the ancient wreck of the old car his gran used to occasionally drive in a very slow and dignified way along the narrow country lanes to the huge irritation of other motorists. It and another rust heap were sinking together into the surrounding greenery, becoming part of the landscape. Some of the cats had made a home in the two old wrecks. Three big elders sat there now, one on a roof, the others on the bonnet of his gran's Wolseley, watching him indifferently. And again, for no good reason, because there really never was any particular good reason for anything but what he and his bottle felt like doing, he lay on his back in the long grass and closed his eyes, and tried to think of some other thing apart from what was left of a body after thirty years in the ground, washed down in the swill like a bit of rubbish. He'd have been at sea then. Didn't anybody miss the poor fucker? Well, no one would miss me either, he thought. It's not that bad. It's not unusual. Then he got ferociously, stupidly drunk. It was getting dusky, bats appeared, first just one or two then a constant skittering. When he got up, his head swirled in a pleasant familiar way. He went out and looked down the lane at the bats swooping drunkenly all along the tops of the hedges in both directions. There was no one about. He walked a little way for no reason. The corncrake grated. Walking back, he got that good feeling, the loose softening perception, and there was his house – hello! – glimpsed from the road through the wild hedge.

You'd think it was derelict. The scent of jasmine came to him. He felt sorry for his house. At heart he was a sentimental man.

The high wall of his garden was covered in toadflax. He ambled over, swinging the bottle, kicked the door open and looked at the garden in the fading light. Two paths crossed in the middle and there was a flaking white bench in the corner where he sometimes sat and smoked. That's where the jasmine ran wild. It had always been there. He imagined the bees in their hives, a hum of sleep. The bees and the bats would outlast him. Are all the bees dying? His aren't. His are just the same old bees, living on like pioneers. The last bees on earth. Nothing much was growing but parsley and spring cabbage and a bit of mint. Down at the far end was the open place where he thought he might build his hen coop and a good run whenever he finally got round to it. Sometimes he worked at his garden in the middle of the night if the fancy took him. It was nice out digging under the moon, the bottle propped in the earth. If only he didn't feel so shattered sometimes. But what could you do about it? It was life. He loved it here. If you stood still sometimes your ears caught things. The trees hissing. Something that croaked and keened under its breath. His ears still listened for a sound from the far wall where the hives stood but it was slightly less than conscious now and fairly tolerable. A couple of times lately he thought he'd heard a new rustling in the woods at night, and he didn't like that. He liked to know what was what. But he often doubted his senses. They'd let him down too many times.

At the back of the house were three circular overgrown red-brick steps, on which he'd scraped his shins when he was three. Foxgloves and Herb Robert ran wild. He sat down and cried, again for no reason. That big orange tom that talked to his feet was snoozing on the bottom step, the one that was scarred with a long gouge on the right-hand side.

'You stupid old fucker,' he told it.

He went back inside, threw some cabbage leaves into the kitchen for tomorrow, drew all the curtains, locked up thoroughly and put some music on. He liked old soul, Motown, stuff like that. He got out his knife and did a bit of whittling. He'd been trying to make a dog out of a bit of pine but it wasn't much cop and the knife needed sharpening and he couldn't be bothered to get up so he lay back and drank and sang along, drank himself to more tears, and talking and singing. He'd lived in this house on and off forever, and almost continually for the past twenty-three years. It had accumulated round him like a soul he didn't want. His things: a few books, guitar, plectrums, pictures that had always been there, CDs out of their covers, vinyls never played because he no longer had a record player. All filthy. He was a pig, he knew. The sugar he spilled last week was still on the rug.

A cat with a big white face jumped up on the arm of the sofa. The stupid ginger one clawed away at the dark red swathes and cataracts of the armchair's side, a magnificent shredding like the hangings of moss in the wood.

In the kitchen he put the kettle on, stood in the big bright space and sang along to the music, distorting his face, '*In the beginning –*'

sweep of strings –

'*you really loved me… but I was too blind, too bli-ind… to really see-ee-ee…*'

The room was like a castle kitchen, with a massive central table and an old doorless pantry painted fifteen shades of dirty cream.

'Which one do you like?'

'They're all fine.'

'Oh come on, you must have a preference.'

'No really.'

His mum obsessing over a colour chart. Every little rectangle looked exactly the same. Cream. Cream. Cream. She was bonkers. She'd go on and on and on till he said 'That one' randomly to shut her up.

'That one?'

'Yeah.'

'Are you sure?'

'Yeah.'

She'd keep coming back at it.

'What about that one?'

Cream. Cream. Cream.

'Yeah, that one, fine.'

'But do you *really* like that one better?'

'Honestly, I like them both, I don't mind.'

Then she'd stand back with a look of profound concern

on her face and he'd lose his rag and walk out and if she followed him, he'd say, 'For God's sake! What the fuck's the matter with you?' and slam his door. Sometimes he'd get a horrible feeling he was going to hit his mum. She just went on and on. On on on. Couldn't block her out. Falling back again on how unlucky she was and how horrible it was being a widow. *Widow.* The way she said it was loaded. She seemed to always wear an invisible set of black widow's weeds, complete with a long black veil.

The kettle boiled and clicked off. He poured water on a teabag. The kitchen windows all down one side were dark. Here and there green eyes peered in. Always a few cats round the windows. He stirred his tea, mushed the bag against the side of the cup. The music in the other room stopped. As if commanded, he stopped too, and just stood there. The following silence felt like something physical slowly pouring into his ears. Beat beat beat, blood in his head. He heard a sound. Outside, neither near nor far.

Click.

His head jerked up. Bastards. The gate at the back of his garden, the one that opened right into the woods.

Quietly he went to the back door and opened it. The woods and the dark night delivered a sudden eerie shiver. Damned if I'm going out there, he thought. The supernatural scared him stiff, he couldn't watch horror films. So he closed the door and locked up, went back into the kitchen and got milk from the fridge for his tea, ignoring the gaping blackness of the windows.

5

Took a walk up to the Wights this morning.

It was such a nice day and the woods woke me up early. Funny, I never used to be able to get out of bed and now I'm up before first light. The birds get going in the dark, the few little whisperers, then the chatty ones; and I lie listening, waiting for the moment when the full chorus begins. It comes along with the light, and suddenly everything's alive. Another night. Got through, I should say, but that makes it sound like an ordeal and it's not, though it doesn't always go easy. But my God, my head's so full! Or rather, the fullness is out there. My head just lives in it.

I got up to the Wights, and sat against one of the biggest stones, and it felt cold against my back. I thought: Fuck you, Long Wights, you never deliver. All that crap about vibrations and earth energies and currents and how you can feel it, well, I never do. *Put your hands on the stone and you'll feel a tingling. Some may experience it as a kind of heat.* Bollocks. I've tried. Nothing. The stones draw down thunder and lightning though, that I know. Wouldn't want to be up here in a storm. This place is full of stories. This is where they brought the nasty old baron and killed him for what he did, boiled him alive or something vile like that. Didn't happen. He lived to a ripe old age. Those old stories, you know, you can bet something really happened but it got garbled. She'd be a lovely fair maid in the ballad – *oh the baron's fair daughter was walking one day* – and the serving lad, the lovely boy, *he's bonny and he's rough*, well, who could resist? Probably had acne and adenoids, poor love, but was the only one who was ever kind to her. She, a pasty plump stammering girl, fourteen, greasy-haired, knicker-wetting. And she got a massive crush on him and couldn't help it. Neither could he.

There were cattle in the meadow and a few sheep nibbled below me. Creatures hummed and ticked in the grass and the sky was deep cloudless blue. The land around here is full of holes, even now, but I know my way around. Somewhere above me is the old storm drain, its sticky black mouth opening to the underground. I went down into the woods. People mostly stick to the paths but I go anywhere, I know all the signs, the curve of a certain trunk, the particular pattern of shading on the bark of one special fallen tree. I went back to my bower. My bower is hung all over with long strands of beads, inside and out, and brooches pinned here and there, and inside I have small round raffia boxes filled with beads and clasps and chains, and an old musical box that no longer plays music. It's full of gauzy flowers and brushed felt and pretty buttons.

After tea and bread and cheese and some wine from my box, I sat for ages imagining the tortoise now, still in the woods but grown to a giant, a prehistoric beast. Beware the Jabberwock, my son. The teeth that snap, the jaws that drool. Time stopped all over again as I sat there – it does, it does –

When it had been dark for some time I thought I'd go see if the cat man was playing music, the poor scruffy man who wears those horrible old baggy trousers that sag at the knees. So I took some wine in a bottle and went to the place near the back of his house where I could sit among the trees and listen. I like that. He plays corny old stuff, things I haven't heard in a long long time, like 'Misty Blue', and 'When the Deep Purple Falls', and 'What Becomes of the Broken-Hearted'. Sometimes, in the dark after a drink or two this heartsick music is unbelievably beautiful. You sit there going, oh remember this one, oh –

He's a sad old thing, his face all frazzled and a look of puzzlement as if someone's just told him off and he doesn't know why or what to say. Poor idiot. Poor drunk. Yes, I can hear it in the distance, so off I go and find a nook, and there are lights on in the house. Weirdo.

Once I heard, played on a fiddly jazz sax, 'Lily of Laguna'. Remember that? Ah no, of course you don't.

She is my Lily of Laguna,
She is my Lily and my rose.

I used to sing it to her when she was a baby.

So there I am lying on my back on Acid Tree Lawn, Holland Park, 1969, the sun hot orange through my closed eyes. A shadow falls upon me and I open my eyes and there's this young black guy with a hooked nose and a long chin saying, 'S'cuse me, love, is this your shoe?'

Me and my friend Fiona had dropped out of university and gone to London. I didn't realise I wasn't clever till I went to university because up till then everyone told me I was (I could *seem* to be clever *sometimes*, I think) and boy could I pass an exam. The trouble was, I wasn't clever, really I wasn't clever, but everyone thought I was. And I wasn't tough. Everyone else was. Tougher, harder. No one else seemed scared like me. I wished I could be hard, but I don't suppose it's all it's cracked up to be. And those intellectuals made me feel stupid. It's a closed shop and I can't be doing with it. I couldn't stand the way they talked, and they were all posh, and if they weren't posh, they were hard, and everybody putting everybody else down as the song says, and I hated it. I'd sit in a seminar feeling dumb while everyone else talked like Malcolm Muggeridge and snortled superciliously. And everyone banging on loudly about oppression and the domination of the few, when it was still all the same, the ones who banged on the loudest were themselves always the ones rising to the top, the strong, the loud, the confident, and no one else mattered. It got harder and harder to hide my dumbness and lack of tough. But Fiona was OK. She was on my Biology team, and when they brought us in the trays of maggots for scientific purposes – we each had our own personal tray – she joined me at the back of the room. Can't, I said, just can't. Me neither, she said. No point in going home, my parents had moved to Halifax and I didn't know a soul there. Anyway I couldn't have lived with them any more. I'd spent years wanting to get away and it would have been a massive capitulation to go back. Mainly it was because of my dad, who'd always

treated me with embarrassed contempt and made me feel
afraid for no reason I could articulate. I don't suppose it
was personal, he was like that with everyone. And my poor
old mother, she just put up with it. What a way to live – no
choice, always in the shadows, always just enduring. My
brother though, twelve now, still at school, stuck there with
all that, though to be honest whenever I did go home, he
seemed fairly happy with his friends and his football and
his scouts. So we went to London, Fiona and I. Fiona had
big grey eyes and tumbling red curls that flowed everywhere
and she could dance like Isadora Duncan. She ended up a
model. Used to see her sometimes in catalogues. And me!
I'm laughing now. Look at me! What a state. Oh, but it
was such fun! To be young and free and stupid and land
in London in 1969. It was a dressing-up festival. Clothes
were like fancy dress. Fiona was a medieval princess. I
had a floppy yellow bow-tie. I just let my hair go and it
went all wild and frizzy like an Afro, and I dyed it black
and painted my nails green, and we lived in a wardrobe in
Fiona's brother's room in a house in Notting Hill. We had
to stay in there in case the landlady found out about us.
Sitting in the wardrobe putting on our smudgy black eyes.
It was a very conscious decision to run wild. It was the first
thing I'd found that I really wanted to do. Oh Portobello
Road and the Dilly. All those pretty people. How hard it
was. No one could be beautiful enough. Inside I felt like the
geek in 'Ballad of a Thin Man', lost in it all, no confidence
at all, but coasting along like a colourful duck on thin ice.
We smoked dope and took orange pills, oh those orange
pills, Christ, I could do with one now – and one night in

the middle of some music thing in a park I looked down and realised I was wearing a Tyrolean milkmaid's outfit. My God, I thought, what the hell am I doing? And on summer days we'd go down to Holland Park and lie in the sun on Acid Tree Lawn. I was lying there one day on my back, eyes closed, when a shadow fell over me.

'S'cuse me, love, is this your shoe?' Prince Charming.

My blue espadrille. The other still sitting there. A dog had run off with it.

Wilf was a chef in a hotel near Euston and worked odd shifts. He had a classic cupid's bow mouth, which he gave to Lily, and he rode an old Norton motorbike on which we took jaunts out into the countryside whenever we could, taking just any old turning to see where we ended up. He was the most laid-back man I'd ever known. For two years we lived together in a room in a basement in Notting Hill, and if ever there was a time in my life when the living was easy, that was it. I sold shoes on Ken High Street. He baked apple cake, ginger cake, perfect angel cake, read sci-fi and watched football. Sex pretty much stopped after the first year but it took us a while longer to realise that all we were was just good friends. In those days, though, you always had to shack up, that's how it was. We were never going to stay together. We must always have known, but we just went on as we were because it was so easy and we got along so well, and every now and then we'd still have sex but it really wasn't lighting up very much. So we decided to split and stay friends, and then I realised my thickening waistline was not only from the apple cake. It was Lily.

* * *

Silent lightning over the tree tops once a long time ago, and me sitting on the bench with my jewellery things. A silver leaf. Things have been a little mad these days. I started back through the trees and – woo! – listen! –

A kind of sweet singing sighing voice made out of tree tops.

Lor-na! Lor-na!

Hello?

6

He'd started sketching again. Tried to draw one of the cats but the stupid thing moved off. He drew a cat and a fiddle. Found some old drawing pencils and a rubber in the cats' room. State of it. Wood. Old pine doors. Plywood boards and planks. He was always intending to build a chicken coop and put it at the end of the garden with a run, the bit where he didn't grow anything. Might as well. Fresh eggs. But he never got round to it. Hey diddle diddle, the cat and the fiddle. The cat looked stupid. Gave him whiskers. A smile. Gave him lynx ears. That was better. And musical notes dancing around in the air about his head. Stupid, he wrote. El Stupido. Then he chucked it all in and went to the pub. Pete Wheeler was there. Eric Munsy, mates once, long time ago. God, what's this all for? They used to go out together sometimes, him and Madeleine, Eric and Josie. What happened to *her*? Big tall girl. No idea. Still skinny as a rake, Eric. Long grey hair straggling over his shoulders, face like a wet weekend. And here we all are, some of us, still kicking about. Eric raised his glass in silent greeting from the other end of the bar. The music was loud but you could hardly hear it, something bouncy and techy, not his thing. Lots of young ones in tonight, someone was having a birthday or something and they were on their way somewhere. Lots of shouting.

Mary behind the bar knew what he wanted and reached automatically for a glass. 'Wild in here tonight,' she said, pulling the pint.

'Aye.'

Mary was in her fifties with long dyed black hair and a trim figure. 'There'y'go, my love,' she said, smiling a crooked-jawed smile and putting the pint down on the mat.

'Ta, Mary.'

He sat at the bar trying not to look like a dirty old man. He always sat at the end if he could, with his back against the wall next to the old dragon banner the schoolkids made out of rags. It had been there for years and was falling to pieces. He drank steadily and quietly, one pint after another. The bright young things talked very loudly. A hearty little roar went up now and then from the darts players way down the other end, and the grey parrot in its cage just sat there looking wise. Pete Wheeler came over. 'Oy!' he shouted over the roar. 'Did you hear about your old ex?'

'What?'

'Your old ex, Madeleine.'

'What about her?'

'Been talking to the police about that body,' Pete said. 'Says she gave some guy a lift around the time it was, you know, when it happened. And he had blood on his face.'

'I didn't think they knew when it happened,' Dan said.

'Yeah, well, I dunno. Parrantly she went to the police. Said she remembered something. It was in the paper.'

.

Long after his time, he thought. He'd have been away.

'So, what then?' he said. 'They find out anything?'

Pete shrugged. 'Oy! Sam!' he called.

His son with the spiky hair came over with his girlfriend.

'What did they say about that body?' asked Pete. 'In the paper?'

'Oh, not much,' said Sam.

'Too long ago,' the girl, a thin little thing in a leather jacket, added. Her eyes had spikes at the corners.

'Don't suppose they'd tell us anyway,' said Mary, who was reaching under the counter for crisps. 'Who knows what goes on?'

'Shouldn't think they'll bother.' The boy's yellow hair glittered under the light like tinsel. 'Not unless they come up with a missing person.'

Pete worked for the water board. 'Really messed the drains up over Copcollar,' he said, his red face sweaty, downing about half of his pint in one go and swaying gently sideways against his son.

'The world's full of mysteries,' the boy said portentously.

'What do they do with them?' asked Dan.

'Sorry, Dan?'

'With bodies? If they're not claimed.'

'Like in Lost Property,' said the girl. 'If not claimed in X number of days...'

Pete must have actually been very drunk because he suddenly threw an arm round Dan's neck and cried, 'See this guy! Wouldn't credit it, but this geezer's been round the world twice over.'

'Have you?' asked the girl, interested, turning to him.

'Merchant Navy,' said Dan.

'Really?' she said. 'My uncle was in the Merchant Navy.'

'In the engine room,' said Dan.

'Really?' She actually seemed interested.

'Not twice over,' he said. 'Not even once. Been to Iceland.'

'Good man,' said Pete, shaking his shoulder, 'what you having?'

More of the same.

'How's the motor?' he asked Sam.

'Great,' the boy replied, scrolling something on his phone. Then they all forgot him. Fat Marlon appeared behind the bar and Mary nipped out for a smoke. Dan fancied a smoke too. All these kids, he thought. He'd have liked kids. Well, maybe not. People who had them moaned about them all the time. Marlon knew his stuff and brought him a Scotch, which he refilled twice more, and Dan sat there till he found himself moving. He'd noticed that. You just did things. You didn't have to think. You were just the man who props up the end of the bar. Your stomach shoves out over your belt. Then you're outside under the Dragon and Hope sign so you must have got up, your body just did it. You're in the lane going home. It's full moon. You're at the end of the village so you start to sing, just quietly. Funny, you get into this state still. I want a dog, he thought, another dog. Wonder what the cats'd think? Couldn't really get one that bothered them. Best go to a dog rescue, get an older, sober one. And he sang: 'Oo-oo-ooh, *baby baby* – *oo-ooh-ooh baby baby, oo-oo-ooh, baby baby...*' like a dog howling at the moon. By the time he got home he was feeling great. Awooooh! 'Werewolves of London' – He checked on the bees, even tinkered on an engine for a while, then somehow lost the wrench, couldn't find it anywhere, so gave up and went in with his head spinning, put on music, got the bottle of Irish from the shelf and banged out some ice.

He came and stood at his back door, looking out on the still night. My back steps, he thought. Here they are. Mine. My back steps. Always. They don't belong to anyone else. My back steps. They were wide and round, concentric circles, very old red brick eroding at the edges, dustified. On the bottom one was a wedge-shaped gouge about an inch and a half deep that filled with dirty water when it rained. His mum had made it with a pickaxe one day when she was arguing with his grandma about money.

They screeched.

His mum: 'So? So? So? You can afford it.'

'That's not the point!'

And he'd screamed his head off because he was only about two and he and his mum had only just come to live with his gran, and he wasn't used to it. Later of course it was normal. She was always too high on emotion, his mum, probably mostly her fault. Everything was drama, slobber slobber emotion or bitter anger or Greek tragedy, anything but an even keel. He remembered the first time he realised the shame of her, once when a man outside the shop, when he was waiting while she bought her cigarettes, leaned down in front of him, his big red-nosed face with all the deep pores and the friendly smile, said to him, 'Listen, son, what's your age?'

He thought it was a funny way to say it: what's your age? He didn't even know who the man was.

'I'm nine,' he said.

'You're a big boy now. You shouldn't be letting your mother show her affections like she does with you. Know what I mean? Not like when a mother kisses a baby, if you see what I mean. You're too big for that sort of thing.'

Then the man had moved away, strolled off across the village green, and he couldn't remember ever seeing him again. He had a feeling he might have been the man who delivered the minerals to Ollerenshaw's. Horror. His soul had curled in mortification. His cheeks blazed. It was wrong. Everyone was laughing at him. Looking at him funny. And after that she'd been too big, and so was he, big son of a big mother, lumbering about, graceless. It was the time after his gran had died and it was just him and her, and she'd still seemed like a big girl, still with her long hair. It had been a good time. But no longer. All ruined. There'd been snuggles and cuddles, and she'd hugged him so tight she'd made him cough, but after that he wouldn't let her. He'd go off into the woods and she'd sulk for days when he got back, and cry quietly to show how horribly he'd upset her. So he'd stay out again and then she'd go mad.

Googly eyes filling up with tears.

Oh, poor Mother!

She was too weak and scared to live out in the world. Couldn't cope. Hunched up in the bathroom, crying next to the bath. Clutching her knees, peering soulfully at the wall with massive pining eyes.

He put his hand down to pull her up.

Fuck you, Mum. I shouldn't have had to put up with that.

OK.

Musico! Get sensible. Make a list. Go into town Friday. Need a few things. He'd never got round to locking that gate. Seemed pointless. Things to do. Things to do, things to do. Make a start on the chicken coop. But instead of doing sensible things he found himself getting sentimental with the cats. Chasing a small tortoiseshell, scooping it up and singing: *Oh what a beautiful pussy you are. You are! You are!* The cat, which had no name, purred and narrowed its eyes at him, wisely. The line down the centre of its face looked as if someone had done it with a precision tool. It wriggled, squirmed out of his arms and fled.

He stopped, struck like a statue under the full moon.

This is no way to carry on.

It's a shame, people said. He wasn't so bad before the drink got to him. It was after he came back from sea. There just didn't seem to be anything else to do. He remembered his bunk. His face in that little mirror. He must have been younger then but it always seems to have been the same face in the mirror, the same one all these years, till now it didn't look like him any more, it didn't look like anyone he knew. It was much fuller and harder and older. He talked to himself and the cats, forced himself on the tortoiseshell again, danced with it. Ridiculous. Sometimes he did ridiculous things like suddenly shout yeeeh-haaah! to the starry sky for no reason.

The cat scratched his hand, jumped down and ran.

'Sorry! Sorry!' he said.

Cold.

Getting cold.

Turning to go in, he stubbed his toe on the wrench that had materialised from nowhere in his path. 'Fuck!' he yelled as it went spinning, tripped over a straying wheel brace and fell hard across the steps, cracking himself bang in the centre of the forehead against the edge of the top step.

7

Oh God, poor fool's knocked himself out.

Well, what can you do? Got to do something. Terrible thing to find the poor fucker's dead and you could have done something. I only came for the music. Had some wine earlier and was feeling nice. Then he comes out and starts making a racket behind his house, shouting and yelling and groaning, then clonk and that awful silence. The music went softly on in the house, I don't know what it was, but honestly, it was sinister, the way one minute he's shouting and singing and the next – nothing.

So of course I had to go and look. I came out of the woods and went into his yard for the first time, and there was plastic tacked over a couple of the back windows, and hundreds of cats all looking at me with wide suspicious eyes. The man was lying face down and half on his side right across the steps, and there was blood on the step and on his forehead; it had run down his face between the eyes, and his eyes were moving about a lot under the lids so he was alive anyway. He was OK. Breathing and everything. Just pissed out of his head. But he looked really uncomfortable, the way the step pressed into his neck and shoved his face sideways, so I thought I should get him a cushion, and went inside. To be honest, I was curious. I felt sorry for the poor old bugger. So I had a little poke around, and it was creepy and depressing. There was a wide staircase with darkness at the top, and on the right as you went in, a massive kitchen that smelt cold and a bit off, with a big wooden table in the middle, deep old white sinks and wooden draining boards. Not much used, I'd say. To the left, from which the music came, the living room, messy and surprisingly cosy with a long sofa and comfy chairs and a TV, and pictures on the walls, the kind of things you saw in junk shops, hunters with dogs, landscapes, boats, nature studies, and a fireplace all laid and ready to light. There were two more rooms, one on either side of the stairs. One was a workshop with tools and wood shavings and cluttered shelves, the other a cat-stinky place filled with old furniture and boxes and a few old doors stacked up against the wall. When I turned on the light there was a scuttling and something dark ran behind a beat-up brown armchair with no seat and scratched arms. 'Hello,' I said, 'I hope you're a cat and not a rat.' Why keep all this stuff? Not many books. Not a reader then. I opened the top drawer of an ugly sideboard. Jumble. A Present From Whitby, a little quaint fisherman's cottage. A lump of rock. A boat with blue-trimmed sails. A pair of cream-coloured kid gloves, perfect and tiny. A brooch consisting of fine filigree intertwined letters, an O and an A and a C. Letters in a bundle. An old telescope. That was nice. I picked it up but the glass was obscured with filth and the mechanism refused to budge. Photographs half out of an envelope. Old black and white of a young woman standing by a swing, grinning happily. An old man and a woman sitting formally, stiff. A lane. Garden. Beehives. The ones out back, must have been there a long time.

Enough. The poor man'll be dead.

I picked up a cushion from the sofa in the living room, took it out, carefully lifted his head and shoved it under. There. Much better. He sighed and opened his mouth, frowned in his sleep. Someone more of a wreck than me, I thought, ha ha.

'Sleep it off,' I said, then, following the theory that you can instil a sense of security in someone by whispering into their unconscious, did what I used to do with my kids when they were asleep. I leaned down and whispered by his ear: 'All shall be well and all shall be well and all manner of things shall be well.'

And he said, 'What?' in a gormless voice, and I ran away.

OK, so I saw him through that and then I went back through the midnight wood to my den, and got the Tilley lamp going strong. Out came my book and my pens and pencils and I went on writing in that frantic heedless way that people do when they try to leave a trace, catch the voices all wanting to be heard, the clamouring past, make the good old times return. They were lost and things went wrong, but the wood smoothed it all out, smeared the past and present into a singularity, and since I came here there have been moments when everything was clear, as if this green world contained the whole of the ground of being, whatever that means. Those were the days, my friend, we thought they'd never end, playing on repeat forever at the gates of heaven or hell or wherever you end up, those days, my friend, we thought would never end, oh but end they did. I wrote down Carmody Square, a big squat full of people running from Iran, from the Irish troubles, from whatever was to be left behind, people with not much money; just anyone who couldn't get a place, and there among them me and Johnny and the girls. I loved living there. This rug on my floor, with its red and brown faded pattern, that's from Carmody Square. We got a whole top floor of a house next to the shop, overlooking the square, with a view towards Vauxhall Bridge. I learned to make jewellery and work silver and sold them under the flyover at the end of Portobello Road. Johnny stole expensive art books and sold them to second-hand bookshops on and around Charing Cross Road. To live outside the law you must be honest, he always said. Eve and Steve lived downstairs. Steve looked like a pirate. Eve's hair came thinly down to her waist. On the main road, the pub had lunch-time strippers who ranged from very beautiful to agonisingly fragile. We had a cat called Lemon, she'd sit on Johnny's shoulder like a parrot and nibble at the glasses he wore for reading. Sometimes the police came round very early in the morning and raided one of the houses across the way, bang bang bang down in the square and the crackle of walkie-talkies. Johnny took the girls out, Lily by the hand, Harry in the pushchair, down to the river to watch the boats, over the bridge, past the Houses of Parliament, back across Westminster Bridge. Then he'd say, You girls, you go off to your room. He was good with kids. Could get them howling with laughter, stuck his arm in a hole in the cliff – It's got me! It's got me! – put my wraparound skirt on to do the washing up, all the mad upside-down faces and stupid walks. At night, Harriet snuggled into his side, zzzzzzz, Lily listening, zzzzz, the Bluzbo stories, night after night how they rambled on, like *Watership Down* only with flies, Bluzbo the plucky bluebottle, evil Zubb his sworn enemy, and a whole fly creation mythology, metaphysics, existential angst, the lot. All in a drowsy room on a summer's day. You should write a book, I said. I'll do the illustrations. He'd do a thing with the guitar strings – God knows how he did that, the strange music of buzzing, slow and lazy then speeding up – compulsion towards the Light, oh the tension, round and round, the madness. And the prolonged drama of evil Zubb's loud death throes, whirling frantically on a windowsill after catching a full face-load of the dreaded Death Mist.

Always ended on a cliffhanger.

More! More! Harriet's face, gap-toothed, anxious and sweet.

No! Time for bed.

Never saw either of the girls kill a fly after that.

I put down the pen, make a roll-up and light it, listen to the darkness outside and dare myself outside. Walk a way to where the trees begin to thin and the sky stares down, lie down and think: Fuck me, this is what it's all about. Nights lying transfixed under trees, watching the stars, no human soul near, the sound-filled silence of the wood roaring. Out here I can play. I see the Great Bear, Cassiopeia. Wish I could remember all the others. Johnny knew them all. I castigate myself for naivety, but in those days it was so hard to see the flaw in him. Some special soul. That was my Johnny. God but he could charm. Then.

There faintly goes the Milky Way. I never saw that in town. It seemed to me that it was very important to look at the Milky Way once in a while. I was tired. That fucking man was in my head, I felt sorry for him and I didn't want to be bothered. I wish he wasn't here, too close to the wood, as if he owns it. Looks like he could hit you. Weird, living alone, drinking too much. Got to be careful, you never know.

8

Stiff and freezing cold, he woke up in the early, still dark morning. Jesus Christ. Hammer in his head. Blood. Fuck.

Dan felt his head. His fingers came away damp and rusty with drying blood. A jag of lightning shot through his brain when he sat up. He remembered the wrench, stubbing his toe, falling. Stupid old fool. Idiot. His stomach lurched when he looked around. He had no idea of the time but there was the vaguest hint of the sky lightening above the trees. Why was the cushion from the settee next to him on the step? He gawped stupidly at it, touched it. It was bloody. I didn't bring that out, he thought. Where'd it come from? Or had he? Must have. But I didn't, I didn't, I know I didn't. Fuck, going mad. Creepy. When he stood, his knees were weak. Oh shit, not again, off your stupid head *again*. Must have gone in and got the cushion, forgot. Course not, makes no sense, if he'd gone in to get the cushion, he'd have stayed in, wouldn't he? Couldn't work it out. 'Go to bed, you fool,' he said out loud. Where are those fucking cats when you want them?

★★★

Sleeping, Dan thought he was in a hole in the mud, his face squashed up against soft dirt, but when he jerked awake with a shout he realised it was just the duvet. It smelt funny. Stinky. Holes in the ground. Must have been thinking about that body. He turned over and fell into a mess of half-awake dreaming, a Bambi deer looked in the gate from the woods, the ghost of handless Jenny walked under the trees down by the Dogwood Beck that ran down the narrow valley between Hothemby Fell and the Copcollar. Mist rolled down from the heights and handless Jenny turned into his mother sitting on the bathroom floor looking up at him with big black suffering eyes. There was a thunderstorm, heavy rain pounding the bedroom window, he was running through the woods, gasping and panting, crashing wild, throwing sticks for Billy, a grumpy little black and white runt with a docked tail and a tic in his head and a terrible flatulence problem. Something crept over him, and he woke at last, fully, flailing, with a cat getting settled next to him and the thought of his old dog Billy in his head. Tears shocked him. How he ached this morning, body and soul. Pathetic.

Should get a dog, he thought, reaching for his watch. Getting on for noon.

Old, he thought, drinking his tea on the back step, stiff all over.

'There you are, you bugger,' he said. The big orange cat sat on the step below watching him. One notched ear was bent over, didn't look right. The cat moved suddenly and made a peculiar little sound as if saying, 'What's up?'

'Come, Puss,' he said. 'Come on. C'm'ere.'

Puss purred but would not come.

'Sod you then.' He drained his tea and sat for a while gazing down into the tannin-ringed grimness of the mug. The eternal cowboy, free and cheerful, swirled his lasso on its side, his colours eroding.

He had to go into town. Things to get. Get in and out quick, he thought.

Half-way there, the car started whining, a high thin nag of a sound that made him want to punch it in the mouth. Town was packed. He went to Currys, Wickes, Wilco, bought some paracetamol from Boots and swallowed a couple straight down without water, relishing the horrible taste. Coming out of the market hall he saw Madeleine on the other side of the road, pushing a double buggy. She was with a tall girl who looked like her. Her daughter maybe, no, grand-daughter probably, Christ, the time gone, insane. Madeleine was leaning over the bar of the buggy, googling delightedly at the little things in it with their kicking legs in pastel socks. She didn't see him. He thought about going over and asking her about all that stuff with the police, but didn't. Nothing seemed to have come of it anyway. Those poor legs in pastel socks waiting to walk and run, fuck, all that long life in front of them, poor things. Baby animals, break your heart. No. Leave her to it, all goo goo ga ga. Instead he popped into the Wagon for a pint before heading off. It was nice and dim and quiet in there, the TV was on but the sound was down, the News with words scrolling across the bottom. Earnest politicians. Fuckem. He sat in his corner, wondering about the whine in the car. Hadn't drunk in here in a good while. Used to come in a lot once. College. God, that's an age ago. He was a drinker even then, before he met Madeleine. Runs in families, doesn't it? His mum always drank but discreetly, in that you never saw her doing it, you just noticed the level in the bottle on the shelf going down, and that was just the bottle you saw, there were others hidden away. And his father's people, the Brooms, they were all drinkers too. They bred dogs in Durham. The Brooms, sounds like something in a comic. Rough-faced men in old pictures, faded. Grey fields and terrier dogs. Never saw a one of them for real. Like people in books, but somehow inexplicably linked to him. She didn't get on with them. She didn't get on with many people. Couldn't stand poor old Madeleine. The way she went on about her, and she never hurt a fly, poor girl. *She looks like a horse.* He just sat there. Should have stuck up for her more. *The face of a big horse. She's got that kind of skin that gets threadveins when you get older.* (Actually that had come true.) Madeleine couldn't eat tomatoes or potatoes. *What's she mean, allergies? Everyone's got allergies these days!* God knows what she'd have made of it now with all the gluten and stuff. Good job she's out of it. *I wish you'd never gone to that college,* she used to say. Car mechanics. Madeleine doing sociology. She had ginger hair that grew longer and longer as time passed, and she never wore makeup at all, just occasionally some very pale pink lipstick, the kind a lot of girls wore then.

9

Perhaps I should get a toad. I'd like that. I picked one up once to put it under the hedge where it wouldn't get stomped on by the horses, and it was scared and put its hands over its eyes and I thought oh you sweet poor little thing. It's not that easy to get a toad though. What do you do? Sit in your doorway and wait for one to come. I'm sure I've read about that, old lady alone, lonely, back door, yard, toad. Hop hop. But they don't seem to come to me. I've seen one or two but they seemed OK where they were, it seemed a huge imposition to intrude upon it and carry it off to my lair. In the old days I suppose they'd have called me a witch, ha ha. You can see how all that happened, can't you?

A voice says, 'Lorna?'

The hairs all over my body spring to attention. But it's only the rain, light rain pattering in the leaves. There it goes, this thing under the skin. It's moving again. I put my thumb on it and it pushes against me like a baby under the skin. It's in my elbow. Go away. Stop. But it won't. I think maybe I have some weird disease. It's cold. I get into my sleeping bag, pull the blanket over and close my eyes. I think I fell asleep, because I was waking up suddenly from a dream thinking:

What if it was all true? You did it. What if it was in you? That feeling – of something a long time hidden, down down down under a million gossamer layers, a memory that lies too deep for the daylight.

Here's a pretty rhyme for times like these: the old woman alone at night in her cottage.

And still she sat and still she span
And still she wished for company.

and

In there came some girt girt legs.
With Ai-wee-ee and Ai-wee-ee-ee –
And sat them on the girt girt knees...
With Ai-wee-ee and Ai-wee-ee –
And still she sat and still she span
And still she wished for company...

Until the whole ghoul is there, girt girt head and all, and says –

I've come for YOU!

There's company here in my head anyway. Those days, those days, that place, the view from the window at night when the street lamp shone on the square. Johnny always had people around him, it was his way. All these people all the time, so many many nights, eating, drinking, the talk going on and on and round and round, hanging like smoke in the air, even when they'd all gone. Cosy with the cats, Lemon and her baby, and the plants and the pictures on the wall. Salome with the beautiful curly-haired head of John the Baptist, dripping blood. Arthur Rackham, trees with faces. And later, very late, all of us talking in the big room, the yellow tasselled drapes of the people downstairs, the TV on with the sound down, getting sleepier and sleepier but it was perfectly acceptable to snuggle down into the big bright floor cushions, close your eyes and drift with the words all tumbling about all over each other like puppies, dialectic dignity democracy new start libertarian positivist boujadiste rule of humanism syndicalism pax truth enterprise republican league justice alliance equal positive law representative georgism blabbadyblabbadyblabbady blah... and every now and then, a tolerant backward glance from Maurice would cause Johnny to quietly implode. No words were needed, no change of demeanour. 'That's interesting,' Johnny would say seriously, 'that you should think that,' his voice strained, a peculiar tightness in the set of his jaw.

Rain's setting in, but I'm cosy here. You know, I was lying when I said I wasn't scared? Did I? I did. But it's not true. I'm alone now, but once upon a time it just about killed me. First time they left me alone in the house at night, God knows where they'd gone, no idea. I remember how time changed and I listened to silence, all scrunched up alone in the corner of the settee, biting my nails, hearing footsteps that might have been, far-away laughter that might not have been. Everything flew apart and I dissolved. Shh. Stay still. It was like fainting when I was very small and a door slammed on my thumb, the dent in my thumb, the dent in reality, and my head turning round and round and dropping into a whirling pit, and the fear and surrender, and the space where thought returns. I had to pull myself back, so I jumped up and switched on the radio. It was dark outside, probably only about eight or nine o'clock but it felt like the middle of the night. I heard a song I'd never heard before, 'Bruton Town' sung by Davy Graham, about blood and murder and sadness. Its mood was piercing in my loneliness. I can still sit still, let that feeling back in and let it creep.

Here you are, I say. Fear. Stare me down. Here I am all alone in the wood, just walk out of the bushes, put your head in my doorway and look me in the eye. That silly young doctor, first of many, all those years ago so happy to explain: you made it all yourself, in your mind, being very imaginative, blah blah blah—

How terrifying that was!

Far better if he'd said yes, you saw a ghost, it happens. But he made it real and placed it squarely inside me, and if that's where it arises, there's nothing you can ever do to get away from it. He meant the Tulpa but he didn't have the word for it. The Tulpa is all yours, that deep soul fear from the void that sometimes spreads itself like a smooth sea over the hour of the wolf. But it's got out, broken away, taken form and is running around out there in the world. Here alone in the woods, how does the Tulpa sound, coming silently through the trees? You made it.

God, you're clever! Look what you made! Think about it. I love horror films, I love the bit where she comes out of the telly, where she's jerking and crawling down the stairs, where the little boy's sitting under the table. I feel so sorry for the poor ghosts. Something terrible happened to make them like that, and they want to tell you. They want company.

Come, little Tulpa, through the trees.

10

The whine in the engine had gone, but he got a flat a mile from home, and wouldn't you just know the damn spanner was nowhere to be found. Grumbling, he slammed the door and set off plodding along the lane.

He could tell at once that someone was there because of the way the cats were behaving. That look they got, all eyes. His high-walled garden gave nothing away.

He stood outside the gate and his spine went up like a dog's. If he could have growled, very low, he would've. Standing very still, he gauged the air and listened but he couldn't hear a thing. Cats were mad, everyone knew cats were mad, saw things that weren't there.

He lifted the latch silently, crept in.

There was a horrible woman with long rough white hair and an old black coat in the opposite corner. Putting things in her bag. Eating his raspberries. She looked like a witch, and the scare she gave him was a huge affront.

She hadn't seen him. She was stealing food, mint, sage, a sheaf of big dark green cabbage leaves.

'What are you doing?' he roared.

She jumped as if she'd been stung and stared at him.

Good. Put the fear in her. She looked weird, her eyes were much too big and she had round high-up cheeks and a sunken mouth.

'What are you doing?' he said again, like a stern teacher who's just caught a kid smoking. She said nothing.

Furious, he moved towards her. 'What the *fuck* are you doing in here?'

She tensed, clutching her bag with bony hands and backing towards the gate into the woods, never taking her eyes off him.

'This is private property,' he said, shaking with anger. 'Fuck off right now or I'll call the police. You're stealing.'

'I'm sorry,' she said, 'you can have them all back, I'm sorry, I'll go now,' pulling all the stuff out of her bag and dropping some, her eyes looking all over the place.

She's not all there, he thought. 'Fuck off!' he said, low down in his throat.

'Here.' She thrust an armload of cabbage leaves in his direction.

'Oh for fuck sake, they're no use to me now! Take them and fuck off.'

She walked quickly towards the front gate, down the flagstone path past the ragged mint and the compost heap, and he walked behind her with his most aggressive gait. She lifted the latch to let herself out into the lane. But that's not how she got in, he knew it. She always came the back way. He knew the sound of that particular latch lifting after dark.

'It was just the outer leaves,' she said, glancing back. 'I didn't think you'd notice. Sorry.'

'Fuck off!' he said. 'Now!'

'I'm going!'

Gone.

For a moment, shocked, he scowled at the gate, then went after and stood in the lane, but he couldn't tell which way she'd gone. That was outrageous, that was, just walking in and stealing his produce. What a bloody cheek. 'I'm going to padlock these gates!' he shouted, but she was nowhere in the road so she must have gone into the woods. How did she do that? There's no way in there. Just disappeared. Crept right in through the undergrowth like an animal. Must be living rough. Must be mad lurking about back there in the dark scaring the life out of people.

It was a terrible invasion. Not like kids, kids he was used to.

Look at this gate, he thought, anyone can walk in any time, ridiculous, should have put a padlock on it years ago, and went back in, pulling the gate firmly to, dragging a couple of old planks from the side of the compost heap and shoving them up against it, determining to come back with a padlock. His poor garden. He'd let it go. Now suddenly he was stricken with a deep pride in it and wanted to protect it. And that's another thing, he thought, returning to the yard, what do you think you're doing leaving all those good tools just lying about all over the place? He grabbed what he needed and walked back to the car all unsettled. It didn't take long to change the tyre, and when he got home, he walked round locking everything up, muttering to himself every now and then: 'Unbelievable! Fucking unbefuckinlievable! What a *fucking* cheek!'

It was horrible. Everything felt spoiled. He didn't want to go out and sit on his back steps tonight. He looked for a padlock but couldn't find one, and that night he couldn't get easy, kept wandering about the house picking things up and putting them down, things he'd kept from his three years at sea, a seahorse, a Chinese bottle with a painting on, a mechanical goose from Alexandria, reminders of longings and disturbance, yet still, comforting as an old jumper. Oh God, don't let me get the willies, he thought, turning on the TV and not really watching some daft murder thing. His mind wandered. What if there's more? A whole colony of mad old witches in the wood, the old kind, mad and wild and dangerous. Her face had had a hard cast. Something stealthy and stary about her. Not natural, living alone out there. Allison Gross who lives in yon tower, the ugliest witch in the north country. Where did that come from? His gran's old book. Probably still somewhere about. He remembered the picture in the big poetry book, an old line drawing. The witch actually didn't really look as ugly as all that, she was just very fierce and wild with black hair and huge sinewy arms and a huge muscly neck and thick shoulders, and she was hanging all over a terrified young man in tight Elizabethan hose, who sat on something like an ancient chest, and stretched himself as far away from her as he could possibly get.

Where did things go? He went looking for the book and ended up going through the boxes in the back room with a kind of horrible fascination at the weird remains. Why were they there? Who wanted these old birthday cards?

No! Throw them! Didn't know that was still there. Leeches, hanging on. You can't pull them off and when you do and you've hurled them overboard, you remember them two days later and think, oh God, that old receipt, the spyglass! The ration card. Those cards, the Jack that looked like Mr Punch. At last he found the book half-way down about the sixth box he got to. I'm going to take this whole lot into town and dump them, he thought. The lot. Go by Tring and Lily-hoo. There you go, another thing remembered from his gran, she used to recite it in a mournful voice sometimes, that and 'Barbara Allen' and 'The Spanish Lady'. What was that thing, Tring and Lily-hoo, something like fuck it all, just throw it up and go, take the country lanes, that kind of roving gypsy kind of thing, by Tring and Lily-hoo. Drawing of a tree, silhouette, perfect oak tree. Oh he remembered the page. Lily-hoo, for God's sake. Did it exist? Who called a place Lily-hoo?

And that was another thing. He didn't much read. Madeleine had always been trying to make him read things. He just didn't want to. The real world was too much anyway. Why would you want more? It had been mad, him and her, so different. She was serious and intelligent, cleverer than him. Why did she pick him out? Because it was *her* doing, no two ways about it. There was nothing nice about him. No saving grace. He wasn't nice. Not good-looking or clever or smart. Neither one of them had really been out with anyone till then. He'd been sitting in the foyer waiting for something, seeing one of his tutors or something, and she was sitting along from him on one of the blue chairs and she turned her head to look at him, not smiling, just looking at him in a serious, inquisitive kind of way. And there he was, him, young, poor stupid boy, a big tough body with a tremor inside and her looking at him like that. She was big and solid and sensible-looking, a very restrained kind of girl who didn't mix freely, and she'd just been there for weeks in the general everyday heave of college. Unbelievable. They'd actually talked once about getting married. He always knew it would never happen, but she seemed to think it would at one point. So she can't have been that clever, can she? And her always lording it with her smartness and reading and such and making him feel small.

He took the book into where the murder thing still burbled on from the telly. It was a big thick book and he couldn't find the picture. There was no index and no contents. Tring and Lily-hoo. Perhaps that was in here too. It was the kind of poetry book that had lots of different departments, Old Tales, Lyrical, Humorous, Nature, Mortality etc. Nice pictures. That one. Ha! He clasps the crag. And all these funny half-remembered phrases clamoured from the side alleys of his memory and still he couldn't find that old song. He found Tirra lirra by the river and Is it even so? And the fleas that tease in the high Pyrenees, but not what he was actually looking for. And he didn't find Tring and Lily-hoo either. Maybe it was another book.

An old black matriarch with wild amber eyes, mother of many, graced him with her presence by the fire. Where was the orange one? He looked around, counted four. On a normal night he would've gone out and stood on the back step and called *puss puss puss puss puss* and usually the old ginger tom would come. Might get clawed but he'd come.

The woods had never bothered him, apart from round the old ruin sometimes. But you just stayed away from some places. It was creepy out there, no denying. Things should be the same, they shouldn't change from day to day. Things shouldn't be there that aren't really there. To be out there, now, in the middle of the night, in that dark wood, you'd have to be mad. You're not supposed to say mad any more, someone told him that in the pub. People are stupid. What else were you supposed to call it? He knew what he meant by it. Not the kind of everyday madness everyone had, no, this was something other, something beyond. To be out there on your own in the wood in the middle of the night, that's real insanity, he thought, and it scared him in the same way that the idea of the supernatural did. Anyone could go mad. Fear could do it. It was quiet but always padding around him like a great invisible bear. Sometimes it ached in his throat and stung his eyes and made the very next second of life unbearable. The scary thing: what if the words come by themselves out of nowhere. What if the picture on the screen changes? The murder thing ended and something else came on. He flipped through a few more pages and there she was, Allison Gross who lives in yon tower. There was the sick young boy. My God, it's still there. The TV screamed. What is this? Someone was getting chopped about, blood spewing. Horrible demon face, how do they do that? No! Zap zap. Couldn't watch anything like that.

There he is. Prrr.

'There you are, you bastard,' Dan said.

The cat narrowed his eyes.

'Stealing my produce,' said Dan.

Produce? the cat said. *What are you talking about, produce? A few old cabbage leaves.*

11

Once a week I smarten up, walk to the car park on the Gully road with my bag on wheels, get the bus into town and stock up. Hit the cash machine. My pension goes in, about the third week of every month. I've got a bar of chocolate I'm saving for later. My treat. I eat two a week. I try and spread them out but sometimes when I've been drinking I go all stupid and scoff the lot in half an hour. I've got a bottle of Cava. The cork popped when I opened it and flew up into the leaves. I poured carefully into the smaller of my cups and drank the Cava down very quickly – that made the cooking go better – I was chopping garlic on my board, I'd got the pan hot. It reminds me, teaching Lily how to peel garlic properly, how you bang it with the handle of the knife. Her in her turn, teaching it to Harriet in the kitchen of our old place. I fried mushrooms and tomatoes and chucked in a can of tuna. I wish I could say the mushrooms were wild woodland ones, foraged knowingly, but they were from Aldi. I tried not to think of the man and his garden and not being able to go there any more, kept pushing away the fear that I was discovered; but it went on in my stomach and throat and chest, and it was horrible. God's sake, I thought, didn't I come in here to get away from all this? Worry, for God's sake, the worry you get from people. Thought I was done with all that.

Now that I live here in the wood, I wonder why I was so scared back then in those old days about never having anywhere to live. All of us, everyone we knew, young, with lives back somewhere else, somewhere out of London, living in crappy little rooms, getting out in the early hours for the first papers of the day, combing through the ads, ringing a million numbers that were engaged or said it had just gone or it was too expensive or way off the tube lines, and once or twice getting as far as a viewing and finding yourself standing in a line of awkward couples not really wanting to look at each other. Leaving Lily at Wilf's and sitting for hours in the housing department trying to get on the end of a futile list, and all around us everywhere, empty places, empty and empty and empty every time you walked past, weeks, months, years on end. And my mother saying it's impossible to be homeless if you have family, not realising the impossibility sometimes of going back. Being without a home is worse in the city than in the woods. Comes back to me a scene under an arched bridge, very first cold light of a winter day, wet white frost on the railings dividing the end of the ginnel from a small ornamental garden. A line of long heaped darkness. Sleepers. The sound of engines as the police vans approach. Funny. I never saw it but I feel as if I did. Johnny told me about it. He cried. Such a heart he had for the mistreated. Soft.

When the food was done, I didn't even feel like it. I ate some because I thought I should and let the rest go cold. I don't eat too bad, you know. So far, no real big problems. Not on the material level anyway. What has me attentive is the thing out there, the thing on the edges, the thing not too many really notice or care about but which will make itself felt at the strangest, most unexpected of times. I used to envy the ones who never heard it or saw it or felt it. I don't any more. I just don't want it to take me too far away again. Then again, sometimes I do, just to see what it's like.

Five a.m., the woods all still: still couldn't sleep. Someone knows I'm here. I can't stand that. Got up and walked.

This countryside is lovely and serene yet there's blood and fear and betrayal. Up there by the Long Wights, where they took the old baron to his hideous death. The stones are bloody. Blood draws blood. The stones draw thunder and lightning.

> One fine day in the middle of the night
> Two dead men got up to fight.

That night there was no thunder, just silent lightning, so fast it was like the onset of a migraine, maybe even imagined.
Flash –
Flash –
Flash –
Two mad little cut-out men in a flick-book, neither of them good at it, mitts up like amateurs. Don't hit me, please!
How these two fought!

* * *

I went back to the cat man's place. He hadn't locked the gate, and he'd had plenty of time. But this time I didn't go into his garden, I went straight into his yard. At first I thought he wasn't in, then I saw a face looking at me from the back window. It had large soulful baggy eyes, very startled and naked, and its hair jumbled out on either side of its round, rather magnificently ridiculous face. I smiled at the face and lifted one hand like a chieftain in an old Cowboys and Indians film. How! The face disappeared, and before I could get to the door, it opened and he stood there. He didn't say anything, just glowered. He was big. We were alone. For all I really know, he's a maniac.

'What do *you* want?' he said nastily.

I stood at the bottom of the steps looking up. 'Just wanted to apologise,' I said, looking into his crinkled sad old eyes. There he stood with an outraged air about him and stains down his jumper, thick neck sloping into a barrel chest. Something was wrong with one of his eyes, it watered all the time.

'That's all,' I said. 'I'm sorry. I shouldn't have gone in your garden.'

'No, you shouldn't,' he said fiercely.

'Yes… I know… anyway, sorry…'

I could have left a note instead. This is stupid.

'The thing is,' I pressed on, 'I was wondering if. I mean, I'd appreciate it very much if you didn't say anything to anyone. About me.'

Still nothing. Stupid to ask, of course.

'All your cats,' I said, looking round, trying to make light of things.

'They're not mine,' he said bitterly.

'Oh! Well. I'd better…'

I can revert to normal, just like that. I smiled at his scowl. 'So, is that OK then?' I said. 'You know. Like, that you don't mention anything? About me.'

His face turned harder. Nothing, nothing. He wasn't going to say anything else, so I just turned and walked round the side of the house, towards the lane, thinking, now he'll go and tell everyone in the village about this mad woman who… and my neck got a creeping feeling. He was behind me. I looked back. He was standing at the corner of the house. When I got to the gate he came lumbering down the path so I got out quick and put the gate between us, but it was OK. He just leaned his meaty arms along the top of the gate, didn't meet my eyes, and said, 'Take what you want,' as if he was telling me to fuck off.

'What?'

'Doesn't make any difference. I'll turn a blind eye,' he said, and walked away.

12

There used to be a horse in the field but it's not there any more. First there were three, Little Sid, Pepper and Lady. Then Little Sid's people took him away. Then Lady – what happened to Lady? Then there was just big Pepper, who was a very old horse by the time he'd left for sea, and gone by the time he got back. Now that was a beautiful animal. Got to ride him when he was fifteen. Pepper belonged to Gallinger who had the farm, but he was past his prime and living out long peaceful days, and when Dan had gone up and asked if it was OK, they just said, yeah, sure, here, take his tack, it's hanging up in there. He'd never caught a horse before, never saddled up, but he'd seen it done many a time; never ridden but there was no doubt in his mind he could do it. What a horse. Turned that great head as Dan approached. Sprayed a greeting from loose wet nostrils. Knew him of course, the kid who hangs on the fence, strokes his face if he gets near enough. Stood quiet and willing as the harness slipped over his head, didn't puff out his belly when the girth went round, swung his head round now and then to see how things were getting along. And when finally the big clumsy boy put his foot in the stirrup and hauled himself up and over, being careful not to land too heavily, Pepper shifted his feet expectantly, raised his head and shook his long ginger mane. Dan knew what to do, dug with the heels, gentle, and away they went walking, just ambling along the edge of the long sloping field. After a while they veered towards the centre, and he pulled on the reins. Pepper stopped. He remembered that feeling still sometimes, there'd never been another like it – like when you read in a book or something – his heart soared. That's what it was like: the high blue sky, the musky horse smell, the distant droning of insects.

Sitting out back, pushing midnight, the big drunk sky. Weary. What was it with him? The way these times kept happening, times when a thought of an old horse could get him maudlin. Fuck, that's pathetic. Time to stop. Funny thing, all that. You just have to forget it. All stupid anyway, all that madness and crying and stuff for nothing. We're all still here. It doesn't matter.

The things he hadn't had gathered round him. Too late now. All that. It was awful, sometimes everything that came into his head seemed set on giving him a pang. Things in the paper. Things underfoot. That horse, Pepper, when he rode that horse round and round that field, at one time rising to a glorious canter, there was no fear and nothing gauche, he was strong and graceful, he and the horse together. Of course Pepper, for all his size, was just a soft old thing a baby could have ridden, but still. And he remembered how, when he got home, his mother had already heard from someone about what he'd done and he'd had to pay for it for days.

Couple of days later he ran into Eric in the village.

'Hello there, Dan. Howya doin'? So how's it going?'

What a fucking stupid question.

'OK,' Dan said.

You want the full story? I've got this pain – here – and my fucking knees creak, and this shooting pain that's really scary, sort of simultaneously front and back, but then it goes away again and you feel a fool going all the way down town to see the doc.

'So-so,' he said.

'Aren't we all?' Eric's frizzy grey hair was tied in a ponytail, his small eyes squinted past Dan's shoulder into the low evening sun. 'Have you noticed anything funny around here lately?'

'Funny how?'

'Seen anyone hanging around?' Eric chewed the inside of his cheek and his mouth twisted to one side and made him look like a flounder.

Don't tell anyone about me, she said. Why would he bother?

'Don't think so.'

'No? No one hanging around?'

'Hanging round?'

'Yeah.'

'Why? Should there be?'

'Just Murph saw smoke in the woods. Like a campfire. OK now when it's damp, but it's supposed to be getting hot next week.'

'Campers,' Dan said.

'So long as they're careful.'

'I'll keep an eye out,' said Dan.

★ ★ ★

He could have laid in wait, got the police, whatever, but when he'd thought about actually doing anything, a great torpor had come over him, and now a kind of routine had set in. He didn't see her, but he knew she came and went, once, twice a week, maybe more, who knows, she was stealthy. And once he saw her stalking in the field, acting crazy, gesturing with her arms as if she was talking to someone. When she turned towards him, he hid behind a tree.

That was it.

Poor bugger, he thought.

She always came when he was out, but one day in the very early morning while he was lying on the settee with a headache crowding his eyes, drinking cold tea from his cowboy mug, having not been to bed, he heard the click of the gate and knew she was coming in from the woods. Still creepy, he thought. Creep creep creep when everything's quiet.

She wasn't there long, couple of minutes. Then he heard the click again when she left. It was only just light. He got up, went to the back door and opened it, looked out. She was walking just this side of the trees on the other side of the stone wall. She froze. He didn't know why he'd opened the door. They looked at each other nervously.

'You're up early,' she said.

He didn't say anything for a moment then, 'Thought you might like to know, someone saw your fire. Smoke.'

'Oh,' she said, and her heart sank. She'd been worrying about that.

'What's it like out there?' he said.

'I like it,' she said, and he went back inside, and she walked on, thinking, funny how it all turned out. He's OK. First I thought I fooled him, didn't want him knowing I came from the woods. But of course he knows.

She went back in the evening to listen to the music. Poor man with his old music. Pathetic, aren't we? All living in the past. What's he playing now? Bob Marley and the Wailers. Not his usual. Oh God, doesn't this take me back! Oh but doesn't it? Twenty-four years old, hearing it for the first time.

She didn't know but he could see her from the upstairs window, had been uneasily watching her listening for several minutes. She was wearing a woolly hat, leaning back against the outside wall of the garden, smoking a roll-up with her eyes closed. It was threatening rain. After a while he went down and approached, making sure she heard him as he crossed the yard.

'What the hell are you fucking doing sitting there?' he said. 'Are you mad?'

'I love this,' she said, not opening her eyes. 'This track.'

Stir It Up.

'For Christ's sake!' he muttered, and she opened her eyes and looked up at him. He was a very angry-looking man. She is completely stark staring mad, he thought. 'What are you doing living out there anyway?' he said.

She thought, then said, 'I don't know. Same as anyone else, I suppose.'

'How long you been out there?' he asked, as if she was at the South Pole.

A shrug.

'You drunk or something?' he said, and she gave a short laugh.

Inside, the music changed.

He felt stupid standing there. 'Do you get scared?' he said for something to say.

She thought again. 'Sometimes.'

The first bat jerked across the sky.

'Fancy a drink?' He looked away.

She thought again, and this time it irritated him that she didn't answer immediately after he'd made the effort to speak.

'Yeah,' she said finally, 'wouldn't mind.'

He jerked his head at the back door and she followed him to the back steps. 'Stay here,' he said, and went in for the bottle. Fuck, bad move, he thought, getting down a couple of shot glasses. When he went out she was sitting on the top step, holding out one hand to see if it was raining. 'It's that funny kind of moist weather,' she said, 'when it's so fine you don't know if it's there or not.'

He sat on the other end of the step, and put the bottle of Jameson's and the two glasses between them. Leaning on the door frame, he poured. The more sociable among the cats came round.

She knocked it back pretty quickly.

'Smoke?' He offered a pack of cigarettes, though she'd just put out her roll-up.

'Thanks,' she said, taking one, and they lit up.

'How many cats have you got?' she asked, smoke flowing from her nostrils.

'They're not mine.'

'Of course they are.'

'They're wild,' he said. 'Not mine.'

'Well, you feed them,' she said, 'and they come in and out of your house whenever they want, so they're your cats.'

A few spots of rain appeared on the steps. Ginger Tom came stalking from the woods, mouthing a silent snarl as he passed en route to the old cars out front.

'Cats aren't like that,' he said.

They sat smoking and drinking in silence for five minutes.

'Better go,' she said.

She stood, brushing herself down as if she was wearing fine clothes.

He stood too. 'You want some runner beans?' he asked.

She pulled the hat more firmly down over her ears. 'Can you spare them?'

'I wouldn't ask if I couldn't.'

'OK,' she said.

He went in and she followed, just inside the entryway, and stood in the hall while he pushed through a door on the right. She could hear him in there opening cupboards and poking around. The hall was wide, a staircase running up into darkness. A coat stand was buried under old coats and macs, and there were a few pictures on the dirty white walls, flowers, dogs, birds, old things that looked as if they'd lived there for years. If you lifted one, you'd see clean white underneath. Where the stairs began, the hall turned a corner. A black cat appeared, saw her and turned back.

'Puss,' she said, tiptoeing after. Round the corner was the original front door of the house with a never-opened look, and another door, open, through which the cat skittered. She peered in. Light through an uncurtained window. Boxes, old furniture, dust, cats. An old-fashioned sideboard by her elbow, its surface covered in forgotten envelopes and newspapers, spent matches. Old pine doors, wood. Doors – old barn doors. One with a wooden knob all eaten away by something, one with a rusted metal latch. One four-panel, almost decent.

'What are you doing?' he growled.

Standing there with a load of runner beans wrapped in newspaper like a bunch of flowers, the pointy ends sticking out.

'Nothing,' she said. 'Looking at your cats.'

'Not my cats,' he said again, shoving the clumsy bundle at her. And he walked behind her to the door, like a dog with rising hackles seeing her off the premises.

13

It was dark when I got back. I lit the lamp and made coffee, put the beans into my vegetable box, spread out my coat to dry. Not my cats indeed. Silly man. The rain was soft and constant like people whispering. I was reaching the stage where I could distinguish the small differences between the sound it made running down the rock, the pitter-patter on leaves, the sucking of the earth. I'll fry the runner beans with spring onions and wild garlic. All night the dripping of leaves. *They will not hush, the leaves a-flutter round me, the beech leaves old.* I loved that poem. *I sat on cushioned otter-skin.* Mad in the woods. *Slowly, as I shouting slew and slaughtered – in my most secret spirit*

Most secret.

grew a whirling and a wandering fire –

I fell asleep and dreamed about a green boy who came and stood at the edge of the clearing and smiled at me. He looked terribly ill. He was ragged and his face, gaunt and plague-spotted, had a sickly drowsy leer of a smile, so pretty.

'How could you not remember me?' he said.

Only I wasn't fully asleep. Somewhere between. I've gone off the rails, I thought. And then I was a little bit more awake, and I knew that things were starting to go funny with me again, it was exciting and I started breathing much faster. It was going repeatedly through my mind, I remember, I remember, of course I remember you, how could I ever forget? And a very old dream came back, more than just vivid or bright, a dream of a whole new order more memorable than many a real thing, coming out of the nether and piercing through the little core that I am or was: a boy dying on a bed with a ray of light streaming out of one eye, piercing through the darkness up to infinity. And I realised it was not the first time that I had dreamed this dream, though I wasn't conscious yesterday that I had dreamed this same dream countless times before.

When I woke up in the morning finally, just as the light came creeping in, I felt ancient. Not that I was stiff or tired or anything, at least not more than usual. In fact I was wide awake and alert. It was my soul that felt ancient. My soul, whatever that is. But the grief of the boy's dying was older still, stuck on a moment in time, eternal. I kept thinking about the green boy and the boy with the light in his eye, thinking how funny that they were real before I was born, because they were always there, even before I knew about them. They just were. And how it could be that way back then, when I was – what? – younger than fourteen because it was definitely before I first came to Andwiston that I first dreamed him, that I had woken up one day with this boy inside me. One sleep that had changed everything, and on his behalf a dreadful grief that crashed the world. Could it be so true and real even though nothing had actually happened? It was just me waking up on another ordinary day.

'It's just one of those nightmare things,' my mum had said when I tried to tell her about it.

But it had seemed more than that. It left a sore in my chest, and Johnny made it better.

I got up and lit the lamp. There was the newspaper that the runner beans had come wrapped in, lying open and wrinkled on the ground, and I saw the headline: Human Remains Found In Mudslide Chaos. I read in the paper about a body coming down in a slurry of mud, how all the road was blocked. And all the while I never knew a thing about it. When I read on, I saw that the dead man's age did not match my particular dead man, and that made me wonder. Who is this, come clawing back up through the sad grey mud? My teeth chattered like mad things, and in the back of my mind a little voice said: You really did it, you made yourself into a witch. Witch, what witch? Which old witch, the wicked witch, ding dong she's dead, green face and pointy hat, skinny like a snake, massive-girthed in black, long dangling jugs and toothless mouth, vile filthy hag sitting on your chest, wise woman gathering simples, a basket of herbs, *la belle dame sans merci,* wild-eyed, crowned with the moon, well my pretty, a bite of this apple redder than blood, the chin that meets the nosetip, bentbacked, stick, warts and all, claw-nails, cloven foot.

That's me. A poor sinner if ever I saw one, said I, standing outside myself. I met the bad kind once, eye to cold eye, Phoebe Twist reaching into the freezer for a packet of fish fingers. Ah, Phoebe Twist! A shock of the unseemly at the back of the shop on Holland Park Avenue, her face lavishly coated with whitish powder that had accumulated in the networks of wrinkles running into the hollows of her cheeks, like silt in a delta. A weird little woman, withered and dry, with an anxious pinched face and bright bulging eyes, eyebrows two thin brown lines painted so high up that she looked permanently shocked. Over them a crescent of sore-looking red skin was dotted with scurf; a few wisps of sparse grey hair tried to escape over it from the brim of a dark green beret with a stalk sticking up in the middle. It's her, it's her, I thought, wait till I tell, but then no, why would I tell, why stir all that up again?

This was a rare sighting. The woman was almost a recluse and scarcely ever ventured forth from her white mews house. Everyone hated her. If they didn't hate her they ridiculed her. She was an old has-been now but way back in the thirties she'd been one of those bland actresses with the look of a strait-laced but handsome teacher, the sort no one remembered the name of but who turned up occasionally in one of those rainy Sunday afternoon black and white B movies. Then she'd married a massively rich businessman and gone on to write a whole boatload of thin romantic thrillers, books full of clever clipped prose in which everyone was wealthy apart from a few working-class idiot comic relief walk-ons. No one read them any more. But she was old now, older than old, stinking rich still but long widowed, a bitter nasty creature who lived alone and spent all her time writing peevish letters to the local paper. Three times she ran foul of us. The first time was when she tried to get Hatchet closed down because she thought the cover of a comic book in the window, a cartoon of two men snogging in bed, was obscene. It wasn't just one letter, but three or four, and the stupid paper printed them all. Pretty much amounted to a campaign. Maurice stuck a photo of her on the back of the office door at Hatchet, a black and white one from the jacket of one of her terrible old books. Someone, I think Pedro, whose real name was Peter, with his monotone and mountain man demeanour, had taken the trouble to go out and buy some darts specially to throw at it.

The second time was when someone took a hose and doused the cardboard box sleepers near Shepherd's Bush Market with freezing water very early one morning. Johnny had been on a late night at Hatchet and was walking back to where he'd parked the car and he saw it and when he came back from there he was in a terrible state, You should have seen it, Lor! Horrible. Men in black, well co-ordinated, fucking fascist vigilantes or something, five of them, six maybe, knew what they were doing all right. You could die on a night like this. And it's getting colder.

'I didn't know what to do,' he said, quivering like a wire. 'I went to a phone box but it was fucked. What could I have done? Just me. They'd have kicked the shit out of me. What could I do? They'd have kicked the shit out of me.'

'There wasn't anything you could do,' I said, and he dropped into a chair and sat with his head in his hands. Sometimes he was just a great big hole of self-hatred, a pit of relished failure. It was hard work having to comfort him all the time. Those were the times when I wanted to walk out until he'd got over it, but I had to stay and go over the same ground with him again and again and again, like walking around with a crying baby dribbling on your shoulder, patting him on the back.

The *Standard* covered it. Homeless charities called for an end to harassment and the police denied involvement. Six men and two women were treated in hospital for the effects of hypothermia. One night the paper featured one of the women and one of the men telling their stories of that night and how they came to be sleeping in a cardboard box anyway, and people sent them job offers and encouragement. Phoebe Twist wrote a letter saying most people became homeless because of the choices they'd made. It's not in dispute, she said, that most of them are drug addicts or alcoholics. They've colonised the area in question and the mess they create is appalling – needles, condoms, rotting food. It attracts rats. Many of the homeless beg and use foul language, spit and urinate and worse. People are afraid. There are places they can go to where they could get food and drink and receive assistance, but they don't use them because they don't want to abide by the rules. *I hear no such outpourings of sympathy for those they intimidate*, she wrote, *and I am left to wonder why people seem more concerned about these vagrants than about their own neighbours and in fact all the residents of this area.*

Stupid old cow, we said, that's just what she would say. Talk about privilege, her with the silver spoon sticking out of her gob. Anyway, what's it to her? Hardly ever goes out. 'Christ, what a fucking hateful pile of steaming shit she is,'

Johnny said, throwing the paper on the floor. 'Can just see her in an SS uniform.'

The third time came about six months later.

That whole area in those days was posh and poor all mixed. I think it's just posh now. There were rich places with security guards on, old estates full of graffiti, big houses full of druggies, hundreds of bedsits, clean white mews and sweeping crescents and lovely grand houses. We used to go shopping in Notting Hill and walk down Holland Park Avenue to Shepherd's Bush when Johnny worked at Hatchet. Quite a few famous people lived round there. Tony Benn. Freddie Mercury. Frankie Howerd. Peter Finch. I saw John Cleese once queuing up at the checkout in the same shop where I saw Phoebe Twist getting her fish fingers. So you could bump into a millionaire one minute and a loser like Melvin Morgan the next. Melvin Morgan asked Johnny for spare change on Shepherd's Bush Green one day and Johnny gave him a couple of quid and they talked for a while. Melvin Morgan was looking for someone he thought he knew, only he couldn't remember the address or even the guy's second name or anything at all really apart from the fact that he was pretty certain he lived round here somewhere. And next day or maybe the one after, there it was – Melvin Morgan's pathetic face in the paper, surly and staring with a slight squint, narrow-lipped. Stringy throat sticking up turkey-like from a dirty collar.

'Fuck me, man,' Johnny said, 'I gave him a quid.'

After wandering around for hours, off his head on booze and God know's what, Melvin Morgan had passed out after being sick in the recess of a gateway leading into a pub yard at the side of Phoebe Twist's mews house. Phoebe Twist was on CCTV going out at one o'clock in the morning with a beret on her head, slippers on her feet and a fur coat over her nightie, hauling the watering can she kept for her pot plants. It was a big watering can and she upended its ice-cold contents all over him. In the morning, covered in a thin film of ice and sick, he was dead. It was on the radio, the evening news. Twist said she thought he was a threat, he was mumbling and making peculiar noises. You would, wouldn't you, lost, off your head, drenched in sick in a doorway? She said she'd asked him to leave twice and rung the police, but no one came. The water was meant to wake him up and move him on. Of course she regretted his death. Of course she hadn't waited around to check on him, she was scared of him. Last she'd seen he'd been sitting up. She'd gone straight back to bed and taken a sleeping pill.

I've sometimes wondered: if Melvin Morgan hadn't looked Johnny in the eyes the day before he died, how different would all our lives have been? Of the great archive of social injustice all around us, stretching back in the endless mirrors of infinity and unfolding still into the future, I've wondered why it was that this particular lonely miserable death shook him so to the core. The effect could not have been more harrowing if the man had been his sworn blood brother. We were all appalled, but Johnny grieved. I've searched what little I knew of his life before me to explain it, and all I keep coming back to is the cold at that school in Oxfordshire, the nine-year-old boy getting up in the winter dark and washing in freezing cold water.

'Cold water,' he said, 'cold water. Cold water, my God!'

Over and over again. 'Cold water, cold water, Lor, can you imagine, freezing to death?'

February for God's sake, wind blasting in from Siberia.

'She killed him, Lor. Murdered him sure as if she'd stuck a knife in his gut.'

The story on the page was depressingly familiar. Twenty-five years old, slow, dim, foster homes, young offenders', prison. Booze, speed, H. He'd been staying on his sister's couch in Leeds, she'd kicked him out, he'd come down to London looking for someone he'd been in prison with.

'And that story of hers, full of holes as a colander. And they would back her up, wouldn't they, the police? Where's the report of her phone call then? Liars. All of them.'

14

O ne of my favourite walks is the track along the side of Gallinger's field, takes longer to get home but it's nice. A hedge runs all the way along on the left, full of the most wonderful wild flowers. The trees spread out their long arms, beseeching the arms of the trees on the other side, but they never get near enough to touch. They put livestock in Gallinger's field, sometimes horses, sometimes cattle. It's about two hundred yards across. At the other side there's a narrow track leading away between the back of the farm and the meadows beyond, and there's a wooden bench you can sit on at the start of this track but I never see anyone sitting there, although, very occasionally, I sit there myself. So I was walking along looking across towards the empty bench and watching the sky darken as the wind came up, when I saw the cold boy again. A whole field away, but that's close enough for whatever he is. He was in with the cattle. It's a very high field, and the shapes of the cattle and the boy were clear against the skyline like black cut-outs. The boy faced the back of the farm. I could make hardly anything out about him because he was so dark against the lowering evening sky. I stood very still and watched him for ten minutes or so, then my ears began to ache from the cold and I walked on. For a while I lost sight of him behind the hedge and some trees, but it was no more than half a minute, and by the time I could see the field again he was gone.

I didn't *want* to see him, I swear. I never want these things to happen. But some things you can't stop no matter how much you want to.

Someone whispered. The rising wind. Some witch must have loosed a knot.

Things are talking to me once more. I'm getting that feeling again.

Again I stood still, the wind in the thin upper branches soft but shrill. Don't talk to me in that stupid voice, I said. Don't just talk crap like the dishwasher at Childhallows. It used to go: shoe me mama, shoe me mama shoe me mama…

I got in before dark, made all well, shipshape and watertight. Let it crash and roar above my trees. I got my head down, tired, but I couldn't sleep. When morning came, the woods were whistling. I had slept, I suppose, because there were traces of dreams and there was sleep grit in the inner corners of my eyes. I didn't go out because the rain came thundering, and the howling of the world outside was like a sea. I got my old books out of their box. *The Family of Man*, MOMA 1955. Photographs. Cornell Capa. A traditional fifties Christmas. No, it's not, it's Thanksgiving. A lecture theatre in 1952. I always look at the people in the background. I look right into their faces. There they all are. Those people in the crowd, dead now for many years. All over the world, the eyes, the same, everywhere you look, there we all are. My cards lay scattered, the Queen of Cups, the Knight of Swords, the Devil. Later the rain stopped, though it was still very windy. I went out and my eyes narrowed with the bitter air. I went back to the ruin and leaned my back against a tree. I just watched everything, shoved my hands up my sleeves and watched, sharp as the eye of a stoat. I started feeling sorry for the baron. Poor fucker, I thought. Boiled alive. No, he got off. He was rich, money talks. Swears. He got off with it and lived to a ripe old age with a ghost and a daughter who hated him. Couldn't they just have hanged him, I thought? I mean boiled! For God's sake. Come on. If that's the way it was, I'm glad he got off. Maybe the boy was a pain. Maybe she was a pig. *Oh the baron's fair daughter was walking one day, Oh but her love twas easy won...* or maybe he was just a brute. No daughter, just a brute that killed a servant. *The father to the daughter spake, hey my love and oh my joy...*

Just a touch. A quick dab on the shoulder, the left one, nothing that might not have been a leaf drifting down, anything really. These things never do go away forever.

Ai-weee and ai-weeeeee.

Still weeping after all these years. The ghosts that stick are the sad ones.

15

Justice for Melvin Morgan!
Underneath, smaller: *She must be charged.*

The usual picture of Phoebe Twist, and under it the start of Maurice's article, which continues on the inside page along with the photographs of her house and the wilting flowers in the doorway where Melvin Morgan had died. I was there when Maurice took those pictures. I ran into him near Holland Park tube station and we walked along together in the direction of Shepherd's Bush Green. It was bitterly cold but he kept stopping to take photographs. He wasn't a bad photographer, Maurice. Took some nice pictures of the streets round where we lived. I had one or two till not long ago. We had a framed one on the wall once. He was a very fast walker, always a couple of paces ahead, and I had to keep breaking into little trots to keep up. When he spoke he threw the words back at me over his left shoulder. Suddenly he veered off from the main road, a quick swerve, a jerk of the head for me to go with him, saying, 'Let's get a picture of this cunt's house.' He apologised for saying cunt. 'But it really is the only word for her,' he said. 'Anything else I could say would be worse.' We went and stood in front of Phoebe Twist's house, in the white painted mews full of window boxes. It was on the end of the row with one side facing onto a small cobbled square.

She was so *near*. Not much of a detour.

Sophisticated cooking smells drifted round the immediate area from the backyard of a fancy pub restaurant, invisible behind a high green paling, and *there* was the cursed doorway, locked, a wintry trail of bare clematis running wild over the top of it, set deep into the wall at one side. In spring it would make a sweet shadowy nook, but now it was cold and dreary and the cellophane on a dozen or so shiny-crinkled withered bouquets, two neat rows of them tied up with thin silk ribbons, shook in the wind. I didn't go over to read the notes. Too sad. Maurice acted like a professional, a quick clatter of fast shots, his fingers white and thick and squidged against one another in an ugly way as he held the camera.

'Fucking murderer,' he said, 'she got away with it,' then we went on our way.

One of Hatchet's finest, that was, rushed out by the next day. The article begins with a number of bile-filled quotes from the woman's letters, then gives a brief account of her privileged upbringing, Admiral father, debutante mother, private schools, horses, hunting, all that stuff. 'Consider now the life of Melvin Morgan,' Maurice wrote. 'You will not find here the genteel airs of the country house, the comforts of a fully stocked wine cellar, the whispers of well-oiled doors opening at the nod of a well-connected head.' Melvin Morgan had nothing, Melvin Morgan had never had anything. Now he didn't even have life because a fellow human being had deemed him worthless. No doubt this woman had given ample pious lip service to the poor of the earth in many a sanctimonious hymn and prayer throughout her long and pampered life. Now this *trash*, this *eyesore*, this human being, Melvin Morgan, was dead.

People have to know this stuff.

Because Phoebe Twist had got off scot free. No charges. Money doesn't talk, it swears. Somewhere in all this there was a song to be made, I thought, something along the lines of 'The Lonesome Death of Hattie Carroll'.

'That's what it's like,' said Johnny. 'Nothing ever changes.'

There they all are, the office at the back of Hatchet, Burning Spear on the sound system and the printer running in the room next door. On the wall: *We must devastate the avenues where the wealthy live.*

One of the local rags has interviewed her. She is deeply concerned about local policing. This whole episode has been a dreadful ordeal for her. She'd never intended harm to anyone, had never done so in her entire life, but she no longer felt safe in her own home where she had lived for more than forty years. And there was her smug face staring out from the page, a large photograph, those insulting eyes all bloated with certainty.

Pedro and Barry. Keyvan. Shiv. Els. What was her name, Polly. Others.

'Why do people keep on publishing her? If they just all stopped printing her letters she'd stop writing them.'

'It's not about the letters. Talk about violence, what's that if it's not violence? It's assault, straight up. I mean if that was anybody else.' Disgusted, Barry the ferret, tossing the paper over to someone else.

The pamphlet had just gone out and Shiv was a bit worried. 'You know,' she said, rolling tobacco in the saggy red sofa, 'you shouldn't really print a picture of her house. What if someone throws a fucking bomb through her window or something?'

'We had to put this out,' Maurice proudly held up his pamphlet as if he was being photographed for an award. 'Letters are one thing, but this here what she's done is bodily harm leading to death. I mean, that is extreme. Anyway, we didn't identify the house—'

'Oh come on,' said Shiv, 'people will know.'

'—and I mean, even if we had, it's not exactly a secret, is it? Everyone knows she lives there. For fuck sake, she even puts the name of the street on some of her letters, I'm sure she does – oh no no, not at all, put out the word, she wants attention, she can have it.'

'Can't say I'd cry an awful lot.' Els. Arched eyebrows, standing up and soaring over everyone else. Always felt like a Munchkin next to her.

'Won't make a difference anyway.' Johnny appeared to be in pain. 'It'll all be forgotten next week.'

Phoebe Twist was becoming Johnny's obsession.

'Serve the old cow right,' said Barry.

'Not a bomb.' Keyvan, striding about like he did, jumping on and off the furniture as if he had worms. 'Dogshit yeah. Through the letterbox. Dogshit I'm OK with. Not a bomb though.'

'You know what?' said Johnny coolly. 'I wouldn't give a fuck.'

'Yes, you would.' That was me.

'It wouldn't be murder, it would be assassination.'

'Cut it out.' Maurice swung his legs up onto the desk, crossing them at the ankle and lying back in his swivel chair. The soles of his Doc Martens were splodged with wads of grey chewing gum. 'You want to go and join Barry's lot if that's how you feel. It's not for here.'

Barry the ferret laughed. He was only moonlighting here.

'You see that?' said Keyvan. 'A parasitical underbelly.'

'And what does that sound like?' Pedro got up to change the music.

'That's horrible.'

'It's all horrible. There is so much horribleness out there. This whole world is fucked up.'

'Vermin,' said what's her name Polly. I can't even remember what she looked like. Her head bowed as she buttoned herself up to the chin. 'That's all they are to them.'

'See anyone else getting away with it.'

Shiv agreed, thumbing her lighter. 'Say it was anyone like us,' she said. 'I still say ignore her. Even this,' waving another copy of the pamphlet, 'you're just giving her more publicity. Ignore. Treat with contempt.'

In truth, the people of Hatchet were more into good works and rhetoric than throwing the little streets upon the great. Mostly.

Maurice sat forward and put a hand on Johnny's arm – strangely, I thought, an awkward moment, and Johnny flinched away.

'Yes, I'm angry,' he said, 'I'm fucking furious. So should everyone be.'

'You're emotional,' Maurice said, 'that's not the same. I'm actually probably much more angry than you are, but I'm not as emotional.'

The way Johnny simmered, taking it as a rebuke. God forbid the master should disapprove. I could kick him. Yes, Maurice. No, Maurice. Do you think so, Maurice? You know, I said once, you're allowed to disagree with him. I know! he said angrily, and his anger was so cold. But the smallest thing, he gets mortified. Maurice has a 2:1 from Exeter and Johnny dropped out of Somewhere-or-other. Who cares? *He* did, for all that he said school was a load of crap and we should have home-schooled Lily, we should be home-schooling Harriet. Fine, but *he* wouldn't do it. Churning out units, he said. Where was the aspiration? The pursuit of greatness unbeholden to the leaden hammering in of Gradgrind facts? Teacher, leave them kids alone, *hey* teacher – leave them kids alone! They're brainwashing you in the womb, he said, by the time you're born you're already fucked. Born into slavery. No choice.

Off they go then about regressive tolerance, a sedate duel.

'We should go,' I said. We were picking up Lily and Harry from Wilf's.

The traffic was awful, the sky like lumpy potatoes.

'Are you all right?' I said.

Of course he wasn't.

'You know,' he stared moodily into the traffic ahead, 'nothing's going to happen. Not a thing. All this deadline stuff, all this talk, all this must publish stuff, it all means nothing. Futile. All of it. Nothing's going to happen. Nothing ever does.'

'What do you want to happen?' I said.

Our voices were carefully expressionless, and the moment was peculiar and loaded for no discernible reason. He was quiet for so long I thought he wasn't going to answer, then he said, 'I want her treated like everyone else, that's all. I want her arrested and tried in a court of law.'

I looked away into the traffic and remembered that moment in the shop when I'd seen Phoebe Twist by the frozen foods and looked into her nasty cold eyes, and I wondered if I could shoot her. Of course not. *Could* not. We turned into Wilf's street, and there was his motorbike covered in tarpaulin and Lily on the steps all bundled up against the cold with her big white fluffy scarf, talking to a large thickset lad with ruddy cheeks. 'Hello, old people,' she said as I got out of the car, and ran back inside leaving the poor boy standing scratching his cropped brown hair awkwardly in the tiny patch of earth in front of the house. Avoiding my eyes as I passed, he swung one leg across the low fence, crossed over onto next door's step and lurched into a dim hall. First time I ever saw Terry.

'Who was that then?' I asked in the car on the way home.

'Who?' Yawning in the back seat with Harriet leaning against her earnestly humming the *Postman Pat* theme tune.

'That boy you were talking to.'

'Oh, that was Terry.'

'Who's Terry?'

'Dunno.' She looked out of the window. 'He's doing the windows next door with his uncle.'

That night, after the girls had gone to bed, Johnny made a fist and hit himself hard in the middle of his chest. 'From now on,' he said, 'I'm not going to feel.'

16

The storms abated, though they were set for a return next week. It was fine but breezy for Fair Day in the big field. All the pretty horses, corralled by the wood's edge. They'd asked Dan to help with putting up tents and waving people's cars to the right spot in the field. Through with the work, such as it was, he got his free crap pale ale in a flimsy plastic container and wandered vaguely about. Nothing much worth seeing apart from the races, such as they were, and they weren't till five. The horses grazed and twitched their skin in the corral. He walked over and leaned on the gate. A fat little Thelwell pony ambled over to say hello.

'Hello, Fatty,' Dan said, and tickled her behind the right ear.

She blew hot nostril air at him, faintly snorting, and he remembered Pepper. A couple of boys were playing music on a raised platform, one had a banjo. I should have learned to play an instrument, he thought. The smell of frying onions drifted over from the food stalls.

'Come on, come on there,' he said to the horse.

'Dan!'

It was Madeleine with her husband, a baldy bloke with glasses whose name he always forgot, and a load of kids, two rowdy boys and a sulky girl who stood looking away over her shoulder with her arms folded.

'Hello,' Dan said.

'It's a bit nippy, isn't it?' she said brightly.

'Well if you want to buy it, buy it,' her husband was saying to the girl, 'but don't make a big deal of it.'

The girl ignored him.

'Dan,' Madeleine said, 'have you noticed anyone hanging round the woods?'

She had on one of those big long scarf things, knotted all fancy, draped this way and that, a mere touch of pale brown makeup under her pale blue eyes.

'There's always people hanging round the woods,' he said.

The kids all had Madeleine's hair, not that you'd know it to look at her now with its wild and faded glory smartly pulled back and bundled up into a frazzled bun on the nape of her neck. Back then, she'd been plainer in a way, the way she dressed anyway, subdued, not flaunting herself or ever trying to be sexy, even though she could have. She just wasn't like that. Now look at these flamboyant scarves, the bright layers of ethnic beads.

'No, not walkers,' she said, her eyes straying to the two boys scrambling about on the fence trying to reach the horse's nose. 'Someone living rough.'

'Not that I've noticed,' said Dan. Oh well, he thought, she's rumbled. Well, it's not my fault, I never said a word.

The husband and the girl wrangled.

'You're just angling for more money,' the husband said. 'Not cool, Fliss, not cool at all.'

'It's my Hothemby family,' said Madeleine, pushing back some frail stray hairs, 'their kids play in the woods. Something got them all freaked out. You know what kids are. They're on about ghosts and so on.' She smiled. 'But I think someone might be living rough and, I don't know, they might need help or something. So I wondered if you'd—'

'Not *seen* anything,' he said.

It was sort of true, he hadn't seen the woman in weeks.

'Oh well,' said Madeleine, 'most probably just kids mucking about.' All smiles and jolly crinkling eyes, and the warm throaty voice, must have been terribly reassuring to her clients or whatever you called them. 'We shall see,' she said.

His mother's spiteful voice: *like a horse; face of a big horse.*

And he'd said nothing.

Don't upset Mum.

Yes she was. She was spiteful.

The husband came up and skulked near her shoulder. Gary? Neil?

'She's after more money,' he said, smiling broadly at Dan. 'Hi, Dan.'

Dan nodded.

'What a surprise,' said Madeleine.

The girl walked away in the direction of the food stalls.

'We're on duty,' the husband said, 'for our sins. Got any change, love?'

'Oh, not again,' said Madeleine, putting her hand down into the deep straw bag she carried, 'you're not giving in to her, are you?'

'Course not. I'm getting a bun.'

She gave him a fiver and he strolled away.

'I can't stand the queues,' she said, gazing after him, 'look at them, it's always like that.' He looked at her, somehow worried, not knowing why. 'Did you know,' she said, 'I got let down by the *Examiner*?'

'Did you?'

'I did,' she said. 'They wanted me to write a piece about when I gave that man a lift because it was around the time when that body was found, so I worked really hard at it, you know – it was like a local reader's story sort of thing – they said they wanted it by Wednesday morning so I worked really hard to get it to them on time, and then you know what? Can you believe? They went and pulled it at the last minute because of some stupid thing about brass bands.'

'Ha,' he said, smiling faintly. 'Did they pay you?'

'No, they did not. They weren't paying me anything anyway.'

He opened a pack of cigarettes, offered. She shook her head then said, 'Oh, go on then.'

'Anyway,' he said, 'that was ages ago. It's not news any more.'

'I know.'

He lit her cigarette and she smoked awkwardly. 'I suppose it wasn't important. No one took any notice of it even when I first told the police. They made me feel a bit of a fool. I just thought it might be important, you never know, with this happening round about the same time as the body, you know, and this man with blood on his face...'

The boys got off the fence. 'Nan,' said one, peering up at her, 'where's Ellie?'

'Somewhere over there,' she said vaguely.

'You think it had something to do with the body?' said Dan.

'Oh, probably not,' she said breezily, 'I just got a bit fixated on it for a while.' She hoisted the bag, adjusted her scarf. 'That's it then, boys,' she said briskly, 'come on now, let's go to the race track and see what's happening.'

The other boy hurled himself backwards off the gate. She caught him under the arms, swung him around. 'It was funny really,' she said, deftly setting him on his feet, 'I never give lifts to lone men, you know, not as a rule. But this one I felt sorry for. I just got a feeling he was OK. But then when he got in I saw the blood on his face and I thought, whoops!'

'Where was the blood?' he asked.

'It was on his face. It was in his hairline by the looks of it and it looked as if it had trickled down past the corner of his eye and down the side of his face and dried. He might not even have been aware of it.'

'Where'd you pick him up?'

'It was all in the paper,' she said. 'Didn't you see it?'

'Probably. Can't remember the details.'

'Where the road comes down from the Wights. He said he'd been to see the stones. He thought they were wonderful. And I dropped him the other side of the village. Do you know?' She grabbed the lads, one on either side. 'I could swear it'll rain later.'

That night, Saturday night. He walked through the kitchen singing: *Saturday night at the movies, who cares what picture you see?*

Face of a horse. Poor Madeleine. Never harmed a soul. All she ever wanted to do was help. His mum could be a real cow.

Weeks. God knows. Poor old Mum. She couldn't help it.

The way she used to walk about, after his gran died, that look on her face. Big wide suffering eyes and a pendulous lower lip. Even when you couldn't see her, you'd hear her, that soft martyred cough in another room, a small stern clearing of the throat that served no other purpose than to say: I'm not happy, it's your fault. She looked at him like the Magdalen, Cassandra, Joan of Arc. Such suffering passion. He shouldn't have had to deal with all that. Obvious now.

God knows it can't *all* have been bad, how could it? The thought of how she'd feel to see him like this, all her love and expectations, every hope, to end up in him, here.

'Sorry, Ma,' he said, and laughed.

He stuck a pie in the microwave, ate it, poured a tot and turned on the telly. He wanted a film. Netflix. He'd seen all the good ones. Pete Wheeler's kid knew how to get any film you wanted off the internet, God knows how, God knows if it was legal. The boy was a genius. Just say the film you fancied and he'd get it for you, just like that. He didn't know what he wanted to watch, kept starting things and getting bored. He imagined Madeleine's house, all trendy and correct. It would be something like that house in *Outnumbered* only tidier. Ended up watching some courtroom thing and losing track because his mind wasn't there. He kept thinking about how gross and embarrassing his mum had been, those horrible dinners. It wasn't fair.

She could say, 'Well, *you* look nice, Madeleine,' and make it sound like an insult.

'How long have you been wearing your hair like that?' Just that. Nothing more.

'Oh, I don't know!' says Madeleine, quiet, a bit awkward. 'It's always been like this,' and then a silly laugh. 'I've never been able to do a thing with it.'

Then his mum would give that tiny snort of a laugh and look away with a sly almost-smile.

And even later, when there'd been that ridiculous marriage talk (he could hardly believe it even now) and she'd got the idea it might actually happen, she'd still been horrible to Madeleine, even when she was freaking her out with all that stupid crap about them both coming to live here with her and having a baby, started talking about where it could sleep, in your gran's old room, till it all made him feel sick. The whole idea of it, that horrible room full of old age and death, the chaise longue and those heavy dusty curtains, the slightly off smell of old ladies who never leave their rooms.

'Here we are, a little sherry. Madeleine? Go on.'

Skipping out for the cake.

Madeleine's face, upset but holding it in. Whispering fiercely. 'She's not serious, is she? Can't you say something to her? I mean, we're not even...'

'Yeah, I will, I will. Later.'

Bloody hopeless.

'It just wouldn't work, Mum.'

'This is a big house, Danny.'

'It doesn't matter! It's just not a good idea. People don't live with their parents when they get married.'

'Yes they do!' She started listing examples then started crying. 'I can't live on my own, you know.' Her eyes filling up with heroic tears. 'I can't help it, Dan-Dan, I just can't. I'm sensitive. And anyway, what about you? I'm thinking about what's best for you, after all.'

'Me? Best for me?' he'd said. 'What are you talking about?'

'Well, think about it! You're young. What if things don't work out and you're somewhere far away all on your own?'

'Oh, for God's sake, Mother, if you could hear yourself. You sound crazy.'

'Oh, thank you! That's nice! Oh, that's a really nice thing to say to me!'

'For fuck's sake!' Into his room. Slam the door. Oh, he was the tough one then!

Should have just gone then, made her get used to it.

17

I had to move.

Shame but it was necessary. Kids hanging round, couple of little toughies. Nearly came face to face with them coming back from town one day. I was off the path, wading through the marshy bit, and there they were, bashing the bushes with their sticks. So I got down low. Got myself all wet hiding, and I think they heard me because they went all quiet, and when I peeked out, there they were, still as statues, listening. Boys with little scared faces, holding their sticks like weapons. A squirrel jumped from one tree to the next, shaking the branches over their heads, and they crashed away like panicked baby elephants.

Highly unlikely they'd ever get near my place, but you can't be too careful. I spent the next few days getting my Bower Number Two ready. I'd had it sussed out for a while. I'd decided I'd always keep at least one other little bolthole ready. I could have two or three. Then I could just keep moving about whenever I wanted to.

My new place is nicer than the old one in some ways – higher up, airier. More of the light gets through, and I'm further up the stream. It's bigger. I had to get a new tarpaulin from town, but I'm all snug again now. And I didn't leave a trace back there. It's like when you move in a town really, just the same: you have to get used to all the new landmarks, the shapes of trees, particular plants, murky patches. It's all falling into place now. Ah here we are: dead fox gully, toadstools, fernyfronds, big bear rock.

When the rain returned I found it to be snug and almost watertight. A little more work and it would be perfect. It's essential that I hone my needlework skills, which were never up to much. Two nights of gentle rain, pleasant enough, but on the third day the wind got up again, and again it spoke in voices, which eventually separated and became two voices arguing back and forth till finally they were screaming at one another. Rain came down again and there was no doing anything with the day, till the next darkness fell, and with it rose the next storm, madder, more spiteful than the last.

A horrible night, trees falling.

The weather these days, thought Dan. Not normal, is it? He took the flashlight and went and stood at the edge of the wood. He even went a little way along the path, shone the light and shouted through the sound of the wind in the trees.

Next day he went looking but had no idea where she was holed up. A few trees were down, their exposed roots raw and stark, writhing at air. The woman's mad, he thought. This is a wild wood. It's not like some little kiddie play area, this is an old wild wood. He hadn't minded for a while, it was even kind of interesting, but now the weather was turning he was starting to worry a bit. What if she was dead in there?

Oh well, he thought, that was *her* lookout.

It rained all that day and all the next.

There but for the grace, he thought. He could imagine sometimes how he could have quite easily gone off the rails. Sometimes he thought he had, when he was doing the whole middle-of-the-night fear thing, or waking up from a knocked-out drink-sleep. But the bottle kept him handy. There was no way he was ever going to do without it.

Couldn't even remember how long he'd been sitting there holding this bottle neck. Fancy ending up like this, he thought. There's that orange cat again. There was about an inch left in the bottle. He wasn't sure of the time. It was all crashing about out there, and the buckets on the landing were filling. He should go and empty them. The worst night yet. That's why the cats have all come in, look at them, taking over. Think they own the place. Christ! Thor's bolt. Something came down outside. He should go and look. He groaned getting into his wellies, dragged on his waterproof, grabbed the torch and stomped out. Puddles glittered all across the yard. Slippery leaves waved. 'Fuck's sake,' he said, hunching his way across the yard. The hives were safe, nothing amiss that he could see. He went round the front. Aha. The bonnet had flown off his gran's old car. Right into the wall – that must have been the noise.

He got back in and built up the fire good and high. Christ, he thought, that woman in the wood. She'll be dead. No one could live out there in this.

Bit grim. Dead in there and nobody knowing. Like the body all over again.

Well, that's her silly lookout, isn't it?

He swore roundly putting the guard on the fire which was blazing up nicely, getting back into his freezing wellies and his wet stuff, hurling himself out into the madness once more, swore himself into the edge of the wood and walked a little way towards the ruin. He was pretty certain that was her patch. He thought she might have mentioned a rock. He could think of a couple, big things near water. 'Hello-o-o!' he shouted. She'd never hear that.

This was stupid but at least when she turned up dead he could say he tried. The flashlight was lurid, the dark terrifying. Any minute there'd be something horrible, a face or something. The wood thrashed its long arms, chattering like a host of spirits, and he cursed the woman. Not his responsibility. The size of this fucking wood, needle in a haystack, crazy. 'Hello-o-o-o –'

He stood still, dripping, turned the light off for a moment just to see what it was like and found it oddly better. Fumbling on for a while like this he clonked his head on a branch, and when he flicked the light back on and shone it round, realised he didn't know which direction he was facing.

'Hell-o-o-o!' he cried. 'Hell-o-o-o-o-o –'

I thought, what the fuck, is it a wild boar or something? What is it? On a night like this? I couldn't sleep because of the storm, I was reading, then all of a sudden this awful bellowing, just vaguely audible under the ai-weeeee and ai-weeeeeeeeee… and I thought it might be a deer or a cow that was stuck, so I poked my head out of the flap to hear better, but it made no difference. It stopped and started and then came closer, and I thought, that's a voice. Someone's in trouble. Oh go away please, go away, but I was all dressed anyway, so I had to put my boots on and stick a tarp over my head and go out with my torch, not far. There was a light bouncing around, more powerful than mine. I went towards it and the voice roared again. Oh no, I thought, then there was a great flash far above in the sky, and a terrible rushing swept through the wood; then a sound like a monster sighing, and a detonation. Another.

Trees, falling, one so close I felt it in the earth under my feet.

The light bobbed towards me. I saw a big bewildered face staring out of a hood, a fierce kind of a stare as if someone had just said something very shocking, or a portal into the ultimate had just opened up before his eyes. The cat man.

'This way!' he yelled, and he grabbed my arm.

'What?'

'Come *on*!'

There was such urgency that I just went with him. He was like Lassie leading me to the injured child. But he was hopeless, blundering about like a bear, and I realised we were going deeper and deeper into the wood.

'Where are we going?' I shouted.

'My house!' he yelled.

'Stop!'

He pulled me.

'Stop! Stop!'

He stopped.

'It's that way,' I said, and we turned round.

There was a huge roaring fire, and all these cats sitting in front of it out of the storm.

'Sit there!' he said, pointing to the settee.

It was as if he was telling me off for something and I didn't know what I'd done or why I was here. 'What?' I said.

He got out of his wellies, scowling down. His hair was on end.

'Stay on there,' he said. 'Don't go messing about with anything.'

'What do you mean?' I said. 'Why am I here?'

He went out. I squeezed onto the end of the settee, leaving a safe distance between me and a big spiky tabby that didn't look too friendly. The cat ignored me. Cat man shambled back in and tossed me a blanket. 'For Christ's sake,' he said, 'wait out the storm. That's no night to be out. Keep an eye on the fire. Keep the guard on.'

With that, he stomped off upstairs and turned off all the lights. A door closed.

I didn't even hear him moving about upstairs, just silence.

I felt uneasy, scared. Of him. He was grim, unpredictable. What if he tried anything on? Stay on there? Don't go messing about with anything? As if I just barged in on *him*. I was kidnapped. Doesn't want me poking around, fair enough, but surely I'm allowed to get myself a drink of water? What's he on about? I could just go straight back home now. But the fire and the cats – but is he OK? I mean, is he all there? The tarp had kept me pretty dry but I was freezing and it took a while to thaw out. I listened for a long time but there was no sound of movement. The coffee table had a patina of round overlapping coffee circles in every shade of brown. On it stood a dead candle without a wick, a mega box of matches, a Coney Island coaster and a lump of pitted black rock the size of a misshapen tennis ball. I gave him another half hour then sneaked over to the sparse, cold, strictly functional kitchen. I rinsed a mug from the draining board, a big brown-stained thing with a fifties-style cowboy twirling a yellow lasso on its side, tried to clean up the inside a bit but the staining was indelible. The water was tepid because I didn't leave the tap running long enough so as not to make a noise. I'd have loved a cup of tea but I couldn't risk the noise of that either, kettles and all and having to look for a spoon, so I stood in the hall drinking tepid water and feeling the stone cold radiators for qualms of heat. The house was freezing except for where the fire was. I wanted to have another look at the room with all the old stuff I'd seen before. I tiptoed to the back of the house, the door was ajar, and I found the light straight away. The switch clicked loudly. I froze. The big bad wolf did not stir. I opened a drawer in a sideboard and saw again the little kid gloves, the spindly gilt brooch and the old binoculars. The drawer underneath held a huge fat brown envelope full of snapshots, black and white and colour. Warily, I withdrew a handful. That woman must be his mother. My God, is that him, surely not. Children. Who? A Present From Whitby. And here, I think it's him, something of the look of him there only all smoothed out and fresh? Not smiling, not looking at the camera, young, nice-looking, surely not, because he isn't now. The jacket faded to grey. Two men on a ship, in uniform. Mountains. The sea. The sea. Snowy plains with far mountains. Him? Maybe. At the bottom of the sideboard, a great brown heavy thing with rounded sides that gave an elephantine impression, was a little door that opened onto a peculiar segmented storage area full of ancient records in scruffy old sleeves, LPs, Johnny Mathis, Jim Reeves, Bobby Darin, Roger Miller, The New Seekers, Rockin rollin ridin all along the bay, I said Hello Mary-Lou, goodbye heart, put your sweet lips a little closer to the foam.

That's what I thought it was.

Put your sweet lips a little closer to the phone.

But for years I thought it was *closer to the foam.* I was quite young and it seemed quite logical really, she was drinking a foamy drink, a milkshake with a foamy top or something, creamola foam, and they were sitting in some mythical thing, a soda bar, in mythical America. I listened to it one night in town, in a little snack bar where I sat with my first boyfriend, the woody smell of his hair, lights outside the window and a wide street, a young girl with thin dirty bare legs sitting alone at one of the tables. Two men in suits came in and sat down with her. One of them was tall and plump and wore yellow socks. He bought her a coffee. The dirt encrusted round her ankles was speckled black.

Poor girl.

I was dying for a wee, but if I went up to the bathroom he might wake. I could go out in the yard but then the back door would make a noise. I sneaked upstairs and listened carefully behind the first closed door. Mustn't get the wrong room. He was in there, I heard his deep breathing heading towards being a snore. I crept along the landing. There were three other doors, all closed. The first one I opened slowly and silently onto blackness, and felt for the light switch. Click. Not loud. A spacious room appeared, empty apart from a very old and worn green chaise longue peculiarly placed in the middle as if on display, a ruined chair collapsed in the middle by the curtainless window, and the curtains themselves piled in a heap next to it, a ripped and frayed bundle with the lining stained brown. The floorboards were bare and a lone bulb hung down in the middle of a high, ornate ceiling.

I wonder if there's a psycho thing going on here, I thought. Perhaps he'll come downstairs in the middle of the night dressed as his mother.

Suddenly I was very cold and ridiculously tired, and unaccountably close to tears.

I found the stark, unloved bathroom, peed quietly and worried about pulling the chain. But I had to, the water was all yellow. Afterwards I waited a couple of minutes but there was no sound from anywhere in the house, so I hurried back down to the fire, and the fire was so beautiful and the cats so asleep, and the night had entered into a stillness made out of chaos, but out there, all out there, not here with me. 'Shove up, you,' I said to the big cat, which spat and sprang to the floor. I pulled the blanket over myself, closed my eyes and listened to the fire burn and the storm rage.

I woke up and the fire had burned down a lot but was still good. The wind moaned, a low worrisome tone. The door into the hall was closed, though I was sure I'd left it open, and someone was standing hesitant on the other side of the door. He's there. He knows I'm in here alone. He's very drunk. But then there was silence for so long that I decided I'd imagined it and went back to sleep. When I woke up again the man was over there, sitting in the armchair, drinking whisky straight out of the bottle. I don't know how long he'd been there.

'So where's your family?' he asked, as if we were continuing a conversation. Perhaps we were.

'I'm sorry,' I said. 'I don't really think that's any of your business. Where's yours?'

It was unreal. The only light came from the dying fire.

'What will you do in winter?' he said, still angry.

I said nothing. I had no idea what I was doing there.

'That's no way to live,' he said.

'Really?' I laughed.

'Have you not got anywhere else to go?'

He put down the bottle, got down on his knees on the hearth and, shoving his hand with a great rattling into an old black coal scuttle, started building up the fire. His big dirty hands arranged the coals neatly and slowly in spite of the small flames that began whispering up around his fingers. I sat up.

'What's this rock?' I asked him.

'Lava,' he said. 'It's from Iceland.'

I picked it up.

'It's very light,' I said, becoming aware of odd purrings, muffled squeakings from a big green armchair to the right of the fireplace.

'Feels like the middle of the night,' I said. 'What's the time? What a strange night!'

'Getting on for four.' He sat back down, drank, swilled the liquor round his mouth.

'I thought you'd gone to bed,' I said.

'I did.'

'Can I have some of that?' I indicated the bottle.

He went out without a word and returned with a glass. Poured.

'Where's your family?' he asked, swiping the outer edge of his watery left eye with his paw. 'Anyone?'

'We're not in touch.'

He handed me the glass. 'Do they know you're living rough?'

This was just nosy.

'I was all right,' I said. 'You didn't have to come looking for me but thank you for worrying about me.'

'I wasn't worrying,' he said. The noises from the green chair increased. The purring became thunderous. A great slurping lick-lick-licking almost drowned out the mewing undertone.

'Someone's having kittens,' I said, and he groaned.

'Oh Christ,' he said, 'not another lot.'

I downed my whisky and fell asleep again, and when I woke up he'd gone. The cat and her new kittens still squirmed and purred and licked, and the fire was just a smouldering pit. The storm was abating, but a cacophonous dripping had taken over. I got up fast, grabbed all my things and wrapped up well, and was home before half past six.

★ ★ ★

The storms were past, and a period of fine dry weather followed.

Well, that's OK, he thought. But if she was still there in winter he was going to have to tell someone. He'd got a bead on her now. While she was asleep he'd gone through her coat. It was a long thick tweedy thing with deep pockets. He found a purse, a really old worn-out leather one with a bit of colour just filtering through here and there. She had a Visa card and some store loyalty cards and loads of bits of paper all crammed in everywhere. She had a bit of silver and some coppers and a five pound note very neatly and meticulously folded like a work of art. And a couple of cheaply developed colour photographs, finely creased all over like ancient faces. Two girls. Big grins in a garden. A pretty girl, looked like Caribbean blood, maybe even Polynesian. A merry-looking girl, any age from twelve to twenty, he could never tell. He felt bad looking at them so he shoved them back in and closed the purse guiltily. A bus pass. Picture. Her but different. So she's Lorna Gilder. Lorna Gilder. Seemed funny her actually having a name. And there was a little book with numbers and addresses in it. He scanned it eagerly. A dozen or so names. One of them was Harriet Gilder. Aha! Could be a daughter or something, a niece. Even a sister. Someone might want to know. Not fair on them. So he wrote down Harriet Gilder's address and email and phone, it was all there, written in elegant longhand in black ink. Quink. He really ought to let this daughter know.

Anyway, if she was fool enough to try and go through the winter in there, he had a number to call. Or give it to Madeleine, someone who knows what to do in these cases. Not his responsibility anyway. He wished he'd never gone out that night, she was all right, she wasn't dying or anything, she was doing OK. Just couldn't get his head round it, the horrible dark of the wood, the wetness, the simple inaccessibility. Might as well be on top of a rock somewhere in the sea far west of the Outer Hebrides.

18

I dreamed I was disposing of your body.

Night, a little drizzly, damp on the air, settling on me. I was driving very slowly down a narrow track in the countryside between high hedges. You were in the back, on the floor. The feeling was solemn but I had hardened myself and was outwardly calm. The path ended where a wide gate blocked the way into a field. I stopped the car, got out, undid the rope holding the gate and pushed it open. The field was muddy, the sky blotched and thick with cloud.

And then I realised how crazy this was. Look at me, my stick arms. I could never dig a hole big enough to bury you deep, not if I dug all night. Even though the ground was soft. I hadn't thought this through.

The sky was heavy. My heart too. The world was heavy.

When I woke up it was in my head, a country tune. I turned it into a country song and went about singing it all day.

Great trees had been uprooted. Walking in the aftermath was strangely painful, the sight of ripped-out roots provoking thoughts of toothache. I stood looking round and the drizzle turned to soft rain. Poor wood. Seen it before, said the wood, with a little nervous blasé shrug. The smell of it all, green and rank; if you were painting it you'd want the blackest green you could get. Talk about aromatherapy. Just stand here and breathe in. It's like being under the sea. Lily didn't like these woods. If you stood still, she said, they closed in on you. She'd think I was mad. Quite the claustrophobe, Lily. She had to talk or whistle all the time she was in here, keep the real feeling of the place away. Never liked lifts, and even small rooms unnerved her. Hated going to the toilet, got in and out as quick as she could, then she'd have to go again ten minutes later. Funny little thing she was, always bouncing around and laughing and standing on her head against the wall. Then when she was eleven she started dressing like a Times Square prostitute going out to meet her pimp. We didn't let her, of course, but she sneaked out like that anyway sometimes. And there's Eve downstairs saying, 'It's only like dressing up, there's no harm in it, she's being creative,' and me: 'Yeah but what about all the predators?' and Eve banging on that when *she* was a kid they could roam for hours unsupervised and nothing ever happened to anyone in those days. Well, you can pull the heavy parent act when they're only eleven, but it gets harder. By the time she was fourteen, me and Johnny had turned into repressive elders. The scenes, the tears, the grindings of teeth, that night, the night of the big melt-down, everyone there watching, and Eve came in with nothing on but her knickers and Lily in those fishnet tights. There was a big demo in town and everyone was going but me. I couldn't stand crowds. You could call it crowdphobia, there's a word for it, no doubt. I couldn't even go to the Notting Hill Carnival or Glastonbury. She was in her room. Harriet was eating cold pasta with her fingers in front of *Play School*. Maurice stood in the kitchen doorway holding a carton of yogurt and a spoon, and they were all there, some in our room, some in the kitchen, people gathering, talking, Pedro carrying the coffee pot, Barry the ferret with his noose and skull t-shirt, a couple of his Class War mates, Keyvan, small and handsome, jiggling about as if he had worms, big Els whose hair dominated rooms, little Shiv I knew from a terrible weekend at Greenham Common. And what's her name Polly, with her big face and lank fair hair, and the dandruff in her parting. The little press had been running nobly all day. Piles of skimpy flyers littered the table. I was thinking how nice it would be when they'd all gone and I could flop out in front of the telly. The bedrooms in that flat opened straight into the main room. Lily came out of the girls' room wearing ripped black fishnet tights, a leather miniskirt and a pair of shiny pull-on black boots with ridiculously high heels. She'd been obsessing over her face at the mirror, loading on makeup till she looked like a badly painted doll.

'Christ's sake,' Johnny groaned. He was good with kids. But with teenagers? Lily's one aim in life at this time was to make herself common as muck, as my mum would have said, and drive him mad. She was perfecting her flounce.

'Y'all right, Lily?' said Shiv.

'OK,' she said.

'Where you off?' I asked. 'Round Jude's?'

'Meeting them in town,' she said, trying to seem casual but steeling for the fight.

'You mean *town* town?'

'Where else?'

'Why didn't you tell us if you were planning on going out? You *never* tell us anything. It's not a good night, Lil.'

She hated being called Lil.

'Why not?'

'It's the demo tonight,' said Johnny. 'Where you going anyway?'

'Leicester Square.'

'No.'

'What?'

'No, Lily, it's a bad night.'

Wouldn't have been so bad if there hadn't been everyone sitting there as if they were watching a play.

'I'm only going to see a film,' she said. 'I'm meeting Jude and Sage down there.'

'*Sage?*' said Johnny, '*Sage!* What's her brother called? Onion?'

'What's the film, Lily?' asked Pedro.

Her face was tight. '*Romancing the Stone,*' she said faintly.

Johnny turned upon me a familiar look. Back me up, it said. Aren't you going to say anything? Am I the only responsible adult in this family?

'It's a school night anyway,' I said, 'you should have told us.'

'We only decided this afternoon.' That look on her face, bravado, insulting disdain, not meeting our eyes.

'It's not a good idea to be around where the demo is,' I said. 'These things can turn.'

'Bit too close to the action for comfort,' said Johnny.

'We-ell,' said Maurice, ripping the top off the yogurt, 'not *that* close.'

'Close enough.'

'Definitely.' I looked at him: there see, backing you up.

'You're being completely unreasonable,' Lily said loftily, her voice shaking a little. She cried easily.

'Not tonight,' Johnny said. 'This isn't a discussion.'

She glowered upon us all.

'Anyway, look at you,' he said.

'Rebel rebel,' said Barry the ferret.

'Give them a call,' I said. 'Say you'll go tomorrow instead.'

I caught a look at Polly, who was raising her eyebrows and making a face at Els. When she saw me, she winked and smiled sympathetically.

'*He* said it was OK.' Lily nodded at Maurice, who was wiping out the yogurt pot with his index finger.

'I'm saying nothing,' he said with a faint smile.

'Well, he's not your dad,' said Johnny, and though she didn't say neither are you, she gave him that look.

'People should be allowed to go and see a film in peace if they want to,' she said, tears forming.

'And they can,' I said, 'every other night. It's this *one...*'

Johnny did about the worst possible thing he could possibly have done then.

Since the Melvin Morgan thing, he'd been disconsolate. For a while after the pamphlet appeared, people had occasionally stood outside Phoebe Twist's house to shout

Murderer, murderer, come out murderer. Her neighbours chased them away. She herself never appeared. The outrage simmered on for a few weeks then evaporated, but Johnny never let it go. He wouldn't talk about it, and he sat up late night after night after I'd gone to bed, stiff jaw, sweet lips, stern brow, the look of a man struggling with some profound emotion eating at the pit of his gut, staring into the fire and brooding over the waters like God almighty. To be honest, he was driving us all up the wall, but Lily in particular, who had no patience with it all. So when he became stern and stood in front of her and said seriously into her burning face, 'People are suffering, the government is rotten at the core, everything decent is threatened and are you really only bothered about going to see some crappy Hollywood film?'

It was tough for her, in front of them all. Tough for me, seeing so clearly how much he was doing this to impress Maurice with his high concerns. Trivial. He'd said the word so many times before it didn't need repeating. She liked boy bands and *Grange Hill* and *Smash Hits*, poured scorn on Shakespeare and Mahler and Marx.

'So?' she said.

He let out a massive sigh through his teeth. 'Love,' he said, 'I don't mean to be horrible, I really don't, but you're only fourteen. There's this big demo taking place right near where you're going, and I don't want to have to worry about you. Look at your shoes.'

Everyone looked at her shoes.

'You definitely can't run in those.'

'I don't want to run in them.'

'It's too last minute, Lily,' I said. 'It's not fair to just spring it on us like that.'

'It's ridiculous!' she suddenly yelled.

'Oh, can we just not have this tonight please, Lily.' I closed my eyes. 'Just for once can you not please—'

'Fucking stupid,' she said, kicking the side of the sofa, 'fucking pointless.'

The talk had stopped and she was the focus of the room. The TV quacked on, and little Harry, oblivious to everything, bounced her loosely socked foot on and off the coffee table, and it was then that the door opened and in walked our neighbour Eve from downstairs with a soggy roll-up between her lips, nine months pregnant and naked except for a pair of sagging grey schoolgirl knickers. Eve was four foot ten. Her belly was enormous, one of the biggest I'd ever seen, too big for her, much too big; you felt you ought to offer to hold it for her for a while. She didn't say anything or take any notice of anyone, just walked in and sat down at the table next to Polly, took a drag on her roll-up and closed her eyes, sighing as if she was snuggling down in bed for a nice sleep.

Lily started sneezing, something she did when she got upset.

'You're really nasty, you know that,' she said, backing away from Johnny with the tears swelling in her eyes, 'a really, really nasty person.'

'Yes, Lily,' he said, 'I'm absolutely horrible.'

'Yes, you are.'

'Oh, Lily.' He looked pained. 'For once in your life could you not please just go along with what I say? Could you not perhaps credit the idea that I'm older than you and might actually know more?'

'No,' she said, and flounced away into the room she shared with Harriet, slamming the door. She really needed her own room but it was impossible.

'Should I be worried?' I said to Maurice. 'Really?'

'Oh God knows, Lorna.' He ambled over, sat down at the table and started drinking the yogurt sloppily straight out of the carton. 'We should all be worried all the time, I suppose.'

Which was no help at all.

One by one they came in from the kitchen and sat down at our enormous table. Keyvan walked round and round the room purposefully as if he was getting somewhere, stopping every now and then to rub his mouth. Some kind of witty banter ping-ponged back and forth across the table between Pedro and Barry. Everyone acted as if Eve wasn't there apart from Pedro, whose eyes were drawn constantly. I sat down next to Shiv at the table. Shiv was short and square and jaunty and could have passed for the Artful Dodger in a tweed jacket much too big for her. 'You still got your Tarot cards, Lor?' she said.

'Somewhere.'

'Ooh – get 'em out.'

'Oh no.' I brushed it off. 'I don't even know where they are.'

He was in a mood anyway now, no point in making it worse. Johnny hated anything like that.

'You've not lost them, have you?' Shiv said. I used to

read the cards for her in the tent. Made it all up. It wasn't serious.

'Not *lost* them. Just don't know where they are.'

'I'd love a reading.'

He was hovering across from me staring, the anger in his face diffused, spreading and drawing in such minor irritations as this. I mean, what was the point of wasting anger on me and Shiv mucking about? God help him, if that bothered him so much, what would he have made of my real moments of weirdness? Nothing strange had happened to me for years. I tried to tell him about the cold boy once but he cut me short. Said it bored him. He came round the table and leaned over me. 'Look,' he said with his forehead nearly touching mine, 'don't make me out to be the heavy father figure here. It's just not fair. Don't you care that she's dressing like that? She's putting herself in danger.' He was right of course. Anything to avoid conflict, that was me. Compromise, compromise, calm down, calm down. They were both right. She should be able to wear what she wanted and walk about like a free woman – Christ, if tribes in the jungle can go naked without raping each other all the time, why the hell can't we? – without having to be afraid. But he was right too, and in practical terms he was more right. There were predators. 'Back me up a bit more,' he said.

'I *am* backing you up.'

'Not really.'

'I am. I'm agreeing with you.'

'Don't be an arsehole, Johnny,' said Polly, sitting smiling at the table.

'When was it due?' Shiv asked Eve, rolling a cigarette one-handed.

'Ooh,' Eve said, closing her eyes again. You could see her eyeballs swivelling under her lids as if she was in REM. 'Four days ago.'

'It's not unreasonable of me to say she can't go out tonight, is it? One night. *One night*. The film'll be on for ages, weeks, she can go tomorrow.'

'Of course it isn't,' I said.

'It's just funny,' Polly said, still smiling. 'Here we all are talking about rebellion and everything, and there she is doing that, as far as she sees it, and what do we do?'

'Don't be crass, Poll,' Johnny said. 'This is completely different.'

Polly shrugged. 'Just saying.'

'I know what you mean, Polly,' I said, 'but this is just about safety,' and she can keep her big nose out of it.

'I was wondering, Lor –' Eve's eyes opened and looked straight ahead. Polly and Eve had the same kind of hair. Polly's lay flat around her head, Eve's straggled down over her swollen breasts. The blue veins on them looked sore. 'Have you got anything I can wear? I'm running out of things.'

'Kids,' said Maurice, as if he knew anything about it.

'It's what I always say,' said big Els, stubbing out a cigarette in the ashtray, 'our kids'll rebel against us by being dead straight. I mean, it's really not cool to agree with your parents, is it?'

'I don't think I've got much, Eve,' I said. Her head was already drooping.

'Oh babe,' she said, 'anything.'

'I'll have a look.'

'That why you've not got a stitch on,' said Pedro, 'cos you got nothing to wear? That bad, is it?' He leaned back on an elbow and unfurled smoke from his lower lip.

Eve ignored him and looked across at Maurice. 'So,' she said peremptorily, 'who are you?'

'You've met me.' He smiled coldly. 'Once or twice.'

Maurice scorned hippies and druggies, all the dope-dealers and mystics. All they cared about was getting high and noodling away in their own thick heads while Rome burned. You couldn't just be silly with Maurice. Or am I remembering this wrong? I think somewhere there's a trace memory of the three of us, me and him and Johnny, having fun once or twice. Yes, we must sometimes have laughed. But mostly what I remember is how serious everything was all the time, because it really *was* true, everything really was a horrible mess, and the rich got richer and the poor got poorer and we were ruled by idiots. Maurice didn't drink or take drugs like everyone else, and neither did Johnny, never touched a drop, never smoked, never lost control. Pure as a baby. You'd never have seen Maurice dance or bop. Well, *I* never did. In my mind, he stands looking solemn before a wall of books, a weighty one balanced open on one hand, the index finger of the other hand pointing down at a silky page. He's fooling around for a photograph, but this is really how he is, the antithesis of frivolity.

'And who's this lot?' she asked.

'This,' said Maurice, 'is Pedro.'

'Hi.' Pedro waved his fingers.

'You look like Lil' Abner,' she said.

Pedro had never heard of Lil' Abner, so encyclopaedic Maurice started telling him about the old cartoons and Dogpatch USA and all the socio-economic factors of it. I went into our bedroom to see if I could find some old tent for her. What does she think I am, a dress shop? I dragged out an old smock dress I hadn't worn in years. I'd never get it back. Didn't get the last one back, a dark blue thing, still, easy come, easy go. It had a plunging neckline, couldn't wear that now, my tits are too big. I went back in and Maurice was telling everyone to drink up their coffee and get out there.

'This any good?' I asked Eve.

She took it from me like a duchess in a high-end couturier. Johnny was getting his coat on and everyone was standing up. Shiv wore too-tight jeans and they looked funny underneath her enormous square-shouldered jacket. Els shook out her curly red hair.

'Where you off?' asked Eve.

'Demo.'

'Ah.'

'You know about the demo?' said Maurice.

'Course I do. Watch yourselves.' She relit her roll-up with someone's lighter. 'Things get nasty. Them police don't care what they do. Bastards!'

Maurice chuckled. 'I'm with you there,' he said, patting Eve's cold naked shoulder.

'They're all fucking corrupt.' She took a long frowning pull on her roll-up and sneezed.

'Damn right,' said Polly.

Lily's door opened. 'I'm going out now,' she said, mincing towards the door.

'Oh Lily, for God's sake!' I said. 'Please!'

'You're not, Lily,' Johnny said, stepping in front of her nimbly and placing himself in front of the door.

'You can't stop me, I'll just wait till you're gone and then I'll go.'

'Enough!'

She started pulling at his folded arms, scratching the backs of his hands with her sharp nails.

'Ow! Fuck off!' he said. 'I'm not moving.'

'Lily, will you *please*—'

'You don't know a thing,' she said, 'you think you know everything but you don't. You're just stupid. I know things too.'

'What?' asked Johnny. '*What* do you know, Lily?'

'I know life's not just about reading books and saying clever things. It's not. It's about trying to be nice to people.'

'Oh, very profound,' Johnny said and Maurice said something about the harm principle, and she screamed and turned round with her face ablaze and tears starting from her eyes.

'You think I'm stupid but I'm not,' she said.

'No one thinks you're stupid, love.' I got up and went towards her but she flounced away.

'Stupid!' she said.

'You've just said stupid three times,' said Johnny. 'Try and vary your language a bit more, Lily.'

'I don't know,' said Eve, opening her eyes and looking

sadly round at everyone as if she was about to say something wise. The hard white belly with its straining navel rested on her wide-apart thighs. 'I don't think this baby wants to be born.'

'Oh please,' I said, I'm not sure to whom.

'Oh for God's sake, Lily,' Johnny said, 'go and blow your nose.'

'*You*,' she said. 'You're never wrong, are you?'

'Of course I am.'

I actually wanted to laugh. Johnny was never wrong. Upon this his identity teetered.

'I'm wrong very often, I'm sure. And I'm not afraid to admit it.'

That was even funnier.

'Well, you never do,' she said.

'If there's even a possibility of trouble...' I said. I don't know why I bothered, they never let me get a word in anyway.

'Exactly!' said Johnny.

Lily suddenly deflated. 'I can't go out now anyway,' she said, wiping her cheeks with her hands. 'My makeup's ruined. Everything's ruined.'

'Oh, come on, Lily!' I couldn't bear them all standing around with their half-embarrassed faces.

'Oh, come on, Lily!' She screwed up her face like a gargoyle, shot a look of pure hatred at me and then another around the room, one that took in everyone. Then she walked proudly into her bedroom and slammed the door hard. Harriet jumped up and ran after her.

'Oh dear,' said Maurice drily, 'the Great Refusal. Ha ha.'

His eyes betraying nothing because they never did. He took a last noisy swig of coffee.

'Oh God.' Johnny stooped to pick up a book from the floor. 'Can't we send her to stay with her dad for a bit? Look what she's done to my hands. Claws.'

At last they were gone, thank God, and it was just me and Eve, who just sat there on the hard chair with her eyes closed and the crappy old smock dress draped over her belly, nodding out like an old person in a care home. Harriet came quietly out of the girls' room and sprawled next to me. 'She's been crying,' she said.

'Oh dear. Is she feeling better now?'

She nodded.

'Should I go and see her, do you think?'

Another nod.

I tapped on her door and went in. Lily was on her bed, reading. The room was a pigsty. She'd redone her makeup, paint thick round her bloodshot eyes.

'You OK, Lily?'

'Yeah.'

I had a horrible Barbie vision of her with breast implants and injections. She looked so nice when she was just flopping about at home. 'Oh Lily,' I said, 'do you really want so badly to look like a sex object? You don't have to do this.'

'Do what?' She didn't look up from her book.

'Make yourself up as if you're off on a photoshoot every time you step out of the house.'

Harriet stood at the door, solemnly watching.

'This is how I want to look,' Lily said. 'If I don't wear my makeup I'm ugly.'

'Oh, don't be so stupid!'

'You're not!' declared Harriet, outraged.

'Yes, I am. It's just a fact. I'm just facing facts.'

'You're not!'

'Well, Terry doesn't think you're ugly,' I said, 'that's for sure.'

'How do you know? You don't know what anybody thinks.'

'He thinks you're lovely,' I said, 'it's obvious.'

'You don't know.'

I lay down on Harriet's bed. 'You and Johnny,' I said, closing my eyes, 'you're as bad as each other. Neither one of you sees straight.'

She started crying again. 'I'm not horrible,' she said. 'I'm not! He's saying I'm horrible and I'm not!'

'Of course you're not horrible,' I said.

'He thinks I'm horrible! He thinks I don't care about things! It's not fair! It's not fair!'

'He doesn't really think that,' I said, and got up and went to her and tried to put my arms around her, but she wasn't having any.

Harriet came over. 'There,' she said, sitting by her side and stroking Lily's shoulder. 'There, Lily.'

'But my *friends* are going tonight,' she said.

'Well, maybe they shouldn't.'

Eve called weakly from the other room. 'Oh God,' she said when I went in, 'I think I'm going to have this baby in your flat.'

You are fucking not, I thought. Got to get rid of her.

Thank God Steve came rapping on the door five minutes later, in a terrible mood.

'Is she here?'

I opened the door and waved towards her.

'Come on, love,' he said furiously, 'I'm going mad here. I need my fucking fix.'

Harriet came out and turned on the TV. It was a gentle nature programme about badgers and we slumped together there recovering our wits. Much later Lily emerged and curled herself away in the corner of the settee, sucking her thumb, covering her face and pulling up her fishnet knees.

19

A feeling of grievance rose in Dan's chest as he stood gazing out of the kitchen window at the drips falling from the eaves. He didn't want trouble or fuss. Never had done. That's the last time I do anything like that, he thought. Leave her to it. And these stupid cats taking over.

'That's it,' he said, and turned from the window. He walked with decisive tread into the living room. 'You!' he said to the mother cat. 'You! Out. Now. You and your kits. You can't have them in here.' Then he stood with his arms hanging stupidly limp, thinking, if I move them will she eat them or something? Or is that rabbits?

He didn't want her eating them. Leaving heads about the place. So he flipped up the lid on the laptop and googled 'moving kittens'. Oh Christ, it's never just a yes or no, is it? He skimmed. Blah blah... oh, it looks all right. Nothing about eating them. She might abandon them. Well, if she does the RSPCA can sort it out.

'Time's up,' he murmured, stooping over the furry mass. Blind squirmy newborns. The birthing chair was covered with a grimy crocheted blanket, now ruined. Oh well, he always hated it. Hippie seventies shite. Look at them. When do they start shitting? Not in here. He tried scooping the whole striped squirmy lot up in the blanket in one go, but the kittens mewed like seagulls and the mother hissed and lashed at him.

'Gaa-a-agh!' He shook her off but she clung to the blanket with four legs, all claws extended. Closing the blanket round them, he bore them away. She hung on, a great weight swinging alongside, something between a snarl and a yowl ululating from her throat, all the way into the back room where all the rubbish was. It was cold in here because of the open pipe where the cats got in and out of the house.

He set them down gently – poor fuckers, five fur blobs – on the floor in a space between the sideboard and a suitcase from around 1958, overflowing with pointless cotton nothings and ancient embroidery silks; my God, what crap, envelopes full of photographs fading away like rocks to the scrape of time, *papers*, what? Oh my God, chuck the lot. What *are* these? *Papers.* Is that what it's all about? Nothing here can be important after all this time. He dumped the lot out of the case onto the floor. But oh look. A ration card. I should keep that. Historical. Look at that. Ocella Morse. Chuck the lot. Chuck the fucking lot.

'There!' He scooped up the kittens, even the indignant mother, and put them in the case, stinky blanket and all.

'Now shut up,' he said. 'I'll give you some food.' He went to the kitchen and poured a bowl of kibbles, couldn't find a spare so gave her his breakfast bowl, filled another with water. Gave them that, pulled another horrible crochet thing off another chair in the living room, gave them that, closed up the room and left them there. Time I did that, he thought. Keep them out. Time I closed that door.

Pete and Eric were in the pub. Eric was settling into the look of a seedy guy trying to sell you something you didn't want. Pete, in an expansive mood, stood everyone a tableful of Nobby's Nuts and seasalt crisps.

Nobody wanted a kitten.

'Take 'em down the animal rescue,' said Eric.

'That's right.' Pete ripped open a packet of crisps. 'They'll take the lot off your hands. And all them others too. They'll be glad of it. And they don't put them down, you know. Not any more.'

It was quiet in the pub apart from the occasional squawk from the old grey parrot. The TV over the bar was on but it was just people talking on a couch and you couldn't hear a thing they said. You could still hear the sound of the wind. This weather, thought Dan. Not right.

'Apparently they buried that body,' Mary said, 'or what was left of it.'

'Oh yeah?'

'Yeah. 'Bout time too.'

'Well,' said Marlon, idling on a high stool reading the *Examiner*, 'I suppose they've got to give it a chance to get claimed or whatever.'

'I think it's really sad,' she said. 'Think, being dead and no one even knows who you are.'

'I should think he's past caring,' Dan said dryly.

Mary leaned on the bar. 'Quite a few trees down,' she

said. 'I couldn't get to sleep last night.' The makeup under her eyes was smudged. A tasteful blue tattoo of leaves and vines crept up the side of her neck and vanished behind one ear.

'Wild near my house,' said Dan.

'I'll bet.'

'Yes,' said Eric, 'the weather's sure gone funny.'

'I wish everyone'd stop saying that!' Pete stuffed crisps into his mouth.

'Because it is,' said Eric. 'Can't change facts.'

'All this doom and gloom,' said Pete, chewing. 'Gets on my wick, it really does.'

'People shouldn't talk and eat crisps at the same time,' said Eric piously, his face all soft and sunken. Dan looked away. Sometimes the music in here was crap, sometimes it was OK. Tonight it was crap. He didn't know what it was, a load of gurgling technotwaddle.

'I'd love a kitten, really I would,' said Mary, moving down the bar to serve someone who'd just come in, 'but I just can't have one.'

Pete gave him a lift back. Neither of them spoke and the headlights, acid white, burned the darkness ahead. Everything in the beam was ghastly and unreal, everything outside it nothing. The tops of the branches in the spindly hedges either side of the road sparkled and crackled.

'There y'go, mate,' said Pete, dropping him off.

'Seeya, Pete.'

The night was black.

The house was dark and cold. The fire had gone out. He lit a fire and lay in front of it, stretched out on the settee.

Hell of a racket coming from that room. Never sleep with that going on.

They *all* want in. Oh miaow! Miaow! Tragic. Trying out for the opera. Sod it. He opened the door and let them in. And of course because they were cats and awkward bastards by nature, they didn't want in any more.

'Fuck you,' he said, went back to the fire and fell asleep. When he woke up, he thought someone had just spoken. The weather was calm and there was only the sound of water dripping, and he had no idea what the time was.

There'd been something, a noise.

He sat up.

But no. Nothing but water, a gentle musical accompaniment. He should get up and go to bed, but instead he fell asleep again.

Time passed.

When he woke – a minute, an hour – who knows? – he thought once more, someone spoke, just now, and strained his ears to catch the ghost of the sound; but there was only a merging of several random small sounds, which came together by degrees and were suddenly clear, undeniable, identifiable: the sliding of a hand on the bannister, a discreet cough, bare footsteps on the stairs.

20

Through the green rank-smelling forest after last night's wild night, to the stream. I have to wash my socks and knickers with a bar of soap. I remember Johnny washing his clothes in a bowl at midnight in Carmody Square. He would have loved this life in some ways. Ideally he'd have been a hobo riding the rails into the sunset but he'd never have been able to take the dirt, God knows what a boxcar would have done to him. Took at least two showers a day, even when we had no hot water. Standing on an outdoor landing pouring cold water over his head, his naked body brown and skinny and shiny in the early morning light. He could have been simpler, it would have suited him. He could have been a mendicant monk somewhere in the East, a sage on a rock in contemplation, with his begging bowl and his long black moustaches dripping down into the purling stream that meanders beside him through the rocks. Too fastidious though. So careful in some ways, so hopeless and careless in others. He'd lose a twenty pound note just like that. You might as well give it to the dog. Oh well, he'd say with his gentle infuriating eyes, I suppose we'll just have to get some more.

And here I am, bashing my clothes on a rock in the stream. Johnny had no patience for drudgery. Life's too short, he'd say. *They live like insects, people, mindless, crawling the surface of the earth, scarcely conscious. Not me. Not me. I'm not afraid to plumb the depths. What else is life for? Life, Lorna! Your life! And you, you, you try to tell me what to do. Well, I don't care about all that. I don't care about cleaning the floor and getting nice towels and hanging them up, all that bourgeois shit. I care about what's really important. Don't you ever try and bring me down to that level. I mean it. I'll never join the herd. Never. You think that's real? That – shit. I'd rather be dead.*

Oh, the end times with Johnny were terrible.

Lily was the reef on which we foundered. For a long time I had denied the obvious. How could it ever end? We were, I believed, old souls somehow joined through the dimensions. Don't even start to ask me what that means, I haven't a clue. Just that for so many years things had remained effortlessly right in spite of our differences, which were never few. They just didn't matter.

Until they did.

I became irritated by the silly piercing look of his eyes. I never used to see that. How did it creep up on me? He was a serious man, he'd always been a serious man. Nothing wrong with that. The politics, we were together on that. Oh Johnny, the world was shit. That's what you said. There was suffering everywhere. The beggars no more than children, babies, at the mouths of tube stations. Polite, a bit shy: 'Spare change please?' Only I was sick of going to bed and hearing the impassioned murmur of the two of them, him and Maurice still rattling on two hours later when I got up to go to the bathroom. Lily called him the Roundhead because he objected to her clothes. He couldn't stand it when she giggled and guffawed, and shouted: Oh my Ga-a-a-a-a-awd! 'Is the Roundhead here?' she'd chirrup, coming in from school and flinging down her schoolbag. 'Is that what that droning is?' He was pained by the way she made stupid kissy mouths whenever a camera was brought out. 'Your friends are facile, Lily.' He'd say it to her in his soft way: I'm sincerely trying to help you. 'They don't know any other way to be.'

She was fifteen when she started going out with Terry, the boy who fixed the pipes in the house next door to Wilf. Terrible Terry, thick as two short planks. Rawbones, we called him. He was eighteen. He worked with his Uncle Dave all over from Shepherd's Bush to Notting Hill Gate, plumbing and painting, putting in kitchens, bathrooms, bits of all sorts. He and his uncle drove around in a green van with Rapid Drain Repairs written on the side. Someone had altered the D so that it now read Rapid Brain Repairs. Suddenly Terry was in and out of our place all the time with his gormless hulking presence and big ruddy face. He didn't talk much at first, but after a while started to regale us with sudden bursts of nervous rambling opinion that veered all over the place and were capable of expressing two opposing views in one sentence. He could bang on about foreigners having it cushy and we're all mugs one minute, and the next be extolling the virtues of multiculturalism. 'Shit for brains,' said Johnny. God knows what she saw in him, we wondered. Maybe it was because he ran around after her like a little dog. 'I want some chocolate,' she'd say, and he'd jump up and dash off and be back in ten minutes with a Wispa. 'Oh ta,' she'd say and wolf it down.

He was too old for her, Johnny said.

But he was harmless.

'Yeah, but get this!' said Lily one day. 'He's done a job for that horrible woman. Phoebe Twist.'

'Phoebe Twist!' Johnny sitting forward, suddenly wide awake.

Oh, Christ, no, not her again. This woman was the Bad Fairy, the one whose face sours the milk and makes the baby cry.

He'd put in a new kitchen and a shower with his Uncle Dave.

'She really likes Terry.'

'Terry?'

'Yeah. She always asks for him, whenever anything needs doing. Not his uncle, Dave. Only Terry. She's got a thing for him.'

'Told you the woman was mad,' Johnny said.

Johnny talked to him a lot at first, eager for news about the Twist woman's horrible habits. She had a big running sore on her leg that stank. 'And she's really dirty,' said Lily, 'isn't she, Tes? If you open her fridge, it's bogging.'

'Yeah.'

'And *she* goes on about other people!'

'She's dead creepy,' said Terry. His cheeks were such bright apple red you could almost see the blood running just under the surface. 'She just goes – brush – brush – brush – all day long.'

'What's she brushing?'
'Clothes. Hair.'

I went to see Wilf. I wanted his laid-back perspective. He knew Terry, I figured. He'd done some work on a stone wall in Wilf's back garden.

Wilf was sitting in front of the telly eating thick beef sausages and baked beans from a plate on his knees. He was a sous chef at a bistro off Queensway now, but at home he lived on kids' food. The gas fire blasted heat. Kids were racketing about upstairs and Jananda was yelling at them. Wilf thought everything was OK.

'He's all right, Terry,' he said. 'Anyway, it's not like she's marrying him, is it, Lor?'

'Do you think he's a bit old for her? Johnny thinks he might be.'

'Nah. Eighteen? What? That what he is? Fifteen, I'd have said. Know how it is, girls mature quicker than boys. No no, Terry's just a kid, you don't have to worry about him.'

'A kid with a dick,' I said.

'Don't say that, Lor.' Gently. 'Doesn't sound nice.'

'Well, you know what I mean.'

Wilf put on a considering face. 'We-e-ell – I *might* be bothered if he was a different sort of kid but I honestly think he's young for his age. Nothing's going on.'

'You seem very sure.'

'Oh, I know my Lily,' he said complacently. 'Believe me, we talk things through.'

It made me feel awful that she talked so easily to Wilf, because she never talked things through with me. Sex, for example – I tried once, she just said, 'How dare you, of course I know what I'm doing, what do you think I am, an idiot?'

'Are you OK, Lor? Things going all right?'

'Oh yeah. They're just driving me mad a bit. It has got worse.'

'Him and her?'

'Yeah.'

'I don't mind if she wants to come here for a few days,' he said.

I should have minded that. I should have wanted her to stay with me, but a few days' peace would have been nice. No chance. 'Are you kidding?' she said. 'Spend all my time wiping arses? Oh yeah! Their eyes light up. Oh look, babysitter. Lily, would you just mind watching Biff for a few minutes? I've just got to...'

'She says I always take Johnny's side,' I said. '*He* says I always take hers. Sides? Sides? What are they on about? Sometimes I just want to scream at them both.'

'Never stops, Lor, does it?'

'No.'

'Life. Just never bloody stops.' He smiled. 'All things must pass, girl.'

'Thought for the day,' I said, getting up.

'Got to dash, have you, Lor?' said Wilf, putting his plate on the floor and reaching out to touch my hand. 'God's sake, girl, you're always dashing off somewhere. Ease off. Send her over. Give yourself a break.'

★ ★ ★

Later when I mentioned what Wilf had said about Terry, Johnny just huffed. 'You know what *he's* like. If the bomb dropped, he wouldn't worry till it actually hit him on the head.'

21

How many years had he been boring himself stupid here? Used to be OK. The old days, when he used to come in with Eric. And Mary, look at her, yellow-fingered Mary, constant fag between her fingers. All those years, and now. Eighteen from the back, fifty-five from the front.

'Do you want that filling up, Dan?' she said, smiling.

'Yeah, go on, Mary.'

'Gonna be another hot one tomorrow.' Marlon, wiping down the bar.

'No one can tell me this is normal weather.' Mary pulled a pint of Old Peculier, her brick-coloured forehead glistening. 'Pissing down one day, scorching the next. It's getting ridiculous.'

'We're doomed,' said Marlon, tossing the rag onto his shoulder, 'doomed I tell ye.'

The pub was quiet for the time of night. Something weird and old and black and white played too quietly to be heard on the telly over the bar. He was putting off going home. 'Where is everyone?' he asked.

'Midweek.' Marlon counted change.

'Here y'are, love.' Mary put his pint before him and he

thanked her and took a swig, looking at the screen over her head. Foreign film, subtitles: *Have you brought your examination book?* Something strange and serious. He kept reading the words because there was nothing much else to look at. An old man was having a nightmare. *You have been accused of guilt.* A soft low hum of voices came from the far end of the room, vague music, the clink of bottles. *But my wife has been dead for years.* The old man was a doctor and he had to examine a woman slumped in a chair with her eyes closed. Rows of weird people watched him. *Please diagnose the patient.* The old man leaned over the woman. *The patient is dead*, he said. She opened her eyes and laughed in his face, and her laugh got wilder and wilder and more horrible.

'Look at that,' said Dan, 'what is that?'

Marlon glanced up. 'I'll turn it over,' he said.

'No, leave it.'

People drifted in. Eric, a few tourists who gathered round the parrot's cage, some lads from the creamery. Dan bought some spicy nuts and they were too hot but he ate them anyway. Marlon changed the channel. Football. He turned the sound up till it resembled a distant roaring that surged along with all the other sounds. If I leave now, thought Dan, it'll just about still be light when I get home. Should have left the light on. No reason not to. But that's giving in. Or go back when it's dark. Dark house, dark garden, dark yard, dark stairs.

So what?

It was half and half when he finally left. A hand lifted – goodbye. Nice night. Twilight coming on. Still warm but that drenching feeling gone. All still. He set off at a brisk pace, the sound of his own shoes intrusive. Passed the old boys' clubhouse, the field with goalposts. Sports day. Her, mum, standing on the sidelines shouting, 'Come on, Danny!' at the top of her voice, clapping her hands very loudly and calling, half whistle, half war-cry. Sports day, parents' night, all those things, she was never really with anyone. Not that she didn't talk to people, she did, but she was never really *with* anyone. Why was she like that? Because she went away? Couldn't be that. Other people did. He was sorry for her, always, a horrible nagging ache that hung over his schooldays. Standing there pretending to be just like everybody else, then soon as she got home changing back into her usual watery wreck of a self as if putting on comfy old clothes. In the door, flop down, at ease: 'Ooh, can you make me a cup of tea, my love?'

Poor weak hand on brow like she's in a silent film, down on her back on the settee, eyes scrunched, turning, tossing, pressing her face into the back of the settee. Long long sigh. 'Oh, my feet!' She'd start to ramble as he built up the fire, drinking her tea, smoking her cigarette. First thing he ever learned – life was desperately sad. Bad. And people were bad. You had to be careful. 'Your dad,' she'd say, 'he taught me that. Oh, your poor father!'

And then, staring straight ahead and growing profound: 'There's no such thing as forever.'

A course in existential dread for a childhood. That's what he'd had.

'But then there is!' Bashing her cup down on the coffee table. 'And that's worse! Don't you think? To live forever?

Oh, that's unbearable! This! Forever! And never getting anywhere.'

Yeah, Mum. Fucking terrible.

At the end of the village, on the verge, the lime tree had one arm hanging down. Look at that. Vandals. Kids. Pulled the arm right off that tree. Let me catch 'em, he thought, good clout round the earole.

It was pitch black all round the house. He felt his way along the wall to the back. It couldn't help but creep back on him, that single brief moment when he'd heard, or thought he'd heard, something on the stairs and gone out into the hall with hackles up and eyes wide open – and there was nothing, nothing on the stairs, nothing anywhere, and the second after it happened, it hadn't happened because it couldn't have happened. A sound, when gone, there's nothing to replay, no proof. It didn't happen.

He fumbled the key in the lock and went in.

And if it was her? If it really was?

Fuck off, Mum.

Lights on. Telly on. Kettle on.

Cats came prowling. The big orange one round his legs. Getting to look old, that cat.

'Yes,' he said to it, squidging the teabag against the side of the mug, 'yes, it is, I know.'

He took his tea and a bottle, a stick of wood and a knife, and went and sat on the back step. It was better out here than in there. He stretched, rubbed his forehead and blinked, assessing his body for pain. There were a few problems, aches, peculiar sensations, crap sight, but it could have been a lot worse. He started whittling. Look at that sky! The universe vibrated, the constellations ramped across the sky. He drew in his breath as if something was rushing at him, looked down, and there in his memory, so clear, was his mum sitting on the blue painted chair in the garden, the one that now stood on the top landing with a bucket on it for catching the drips when it rained. She'd been in one of her weepy dreadsome moods and he'd made her go outside, saying look, it's a nice day, the primroses are out, look, you'll feel much better if you get a bit of fresh air. You go out and I'll put these sheets in the washing machine and get you a cup of tea. Here. I'll put this chair here. He'd brought her out a sandwich and a cup of tea, and a bit later when he got back in, looked out of the kitchen window and saw her holding the sandwich half-way to her mouth, head turned slightly towards the house. He thought she was probably crying, he just knew she was, and there was not a thing he could do about it. It made him want to cry, not that he ever did. Ever. And she was looking at him with this look, this look of wistful reproach and loving sadness. How did she always manage to make him feel so mushed up and bad? That jacket he hated. She spent all her money on it one Christmas, bloody awful it was and he had to pretend to like it, used to wear it down to the bus stop then take it off, try to carry it without letting it be seen, impossible. What she want to go and get a thing like that for? Just showed how much she really knew about him, didn't it? Buying him a jacket like that and thinking he'd wear it. Didn't know him at all if she could even *think* he'd wear it. And she was so pleased. Her face when she gave it to him. He still cringed to think of it.

Still, shitty as everything turned out, there'd been good things.

He wished she'd stop. Just be normal.

Jesus, though, what if it was? Her on the stairs. Stop thinking about all this. Drink.

Couldn't handle that.

Oh that's unbearable! To live forever. Nah, she wouldn't hang around. Couldn't wait to get away, could she? Why would she want to come back? But the sound on the stairs kept replaying in his mind and his heart was tight. The terror of eternity came down and sharpened his mind. All those times you feared death and found comfort in the fact that it had not yet arrived, it still would one day. Tick. Tock. Stop any time. It happens. The next second.

Just fuck off. Whoever – whatever – you are. Leave me alone. I'll live till I die.

He drank. He'd just sit out here at the back rather than going back into that haunted house. But maybe she'd come out behind him and take him by surprise. What would he do? Really, what would he do if here he was sitting on the step and suddenly there was just this touch, this cold touch, just there on his shoulder? What would he actually *do*?

'What more do you want?' he said out loud. 'I'm sorry. I really am.'

Was it really all his fault? What didn't he understand?

No life of her own but no need to take mine. So he'd got out in spite of all her wiles, taken the high road by Tring and Lily-hoo, gone to sea and sailed away, and one day the news had come that she'd got the tow rope out of the shed and strung herself up from the top of the garden gate, the one round the side by the beehives. She'd been there three days before the postman found her. After all, she hardly ever went into the village and no one ever called round. He'd had to come back and sort everything out, then he'd gone back to sea for another year or so and the house had been rented out to holiday people.

The dark quivered. Time for ghosts to walk, handless Jenny by the Dogwood Beck, her husband cut off her hands for being lazy. The woods, one great black mass, shifted and swelled.

Christ! Stop! Send yourself insane.

Go to bed. OK, you can leave the light on on the landing.

22

Then suddenly, days of heat that filtered their somnolence down to me under veil upon veil of brightening leaves. And I caught a cold, which I hate, particularly in glorious weather. The best thing to do was stay in my nest and sleep and drink hot water. If it gets worse, I thought, flu-ish, I'll go to the old cat man and get some pills. He'll have some. Or he'll get me some from the village. He will. He likes to look after things. He doesn't think he does, but he does. Lying here with all of my blankets wrapped round me, protected from the heat under the cool green, my sore eyes couldn't read, so I just closed them and drifted away.

There's a sound and the mind runs and strangeness is imminent. I can feel it and there's nothing to be done but let it run its course like weather till it gives way to normality again somewhere down the line. Listen to those cats. Like wailing babies. Such fierce misery. Hear them sing along to these memories.

I was walking up from town, me and Eve and her baby in

the pram, and Harriet skipping and dancing alongside and the sky piling up clouds.

'Ooh, look at that,' said Eve, 'well, he's a sweet little thing, isn't he?'

Mark Gaunt his name was. Gaunt of name, gaunt of face, with a bony jaw and milky, freckled complexion. They were at the door, he'd walked her home from Drama. Trust Lily to go from one extreme to the other. The boy blushed like a maiden when we walked up.

'Coming up?' I said, holding the door open for Eve to get the pram in. 'I got some little Indian sweet things. Come on up.'

They dithered. 'Johnny in?' she asked.

'Not that I know of.'

So up we all went, and Eve and her baby came in too, and I made tea and coffee.

He was a funny little thing, fragile, fairish, very quiet. He came into the kitchen and drank his tea and said hardly a word. Lily ignored him completely once he was in and played about with Harriet, rough old stuff like they used to do when they were much younger, rolling around on the floor, handstands, headstands, showing off for him, look how spontaneous and wonderful and playful I am. She didn't bother to introduce him so we introduced ourselves and asked his name and tried to make conversation, working our way through the Indian sweets while the baby slept in her pram.

'Here,' I said, 'these are lovely. Quick before they all go.'

Smiling, he dragged his eyes off Lily and shook his head.

'So,' I said, 'are you in the play?'

'I play Alan.'

'Oh. That's a big part, isn't it?'

'Well… quite big.'

His voice was clear and low and extremely posh. It sounded weird in our house.

'Can we come and see it?' asked Eve.

'No!' said Lily.

'Huh,' I said, 'hark at her. All we have to do is buy tickets, Lily.'

'I can't do it if you lot are sitting there looking at me.'

'Bloody hell, you'll have to get over that.'

The front door downstairs banged closed; Johnny's familiar tread was on the stairs, the way he rushed up the last flight.

'Oh fuck fuck fuck,' said Lily.

'Lily!'

The boy giggled soundlessly. He had the face and demeanour of a twelve year old.

The key turned in the lock. Johnny came in smiling with his hair in a mess as if he'd just shoved his fingers through it and left it sticking up. His eyes went straight to the newcomer.

'This is Mark,' I said, 'he's a friend of Lily's. From Drama.'

'Daddy,' said Harriet.

Mark stood up. 'Very pleased to meet you,' he said, holding out his hand. Johnny glanced down, surprised, then took and shook it too vigorously, a big smile on his face. The boy looked subtly unnerved.

'Grab one of these before they're all gone,' I said, pushing the round milky sweets in Johnny's direction. He stuffed his face, one, two three, one after the other. Something about Mark seemed to amuse him tremendously and not in a good way.

'Acting, eh?' he said.

'Yes,' said Mark, and Johnny stifled a splutter.

The two of them sat down, Johnny still grinning manically. Harriet leaned against Johnny's knee. Lily stood behind his chair. There were two sweets left. 'Want one?' He slid the plate towards Mark.

'No, thank you.'

'Sure?'

'Yes, thank you, I'm sure.' Both of them blushers, Terry and him.

'Tea?'

'I've still got some. Thank you.'

'So sorry,' Johnny said with that awful smile, speaking like an old Pathé newsreader or a member of the aristocracy, 'I'm afraid we've completely run out of cucumber sandwiches.'

There was one horrible moment.

'My God,' the poor boy said, looking over Johnny's head at Lily, 'is my accent that bad?'

She grabbed Johnny's head by the curls on either side and shook it backwards and forwards as if she wanted to pull it off. It made him laugh more. 'You bastard!'

'Ow!'

She stood back then whacked the back of his skull with the flat of her palm.

'Fuck's sake, Lily,' he said.

She ran round the table, grabbed Mark by the arm and

hauled him up as if he was a child. 'We're going,' she said, dragging him after her to the door.

'See you later, Lily!' called Johnny with laughter in his voice.

Slam.

'Oh God, that was awful,' I said, 'that was really embarrassing.'

'Oh come on.' He laughed. 'I was only mucking about.'

'That was really rude,' said Eve.

'So is she two-timing them?' he asked.

'I have no idea.'

'That Drama lot,' he said, 'load of toffee-nosed twats, from what I can see.'

'Don't be such a meanie.'

'What awful middle-class farce have they got them on now?'

'*Time and the Conways.*'

'It's just the airs they give themselves,' he said. 'It's not proper acting, is it?'

'Oh, shut up.'

'You know what I mean.'

'Well, I think it's a good thing for her to do,' I said.

'Yeah. What you moaning about?' The baby was mewling and Eve started getting her things together.

'Well, here's a to-do,' said Johnny, pulling Harriet up to sit on his knee. 'Our Lily's got herself a nob.'

Next time we saw the Hatchet lot Johnny said, 'You ought to see this creep Lily's going round with. Young Lochinvar.

You ought to hear him,' and he went off into his best haw haw haw splutter splutter upper-class-twit-of-the-year voice. He was good at it.

Everyone laughed.

'He does this,' I said, 'it's not funny. Takes the piss out of the poor boy to his face. It's embarrassing.'

'Oh come on,' he said. 'No one has to talk like that.'

Everyone was laughing.

I was laughing.

'He can't help his posh voice,' I said, 'you don't choose your parents.'

'Some say you do,' said Shiv.

I don't know what got into me that night. Everything started getting on my nerves. I lay on my back on the floor taking no part in any of it but listening to the conversation, which I'd heard several times before.

'We live in a terrible world.' Maurice's noble, serious face moved slowly from side to side as he idly kicked against the floor and his swivel chair went this way and that way, a wall of books behind him. The music was low and sinuous. 'What if a terrible act served a deep historical purpose?'

They were talking about bombs. Not to hurt anyone, but property was fair game.

Barry the ferret wasn't so sure about the property only clause. Depended on the target.

'Where did love and peace get the hippies?' said Barry. 'Look what they did to Wally Hope.'

'Face it,' said Els, 'who wouldn't have given a secret sly little snigger if they'd got Maggie in Brighton? I'm being honest, I can't find it in me to shed a tear for some people, I really can't.'

'But what about the hotel staff?' Keyvan was opening another bottle of wine.

'Aye,' said Maurice, 'there's the rub.'

Johnny said it wasn't simple.

'Sure ain't.' I laughed.

Maybe my tone was harsh because he shot me a nasty look. 'All I'm *saying* is,' he said, 'there's always a bigger picture.'

'Well, of course there is.' Maurice stopped swivelling and leaned forward in his chair with his toes turned in. 'A question, Lorna. Can you imagine one single circumstance in which violence might be justified?'

'Of course. If a madman was threatening my kids with an axe...'

'No no, that's too obvious. Let's say there was some situation where, say, by taking the life of one innocent person thousands more could be saved. And it was your decision, what would you do?'

'I have no idea. It's a stupid question because there are a million million other things to take into account like who is it, why is this, what if it's a child, a baby, what if a million things, how can you...'

I got all flustered. I couldn't argue like they could. I'd think of the right answers later. Instead of some reasoned philosophical response, I said, 'Fuck off and blow something up then.'

I often remember that moment.

Maurice laughed. 'Not me, Lorna,' he said.

'You're all just wanking,' I said, sitting up, 'you realise that, don't you? You'd piss yourselves if it came to it.'

Polly and Shiv laughed, but Johnny gave me a hurt look. I laughed too. 'Come off it,' I said, 'you know damn well we're all much too nice for all that. We just like wanking off on it.'

I said 'we' but I meant 'you'.

We didn't talk much driving home. Johnny was totally sober as always and me a silly stoned fool in the passenger seat. A well yawned between us. Somewhere around Vauxhall he started mumbling in the tone of someone delivering an ancient curse. 'We talk,' he said, 'and we stick up a few flyers and print our little rag and paint a few words on a few walls and stand around chanting and throwing eggs, and no one takes a blind bit of notice. Everything still goes on the same for ever and ever and ever.' I thought about dear old Wilf and how he didn't give a fuck about politics. Never voted. They're all the same. This old fart or that old fart. Who cares? No wonder he and Johnny never really hit it off. Civil, but that's about it. I put my hand on Johnny's knee as he drove and said, 'Ssh.' I didn't want to have a row, and there was a lump in my throat because everything felt wrong, not just me and him but the whole world. A thought of the woods at Andwiston passed through my mind. To be out of the city, quiet, away from strife. He looked so forlorn and like his old self when we got home that I tried to give him a cuddle, but he wasn't in a cuddly mood. That all seemed to have gone by the wayside. I went into the bathroom and looked at myself in the mirror. I wasn't going to cry. It was never going to go back to how it was. I went to bed and he sat up alone reading and listening to music, some kind of twitchy jazz, doodly-doodly-doodly-doo. More and more these days, his music was Maurice's music. When I woke up at about half past two he hadn't come to bed. He'd gone off somewhere with his guitar to some open mic club. He could easily get someone else, I thought. Guitar, nice mouth, deep eyes.

23

A long low moan very very close. Half cat, half dog. Fox?
Not a cat. My goodness, what is that?

Again. Smooth-throated, sustained, rising into a mournful
ululation that faded and hung on the silence. The cats don't
come here. Whatever it is it's right outside. I sat up and
listened. Nothing. Unless it still sat, motionless with crossed
cloven feet outside my outer doorway. How could I sleep
after that? Must be close to morning, I'll wait it out.

Hours later I woke up to the sounds of people echoing
through the woods, got up and crawled out through the
leaves. Nice day, they were all out – shrill-voiced kids, steel-
haired women with walking poles, barking dogs, knobbly
knees in shorts. Backpacks galore, all seeking shade. Litter
louts. People are the strangest beasts. They're so irritating
and ugly. I remember once Johnny looking out of the
window in that place we had when we first got together,
watching the people going up and down and saying,
'Sometimes you know, I despise them, each and every one,
each of their pathetically accepted little existences, every
one of them squandering this single chance to actually live.'
It was horrible but I knew what he meant. In Crawley, that

last place, I found myself doing the same thing, looking out of my window, thinking how horrible we really all were. I am. Things just pop into my head, nasty mean things. State of that, I think. I wouldn't go out with *that* on if I had an arse like that. Listen to their stupid laughs. Look at their fat chins. God he's put weight on. Christ she's aged. Don't we all just get uglier and uglier. Don't we stink?

I don't want them near.

A woman's voice kept recurring, quite close in the end, calling out, 'Hello! Hello! Where are you?'

Thought I was going mad. Surely, I thought, I'm imagining it, she's not after me. Going mad, ha ha, that's a laugh.

I crept further out, slithered through the leaves and the ferns and saw her on the path, just standing still, cupping her mouth, calling again. For a moment more she stood there before striding suddenly away in her walking shoes, the tops of her socks folded over, eminently sensible with her bottle of water and cardigan tied round her waist. She carried a stick, not one of those professional ones, just some old stick she'd picked up.

Cat man told. He must have told or why is that woman here?

I went back, drank some tea, ate some bread and said, yes, I'm up to it, get away from here, go high up, right up past the stones. High as I could go. I got away from them all, there was no one up here, though I could see them down below occasionally passing along the track. I was breathless. My nose was all stuffed up again and my eyes ran. Shouldn't have done that, stupid going so fast, it's much too hot, I'm drenched. Stink.

This place is full of holes. They're pretty much all fenced off and made safe now, but back then it was all open. All kinds of things got chucked down there. In fact, right underneath me, I know, is a great cavern. I know because I was in there once before the rise of health and safety. I lay down and closed my eyes. A little warm breeze ran across my face. I was kind of scraping away at a feeling, not quite knowing what it was. I thought I was still dreaming, that I was really still down there in my nest, then other places flashed through, the places where I go sometimes when I dream, a long high shoreline, the sea far below on the left, an old croft with tall grey houses all round, the bombsite filled with heaps of masonry rubble, some higher than the height of a man, and the alleys and cobbles, and a house like a tower where someone lived, set back from a green country road that went down and then up, a switchback through a beautiful valley by the side of the sea. But I couldn't stay there too long and when I opened my eyes I wasn't sure what I'd see when I sat up and looked around. I thought those other places were real because they seemed so.

But I was only on the heights, same as ever, and my head burned so much I thought I must have a fever.

I felt awful when I came back down, so I got back in my sleeping bag and gave up on the day.

'What's going on with you, Lily?' I said. 'Is it fair on them both?'

'Who?' She got up and sauntered to the open window,

tossing her keys up and down in her hand. Terry was due but she was supposed to be going out with Mark tonight. 'God's sake, I'm not marrying them, Mother, they're just *boys...*'

Terry still came round and they played music in her room with the door shut and wouldn't let Harriet in. But Mark was the one whose name she wrote in various elaborate scripts on her school books. After that first time we only ever saw his pale face when he dropped her off at the door or called for her sometimes and waited silently on the settee if she wasn't ready.

'Does he still do jobs for the old bag?' asked Johnny.

'Oh yes. Now and again. Her toilet's always getting blocked up. She puts things down it.'

'Things? What kind of things?'

'Horrible things. Clumps of hair. Mouldy food.'

'Do they even know about each other?'

'Shut up, Mum. Don't say anything stupid, he's here. Tes! Here!' She leaned out and threw down the keys. Soon we heard the familiar tread on the stairs.

'Did you bring it, did you bring it?' she cried as soon as he came in.

He had been summoned. A CD he had that she wanted and must have *now*. Fool of a boy. 'Great,' she said, grabbing it, not looking at him.

'Sit down, boy,' Johnny said, 'have a cup of coffee. And while you're at it, Lily, make a whole pot.'

'Ha!' said Lily but did as he said.

These days you could almost have believed he liked Terry but actually the main attraction was Phoebe Twist. Johnny was still fascinated by her. 'Seen anything of Irma Grese?' he asked.

Terry didn't know who Irma Grese was but knew it meant Phoebe Twist, along with Cruella de Vil. He had mentioned that she watched TV in the afternoon. 'So, go on,' Johnny would say, 'what does she watch?'

'Quiz shows and things. You know. Those talk things.'

'And she smells?'

'Well, she's got a sore on her leg. That's what smells.'

'Ugh!'

'A big ulcer.'

'Doesn't she get it seen to?' I asked.

'She's got this nurse or someone who comes round sometimes and changes the dressing.'

'Must be awful to be old,' I said.

'The fridge is the worst,' said Terry, 'and the utility room. She's got all sorts round the back of her washing machine.'

'See what I mean?' said Johnny. 'These posh fuckers. Filthy.'

'When you open the fridge,' Terry said, 'you have to hold your nose. Smells like someone farted.'

'Please God she'll get food poisoning one of these days,' Johnny said.

'And she drinks sherry all day,' Lily said, 'all day.'

'You'd think someone like her would have a cleaner,' I said. 'Money she's got.'

'Ah but she's not right in the head,' Terry said with a faint grin. 'She does have a cleaner but she won't let her in. Says she wants to rob her.'

'Ha!' said Johnny. 'And *you* don't?'

'No,' Terry said. 'I don't.'

'So why does she let you in? What's so special about you?'

'Well, it's only when she needs something doing. She blocks everything up all the time, see. Toilet. Sink in the utility room. Honest, she's bonkers. Anyway, she's used to me. She likes me.'

'You?'

'Yeah, me. And I sort her telly out for her.'

'What's wrong with it?'

'Nothing. She just fucks it up all the time by pressing all the wrong buttons. Honest, she's mad.'

'Anyway,' said Lily, 'enough. I've got to get ready. You'd better go now, Tes.' Without a further glance at him she headed off into her room to start the long process of dolling herself up for tonight. She was going out with Mark. Poor old Terry. No idea what he was up against. I felt sorry for him sitting there with his flushed cheeks and slow blue eyes. He stayed a bit longer looking superfluous, then got up heavily.

'See ya,' he said.

'Bye, Terry.'

'Bye bye, Terry,' said Harriet.

Johnny ignored him. 'No self-respect, that kid,' he said when he'd gone. 'Christ, she can pick 'em.'

24

When I was down to a crust I got up. I looked in the mirror. God, is that me? Those hollow cheeks. Those vacant eyes. The skin all softening and the hairs all grey. The dirt.

Strange me.

Something told me I had to go and talk to that man. So I went. It was about eleven in the morning, nice weather. I waited in the woods for a while first, making sure no one else was there, watched him lumbering about in the yard, big shoulders, graceless. He wore a cap and what was left of his hair had grown shaggy under it. The cats were sitting about like mandarins. After a while he went to work on a grey car that was parked by the shed, hanging over the engine in his baggy old overalls. He didn't see me till I was right there, and 'Hello,' I said. He jerked up as if he'd been shot.

'There's a woman walking round in the woods,' I said.

And the fear or whatever I thought I saw was gone and he was just the grumpy old sod he always was.

'I'm sure there's lots,' he said, sticking his head back into the engine.

'She was just standing in the same place for ages calling out. She knew. I'm sure she was looking for me. Did you tell someone?'

'Of course I didn't.' He sounded indignant.

'How else could she know?'

'Are you thick?' he said. 'You leave signs. There's smoke. You're not in the wilderness, you're in a wood. There's people all around. What do you expect?'

I hated that. I could have killed him. Till then I'd been living in my faery realm. It vanished with a horrible sound like a deflating balloon and the terrifying world rushed in, flicking from grey to technicolour in a fraction of a second.

'I know her,' he said then.

'Who is she?'

'She's a social worker. She'd already heard about you.'

Why was he angry? Some people just were. He was like a big bull, breathing heavily down his nostrils.

'You told her about me.'

'I did not.'

'You must have done. How else would she know? *That* part of the wood? That particular direction she was looking in.'

'Oh,' he said, chucking something, some tool or other, maybe a wrench, up onto the roof of the car, 'she doesn't mean you any harm.'

It was a horrible moment. Everything changed like a light turning on or off, I couldn't say whether it brought darkness or light. Like a sound starting up in your inner ear.

'So you did tell her,' I said, betrayed. 'You said you wouldn't.'

It was horrible and bizarre because from the corner of my left eye I saw things starting up, scarcely even aware of themselves, things from the other place.

This other place, Lorna, this other place. Can you tell me some more about that? Can you tell me where, for example, it exists?

Oh Dr Walse here you are after so many years. One of the many. Dr Semple, Miss Farrell, and you, Dr Walse, you used to pluck at your wattles, pull them out like bubble gum and twang them back into place. Again and again. I suppose it was like biting your nails. And you wore bottle-top glasses and everyone made fun of you behind your back, did you know, I wonder? I smiled.

'Oh, not at all,' said Dan, though by this time I'd forgotten what he was referring to.

He gave me a funny look.

'Are you all right?' he said.

Of course.

'Have you got a cigarette?' I asked, knowing I shouldn't but craving one. I hadn't had one for nearly four days. Just goes to show I could do it.

'I didn't tell her where you were.' He scooped out three cigarettes and handed them to me. I have to give him that: he wasn't a mean man. 'What makes you think she couldn't work it out for herself?' he said. 'She's not stupid.'

Sounded like he really knew her well.

'Can I have a light?'

He got out a lighter and handed it to me, seeming annoyed.

'So you know her,' I said, lighting up, 'and you said something to her.'

He sighed. 'If you insist.'

'What did you tell her?'

He slammed the hood down and snatched back his lighter. 'Oh, for God's sake! No more than she already knew. She said is there someone living in there and all I said was I don't know, there might be.' He grabbed the wrench from the roof of the car and started walking back to the house and I followed. Like a dog, the big orange cat came too. That beast needed a good grooming. Full of fleas, the lot of them.

'So I have to go,' I said.

He turned and gave me a sour look. 'Listen,' he said, 'she only wants to help. What are you worried about?'

'I told you.'

He was at the door by now. The cigarette tasted good and pure and fresh and rushed into my lungs.

'I don't want anyone hanging round,' I said. 'I don't want to be moved on. I'm not doing any harm.' I was all shaky. I couldn't help it, I sat down on the back step and my forehead was cold and wet.

'It's not your wood,' he said. 'It doesn't belong to you, does it?'

Nothing more to say. Later I'd decide what to do. The whole thing had always been madness. I could go back to that place, the betting shop and the carpet shop opposite, the sheer hopeless mundanity of it all. Grow old there, *really* old. It was one of those times when I envied sincerely people with faith. I had none, not really, no matter how hard I sometimes tried, and I did, many times. I know I don't have it because of the fact that I'm always scared. That view from the window, the polite dove-grey sky over the street, the grinning leer of the cardboard buffoon mugging it in the betting shop window, all of that, to me, is more terrifying than the wood in the middle of the night.

The orange cat sat across from me, watching me with a grim, slightly concerned look.

'What's the matter with you?' the man said, not nicely.

'I've been ill.'

There was a big gouge in the back step, spoiling the pretty weed-sprouting symmetry of the semi-circle. 'I wondered if you could get me something from the shop if you were going into the village.'

'I'm not.'

One of the cats had caught a vole or a shrew, I couldn't tell what. Oh God, I hate that. The poor little thing with its heart beating visibly and furiously, the darling thing. The sweet little black and white cat with his four white socks. Two steps below my feet, the Roman Games.

'Oh fuck sake!' said the man, stomping back down the steps and seizing the cat by the scruff of its neck. 'Let go!' he roared, but of course it didn't, till he physically prised its jaws open and the vole or whatever it was fell out and tried to run but couldn't. Instead, it just hobbled and crawled like a bad actor in an old western.

'Gaargh!' said Dan, throwing the cat away to land on

its feet with wide eyes and prickling hackles in a patch of clover. At the same time he brought the wrench down with all his weight on the head of the poor vole or shrew or whatever it was, so suddenly that I flinched. It splurted. It was like a horror film.

'Here, you half-wit,' he said to the cat, slinging it the corpse.

'What is it you want?' he asked, stomping back up the steps past me.

'Paracetamol,' I said. 'Milk.'

'I can let you have some of that.' He kicked the door open. 'I'm not walking all the way down to the village.'

I stubbed out my cigarette and watched the cat eat the vole. It seemed very tense, pausing in its biting and chewing every few seconds to look around suspiciously, stopping once or twice to hurl the body in the air with a delicate toss of the head before pinning it once more with a front paw and returning to the feast. The man came back with a carton of milk and a strip of paracetamol. The carton was about half full, I guessed. I swigged some milk down with two of the pills, sitting there on his back step like some old tramp he didn't want to let in the house. Which is, of course, what I was.

'Thank you for this,' I said.

I sensed him standing behind me. 'Look at that,' he said. 'Cruel creatures.'

The cat's tail gave the occasional slow flick.

'Cats don't know it's evil,' I said. 'We do.'

'You look terrible,' he said.

The trees were waving their tops in that old slow way,

the way they did when things were changing. A big lump in my throat pushed heat up the back of my eyes.

'Is it the flu?' he asked. 'I don't want you coming in with flu, I don't want to catch it.'

'I think it's just a bad cold.'

'Well, I still don't want to catch it.'

I started getting up, stiff all over. I didn't want to groan like I usually do, not in front of him. Funny, isn't it, the way we cling on to dignity? 'I don't blame you,' I said. 'Actually I think I'm on the mend.'

He said, 'Come in the kitchen,' which made me laugh because it reminded me of Robert Johnson singing 'Come On in My Kitchen' in his gorgeous distant voice. Because of the peculiarity of my state this made me tearful, a feeling I knew I must vanquish. I sat down at the spartan wooden table that took up most of the room. Poor room, with nothing on the walls, and bare windows and the smell of controlled damp. He made Irish coffee, and put honey in it. 'Honey's good for it,' he said, 'whatever it is you've got.'

I laughed.

'You sound like Barbara Cartland,' I said, but he didn't know what I was talking about.

There he sat, awkward in his own space, electric, constantly looking down.

'Is this your honey?' I said. 'From your bees?'

'Yeah.'

'That's nice,' I said. 'I mean, it's a nice thing to do.'

'What?'

'Keep bees.'

He didn't reply, just sat down and lit up a cigarette. 'You shouldn't be smoking,' he said, 'not with a cold.'

'You're right.'

He just sat there like a big lump after that, and I couldn't think of anything to say. The Irish coffee came in a large mug with spots on. He'd done it really well so that the cream on top covered everything. Honestly, you couldn't have got it better in a bar, and it was lovely, sipping the hot whiskied coffee through the cold cream.

After a while I said, 'This is a nice old house.'

He looked surprised, as if I'd said something personal.

After another while I said, 'How long have you lived here?'

He thought about this. 'A long time,' he said, gazing at the window, where the cat now sat licking its chops.

'What, like since you were little?'

It began to rain softly on the windows.

'On and off.'

'Was it always like this? With the cats and all?'

'Oh no no,' he said. 'Not then.'

We sat in silence for a while and I wondered about who'd lived here, and why he was on his own.

'Must be nice,' I said.

He looked at me but said nothing.

'The honey. Your own honey. Must be nice.'

He stumped out his cigarette and lit another. His eyes narrowed.

'So when did all the cats come?'

A long pause, then, 'It was empty for a time,' he said.

'The house,' he said.

'They colonised.'

After that he said nothing and smoked meditatively.

'This woman,' I said, 'who is she?'

He raised his eyes and sighed as if I was a real nuisance. 'She's just this woman, you know – just this woman who likes to help with things – you know – just like you know – like if she thinks someone needs help—'

'I don't need help,' I said.

He shrugged and said, 'You say what you want.'

'What does she know?' I said. 'I don't want someone coming telling me I can't live there. I'm not doing any harm, it's ridiculous.'

I might as well not have been there. Reasonably enough, he wanted me gone.

'Fucking busybodies!' I drained the mug. 'Can't leave anyone alone.' Next thing I know there's stupid tears running out of my eyes.

'Fucking hell,' he whispered, got the whisky bottle from the shelf and plonked it down in front of me. I grabbed it and poured some into the coffee dregs.

'Bloody ridiculous!' I wiped my face with my hands, downed the whisky and poured some more. 'You know,' I said, 'I just don't care any more.'

He filled up the kettle, his back to me. 'Is it so terrible to you,' he said, 'that somebody might actually be wanting to help?'

'I just don't want it. I just don't want her coming round.' And for good measure, like a child: 'I hate her.'

'Good for you,' he said unpleasantly, plugging in the kettle before sitting down, pouring himself a big drink and knocking it back fast. 'You don't know the woman,' he said. 'How can you hate her?'

So I felt ashamed and hated him instead.

'Can I have some more?' I said.

'No.' I heard people in the woods, very far away, high voices. So vague they could have been birds, or a distant machine. I got lost for a while in following them in their eerie fluctuations till it seemed they were threads mingling and dispersing, an auditory manifestation of flocking starlings. He was talking all the time but I wasn't taking anything in.

He was saying something:

'So what's your story?'

'I haven't got one.'

'Everyone's got one.'

'OK then, what's yours?'

He hesitated then said, 'None of your business,' with an embarrassed sneer.

'Did you always live on your own like this? Or was there, you know, like were you ever married or anything? Have you got children?'

'No!' As if the idea was ridiculous, and he turned his face away and looked at the far wall. The kettle boiled and turned itself off but he ignored it.

'So did you grow up here?'

'Yeah,' he said, 'I did.'

'With your mum and dad?'

'No. Just my mother. And my grandmother.'

'I have two daughters,' I said, and he nodded as if he already knew.

Something hit the floor in the room above. He jumped like a nervous dog. There was one peculiar silent moment as we both looked at the ceiling.

'Cats,' he said.

We sat listening. There was something tight and strained about the air, that subtle change I well knew. I knew because of that dreadful tingle and the urge to run outside that something was upstairs, but I faced it down and stayed put, and there we both were, frozen.

There was a bang on the landing, one loud dark thud.

'Christ's sake!' he said, leapt up and dashed upstairs with a look of outrage on his face. I ran outside and stood in the yard looking at the house. No way was I going back in there. I'd get back in the woods quick. I expected a face in one of the windows above but there was nothing. Then he appeared at the back door. He stood for a minute then came out and walked towards me. 'Nothing there,' he said.

'Cats,' I said.

'Yeah, cats.'

Like me, he turned to face the house and we stood looking for a while at the blank windows and the open door.

'I heard someone on the stairs,' he said.

'Just now?'

'Couple of weeks ago.'

'Someone,' I said.

He shrugged and walked back inside, and after a moment I followed. The feeling was still there in the house but far less so. He was in the kitchen. 'I'm going now,' I said from the doorway. He was rinsing a mug at the sink, looking out of the window.

'*Yesterday, upon the stair,*' I said, '*I met a man who wasn't there.*'

'Shut up,' he said.

'*He wasn't there again today, I really wish he'd go away.* It's a poem,' I said.

'Is it now.'

'Who do you think it was?' I asked.

'Probably my mother,' he said, casually tossing a grimy dishcloth onto the draining board. A chill went through me. Other people's ghosts are so much scarier than mine. I went out into the hall and looked around, at the dirty yellow walls and the open doors, up the wide stairs with the dusty handsome bannister. When I looked back he was leaning in the kitchen doorway watching me.

'Oh,' I said, 'she's here too, is she?'

He scowled and turned away, as if he'd wanted me not to believe him and resented me for making it seem more real.

'You're a grumpy old sod, aren't you?' I said.

He ignored this and went back into the kitchen.

'What's your name?' I said, following.

'Dan,' he replied. 'I know yours.'

That got me. 'How?'

His back was to me.

'*How?*'

'Never mind.'

That was childish.

'I didn't tell you, did I?'

'You must have done.'

He sounded guilty.

'You've been in my purse,' I said.

'You come in my house,' he said, 'I've got a right to know who you are.'

'*I come in your house!* You *made* me come in your house!'

The monolithic stupidity of the back of his head, his round shoulders, his stolid silence.

'Tell you one thing,' I said, 'I won't be coming in again.'

'Good,' he said, turned and walked past me into the living room and stood looking down at the fire.

25

Can't have this. Pull yourself together, woman. Up! What are you, fool, special?

I will try, just for one day, to behave like everybody else. I shall get up, have a wash, comb my hair, sweep my rug, walk into the village. I won't buy a newspaper, they're what drove me mad in the first place. Don't even want to see the headlines. I did all these things, and then I set off, and my heart was scared and thumping by the time I reached the wood's edge. Because soon, maybe today, people were coming, and then things would be wrong again. I walked along, until I reached the part where there's a row of new houses on the outskirts of the village. These weren't here when I first came. Interlopers. The windows winked at me. In the village I stood for a while at the very spot where we parked our car that day, and I could smell the back seat with its fumes and smell of sick and I could see the backs of my father and mother's heads, my father's neck red and angry, hers covered with thick brown hair that curved into the hollow then out again. Then I saw the back of my little brother Tommy's head in the wood, and his little boy voice sang to me: *a pig is an animal with dirt on its face...* as he pissed on a tree.

There were plenty of people around in the village, and horses grazing on the green. It's a pretty place. No one took any notice of me. Outside the pub there was a bench. Two young girls were sitting on it, waiting, I think, for the bus. I know that bus. Through the village and out the other side it goes round a big bend and on past where Dan lives and past the farm and the old cottages, and stops the other side of the narrow bridge going over the stream that runs down from where I get my water. That's where I get on when I go into town for my cash, my bag of stuff, toilet paper, salt, blue soap in a bottle, eggs, whisky. And I get off there too, coming back. It's worked out fine.

I could scream at that woman.

I wondered if I looked like some old tramp. Too open, too raw, the cold air in my throat. I didn't know where to go, straight across the green where everyone could see me, or just walk on up the road and out the other side. Go round the edge. Stop. Go in the shop. Go on.

Ollerenshaw's. Ting!

A woman was being served at the tiny counter, across the papers and the little box with strange bright toffee lollies sticking up in spikes, and the Tic-Tacs and chewing gum and lighters. It was all ineffably strange, all the colours jumping about next to one another, and a million different forms of lettering all over the walls and the shelves, even the doors of the glass cabinet. And there was a man, a little farmer with a wonky eye, and a thick-necked girl with narrow eyes and a mouth that chewed, though I don't think there was anything in it. The people were all strange and looked at me as I entered. Cold eyes they have. I don't think they like me. I'm a terrible, bad person, I know, but am I evil? I am maybe. How can they tell? It's written on me.

The old man behind the counter was thin and stooped and grey all over. His eyes flicked at me and away. My head felt hot inside. It may explode, just burst and splatter them all with my brain. The woman went out. I concentrated on the chocolate and my mouth watered. I felt like gorging on thick sweetness. A tube of Rolos, Wispa, Ripple, Cadbury's Whole Nut. The farmer bought his paper, and the girl looked at me with the steady indifference of a cow looking over a hedge. I smiled at her to see what would happen but it made no difference to her face. Nothing would have. I was just something to look at. The man left and she said in a raspy voice, 'Any bread later, Bob?'

'Come in after one,' the old man said, so she bought one of those awful magazines, the sort Lily used to get, and went out, pushing rudely past me as if I wasn't there.

'Yes, dear?' the old man said, not looking at me.

From the corners of both eyes I saw the rippling of things speeding up. Smiling idiotically, I picked out Rolos, Wispa, Ripple, Cadbury's Whole Nut, and laid them on top of the pile of newspapers.

He said something, probably the price but I didn't catch it, so I just laid a fiver down. This will never do. If it's this bad here, however will I handle town? It's that woman's fault.

'Anything else?'

'No.'

I dropped some of the money on the counter as he gave me my change.

'Whoopsadaisy!' he said.

'Thank you,' I said, shoved everything in my pockets and left.

I did all right.

It started raining lightly, and oh it was good to be in the wood, but my journey back through the fringes and depths was washed with sadness. More change. All the time. God knows where to now. But look at all those people living every day – if they can do it why can't I? That man standing there every day. Ting! *He* manages, doesn't he? I haven't grown up, have I? That's what my parents said. I felt like that when I was thirteen and I still do. What is *wrong* with me? I came home and lay in my nest listening to the gentle patter on the leaves and wondered why they couldn't all just leave me alone. I ate chocolate, half the Whole Nut. Save the rest for tomorrow. I was glad I'd cleaned my rug, it made everything seem good. It was a nice one, I've brought it around with me wherever I've gone for years and years; I can't remember where it came from, but I know I had it in Carmody Square. It's brown and blue and red and green and looks as if it might be Turkish.

I just lay and lay and lay and tried to drift away. Lily came in my head, eating a pink shiny chewy thing, slowly peeling the paper off it, but some of it's still sticking to the toffee. It makes my teeth ache to watch her.

'Remember that poor man that died?' she says. 'Guess what?'

The screech owl woke me.

It was pitch black.

Lily was flopping about alternately sucking her thumb and smoking. 'As soon as I turn seventeen,' she said, 'Terry's going to teach me to drive.'

'How many is that a day now, Lily?' I asked her.

'Only about five.'

'And the rest.' Johnny was playing Chinese Chequers at the table with Harriet. Harriet was winning.

'Five too many,' I said. 'Can you please not blow it in this direction?'

'Why?'

'Because of Harriet.'

'Harriet likes it. Don't you, Harry?'

'I don't mind.' Harriet skipped over another two of Johnny's pieces.

'He's got a driving job now,' Lily said. 'He really likes it.'

'Really? What kind of a driving job?'

'Delivering to shops.'

'What does he deliver?' I asked.

'Anything. He drives a van and he's got his own car now too. It's a really good one.'

'Lily,' said Johnny, 'I have absolutely no objection whatsoever to you learning to drive. I think it's a good idea. But wouldn't you be better off getting proper driving lessons?'

'Yeah, but I don't have to pay Terry.'

Oh well. Johnny and I exchanged a look. She won't

be seventeen for another six months. Time enough to discourage her.

We were supposed to be going to Maurice's but I didn't want to go. I was sick of him swivelling in his chair like our professor, idly tossing the fruits of his knowledge at us in his munificence.

'You've changed,' Johnny said, 'you're no fun any more,' when the girls had retired to their room to play with makeup.

We were always arguing these days, sotto voce.

'No fun,' I said, 'where's the fun in another boring night at Maurice's? If anyone's changed, it's you.'

'That is not true. You're too easily influenced.'

'Me? That's a laugh.'

Not that we ever did have much of a laugh by then.

'You used to be far more open to ideas.'

'You mean I agreed with you more?'

'That's one thing,' he said. 'You don't take my side.'

'Your side? I don't even know what you mean.'

'Yes, you do, you and her, you gang up on me. That's how it feels.'

'We don't.'

'It's always the two of you having a go at me, all the time, and I'm sick of it.'

'What, you mean just because we don't always agree with you?'

'I don't expect you to, you know that, you twist things, I can't open my mouth but you twist everything I say.'

'No, *you* twist things.'

On and on we went, stupid. I said he was a big baby. I hated it when he got like this.

'I hate it when you get like this,' he said, and went off to Maurice's on his own.

When did I first look in his eyes and find him gone?

It was across the room, he was lying full length on the sofa watching something on the TV. I'd come in from somewhere, the shops or something, loaded down with stuff. He turned his head slightly towards me. There was a sneer above his mouth. He lifted the mug of tea to his lips and in that moment I realised how profound and irreversible was the coming change, and how complacently I'd ignored its approach. It wasn't sudden. People often say 'It came out of the blue.' Ah no, the signs were there, they just never came into focus. That day when I came and he looked at me like that I knew that he'd started to hate me but hadn't realised and was still calling it love. He never came back, the old Johnny, the one with soft brown eyes and humour. In all those years, even in the sulks, the snappishness, the irritating smugs, still they were his eyes, shielding hurt feelings, slicked over with pathetic bravado. Now they were hard. There hadn't been evidence. In early pictures of him he smiles, his eyes twinkle. In his later photographs he aspires to remorseless severity. Oh serious man! I only have one from his early life. He's sixteen and completely gorgeous. He carried nothing forward.

And when did I first feel afraid? Not afraid in the sense of terror but deeply and with anguish, the way I thought it must feel to be aware of prolonged coming heartache, as if someone dear had just been diagnosed with a terminal illness. That sort of fear. Bang went the shutters, down came the grille. The time came when I couldn't say what I thought or do what I wanted, because if it wasn't what he thought or wanted to do there'd be a row. He told me I had no moral compass. And soon there came a time when only the new Johnny looked back from his eyes, and they lost their beauty but gained a formidable depth, controlled, noble and steely. It was the cause, it was the cause, my soul. It was a kind of stern vandalism in him, a haughty disdain for the stupid, the fallible, the lazy. Life was serious, not for calm but striving, and what kicked in was a terrible hard master like some old god.

Anyway, he changed.

And, you know, you pretend. You carry on, because if not, it's a tragedy, and even at its worst you'll get a sudden memory like a punch in the gut, Johnny watching cartoons on the TV, such a kid. And I'd cry and lose myself in books.

I did go back to Maurice's once or twice more. Both times I noticed something that must have been happening for a while now but that I'd never been aware of. Maurice sidelined Johnny. All his great thoughts were addressed to the others, and when Johnny spoke, Maurice just went on talking over the top of him. Poor Johnny. Too emotional, loose cannon, a drain on energy. And after all, what had he done wrong? Nothing. He'd just become a different person and it was noticed. This is it, I thought, this is why he seethes and sulks, why we are falling to pieces. 'What a bunch of silly little jumped-up revolutionaries,' I said when we got home. 'Who are they? No one. Words words words. They are not your real life, Johnny.' You should have seen the way he looked at me. Traitor. Apostate.

'Lor... I really want to understand... is it me?... I just want to understand.' Pained eyes, but the hardness gleamed through. 'What is it I'm not getting? Don't you accept that there are terrible injustices in the world?'

'Of course I do. Why are you saying this?'

'I'd die for this cause.'

I looked at him and wanted to laugh.

'Saint Sebastian,' I said.

'I'd kill for it.' His eyes were very serious. 'There are some totally hateful people. I mean, really *bad people*. People who've really hurt people and done dreadful things.'

'You're not Saint Sebastian,' I said, 'you're the good Samaritan. That's what you were when I met you.'

'Don't worry, Lor,' he said, smiling. 'I wouldn't kill *you*. Anyway, what are you on about? Why are you bringing the Bible into it? What have those old fairy stories got to do with anything?'

'Have you read the fairy stories?' I said. 'The real ones? Horror shows.'

'Exactly!' he said. 'And what happens to the wicked? They dance in red-hot shoes forever.'

'Just think of those people at the wedding feast,' I said,

'eating their dinner while this woman dances herself to death in red-hot shoes.'

'Ah,' he said, 'but she was a nasty piece of work, that old queen. Think about it. She had to be stopped.'

26

She was there again. 'I've got some chocolate,' she said, 'would you like some?'

She didn't look right. She was keeping her eyes on the ground.

'I can get my own chocolate if I want any.' He stood at the top of the steps looking down at her standing in the yard with a carrier bag in which it looked as if there was a bottle. 'I've got things to do.'

She looked off to the side with her mouth open.

'Did you hear me?'

'Oh sorry,' she said dreamily, 'bad time, is it?'

'Look,' he said, raising a hand as if to ward her off, 'you can't just keep turning up here.'

'I know. I just wanted to find out if you'd seen that woman again.'

'Madeleine.'

'Is that her name?'

'Yes. No, I haven't seen her. So now you know. So now you can go. Why are you looking down all the time?'

She looked up. 'Am I?'

'Yes, you are, you're looking really weird.'

'I'm feeling a bit scared,' she said. 'I just wanted to get out of the wood for a bit.'

'Oh,' he said derisively, 'back to nature's wearing a bit thin, is it?'

'Just need to let the feeling pass,' she said, turning to go, 'that's all.'

'What's in the bag?'

She turned back. 'Just wine,' she said.

Pathetic, she was. Worse than me, he thought. It was a funny feeling being stronger than someone. 'OK then,' he said and motioned her in with his head. The fire was all laid and ready to be lit. He grabbed the matches from the mantelpiece for something to do but it was too early to light the fire so he put them back. When he turned she was sitting on the settee. Won't be able to get rid of her, he thought. The woman's completely mad. He didn't know what to do so he got his own bottle of whisky from the kitchen and set it down on the low table. Each recognising in the other a fellow piss-artist, they sat in grudging tranquillity till she'd polished off the best part of the wine, then she started rambling like a maniac. She said there was a ghost boy in the fields. As if he wanted to hear that, what with all the shit he was already putting up with. Then she held out her arm and said, 'Look. See how it moves under the skin?'

He couldn't see anything.

She said she'd seen this boy all her life and before that even.

'You're not making sense,' he said.

'I used to be in this place,' she said, 'it was an institution,

I was there for six months. And the first thing I saw when I walked in was this big sign that said: Stop Making Sense. That's from Talking Heads.'

'So you took it to heart.'

'What?'

'Not making sense. You took it to heart.'

'I suppose so. Don't you believe in ghosts?'

'No idea,' he said. 'Don't let's start on about ghosts, no wonder you're scared. You're out there all on your own. I don't mind telling you, I couldn't do it, you start thinking about all these things and next thing you know...'

She stood and paced, straight-backed, hugging her coat round herself. 'We're all here,' she said, 'wandering around in this place, the cold boy, the baron, your mum, and that other one, the one that got washed down. What d'you think about that?'

'What are you fucking talking about?'

'The man that got washed down. You know. All that rain.'

'I think it's a shame,' he said.

'It is. It's dreadful.'

'And perhaps we'll end up here too, why not? All of us ghosts, wandering around together wondering what to do, wandering and wondering.'

She laughed. 'Still, we won't be lonely,' she said. 'The Lord is in this place. How crowded is this place.'

'I think you ought to shut up,' he said. 'I think if I was living out there in those woods I'm damn certain I wouldn't want to be thinking about things like that. It'll drive you mad.'

'Me?' she said. 'Mad?'

Both laughed.

She drank more. She *demanded* it, my God, she was worse than him. He even went out and got another bottle from the village. The pub was open and Mary gave him a bottle and said he could pay her tomorrow because she knew he was good for it. 'Go on, Dan,' she said and winked at him and smiled. She was quite fond of him, Mary was. For a moment he stood and looked at her with his big moist blue eyes, and she looked back and smiled and he thought about telling her about this woman and how she was bloody mad and it was beyond him, he didn't know what to do. A bottle of Talisker. Good stuff. He just paid and went, and walked back down the lane.

She was singing when he got back. He heard her from the yard. She sang liltingly and vaguely out of tune but just about OK, something he didn't recognise.

'Here.' He put the bottle down.

'Oh lovely!' she said with a big smile.

Oh fuck it, just fuck it, he thought, and poured himself a good shot and downed it and poured again.

'Listen,' he said, 'that woman who was looking for you? Madeleine? She's OK. Why don't you at least talk to her?'

She looked away and her eyes glassed over.

'She's OK. She means no harm.'

Poor bugger, he thought.

'Oh, people never do mean harm, do they? Everyone thinks they're doing the right thing but they're all doing harm anyway, aren't they?'

'She's a good person,' he found himself saying, suddenly

loyal to Madeleine. 'She'd help anyone, she would, and not think about herself. She's just like that.'

The woman was looking into the unlit fire as if it was ablaze.

She smiled. 'What if it was me?'

'What are you talking about?' he said.

'What if it was me and I lost my memory.'

'I don't know what you're talking about.'

She laughed and lit a cigarette. 'I feel so much better now. I don't know if it's the paracetamol or this.' Picking up the bottle and sloshing it about. Then she said, 'What if I was a murderer? What if I'm a serial killer and you don't know?'

He shot her a disgusted look.

'I used to put my victims down the old mines.'

'If you're going to start talking weird, you can go,' he said.

He got down on his knees and flicked a thumb across the lighter and held a flame to an edge of paper. Whoosh it went, the yellow fire running, and the whole thing went up beautifully. He'd always been good at lighting fires. Some real skill there, even in that stupid moment he recognised that and felt proud.

'Did your mother die in this house?' she asked.

The wood was catching, the kindle crackling away, heat pushing out at his face.

'Yes,' he said, 'hanged herself,' sitting back and watching for her reaction. It was strange. She was looking into the fire and letting it burn her eyes till they watered.

'Not in the actual house,' he said, already wishing he

hadn't told her and wondering why he had. 'It was round the back where the hives are.'

'It's awful when things go mad,' she said and looked up at him.

He went out just to get away from her, stood in the kitchen pointlessly, not knowing what to do. He didn't want to go back in but soon he realised if he didn't go back it would only make things worse. Must tell her to go.

'By the way,' she said, when he went back in, 'what happened about the body?'

He felt tired when he looked at her.

'The one that came down.'

'Nothing,' he said.

'Nothing at all?'

'Buried, I believe.'

'No one claimed him then?'

'No.'

She looked at the fire again. 'To think of that!'

Then she was off crying and it was awful.

'Come on now,' he said, but she went on. Fuck sake, on and on. She was having a full-blown nervous breakdown in his house and he couldn't handle it.

'You shouldn't be in there in the wood in this state,' he barked.

'I'm not in any state.' Her voice was steady.

'Of course you are.'

She pulled herself together visibly.

Thank God for that, he thought, but she had to go and ruin it by saying 'My head hurts.' She stood up and held her head as if trying to keep it on.

'You've drunk too much,' he said. 'Stop now.'

She sat down again. 'It's like waves inside my head.'

'Are you going to be sick?'

'I don't think so.'

'Listen,' he said, 'I think what I'm going to do is this – I think I'm going to ring Madeleine – I think I'm going to ask her what I should do.'

'No!'

She jumped up and ran out all woozy as she was, leaving the back door open. He pulled a face: oh what now, get up, close it, don't let her in again. It was going dark. He was glad she'd gone, so fucking glad, she was no responsibility of his, but what if she fell over in the dark and died, would that make him guilty? Was it too late to call Madeleine? He closed the door, sat down, turned on the telly then lowered the volume right down and went out after her just to make sure she actually got back. She hadn't gone that far, and she was making a racket, crashing about. She moved ahead, always just in sight through the trees, never getting the way wrong or having to retrace her footsteps. Walking fine, seemed OK. She came to a thick green overhang of ivy and ducked under.

If he followed she'd hear, so he got as close as he could and listened, and after a while lifted up a strand of foliage – a little more, a little more – and a little more. There was a trail inside, a burrow, the kind an animal would make.

So now he knew exactly where she lived.

Somewhere deep inside a light glowed through the leaves. She's a tough bugger anyway, he thought, letting the thick ivy fall. September coming. Then winter. She can't be

in there when it snows. When he was as sure as he could
be that she was safe he set off home. Once he looked back
but there was no sign of the light, so he walked on, and
the next time he looked back the wood was just as it had
always been.

27

Feels like the true depth of night, three o'clock, the strangest time of all. That's when I often wake up and feel everything sharper than ever. It's going strange again. Anything could happen. And my heart starts hammering like crazy. Three o'clock in the morning, dead of night in the middle of the forest. That's when you drink your own soul to the last drop. That's when you get up – ouch! – here at this silly infirm side of life, back and legs aching – and find – strange! – moonlight filtering through even here, making the wood black, soft silver, deep blue. What wouldn't I give for one second of sweet repose? I carry a lidded basket of souls sleeping in swan's down. That's where I put them. Lily in her red dress with a red paper flower at the side of her cloudy black hair. Her dark hair, the red dress. I put us all in. The cold boy's gone in there too now, no matter if he's a ghost or a glitch in the brain. That old memory, that known thing that ached your heart and made you cry in your sleep, the light in the eye, the lost one.

I set off with the basket over my arm into the darknesses where I dare not go.

★★★

I could see Lily through the open kitchen door, fridge open, swigging something out of a carton. 'Tuesday,' she called. 'Next week.'

'Tuesday? Wait – no – oh, OK. Hang on.' Terry, fixing up a date with Lily, got out a diary, one of those tiny pocket things, and consulted it with all the seriousness of a businessman with a heavy schedule.

'Busy man,' said Johnny, lying on the settee peeling an orange for Harriet.

'Can we do Thursday instead?'

'Oh Terry! Tuesday's ideal for me.'

'Can't do that,' he said. 'Let's make it Thursday, yeah? Thursday next week OK. Is that OK?'

'Why?' she said pettishly.

'Doing a job for the old girl.'

'Twist?' said Johnny.

'Yeah.'

Lily heaved an exaggerated sigh.

'I'm driving her to Dorset next month,' Terry said.

'Oh really?' Johnny tossed the orange over to Harriet, sat up and wiped his fingers on the cushion, then picked up his guitar. 'What's in Dorset?'

'Her son. I have to drive her down and then go and pick her up a week later.'

Johnny burst out laughing. It was funny, Terry the chauffeur.

'The son!' said Johnny. 'Another scrounger. And she's letting *you* drive her?'

'Yeah. I'm a good driver.'

'He is, you know,' said Lily.

'Anyway, she knows me now, so I'm all right.'

'Can't she get the train?'

'Doesn't like 'em.'

'I thought she never went anywhere,' I said.

'She doesn't. Hardly ever. Anyway she's paying loads, so I'm OK. I do a good job.' He laughed. 'She doesn't like him. Her son. He's called Douglas. Oh him! she says. I know what *he's* after!'

... but I... do go anyway alone through the trees. Follow the silver trails, which cross and turn. To the ruins where the cold boy lives. I sit still, alert for whatever may come, angel or demon. Nothing comes. I have come to these trees to die, I thought. My trees, my trees, clinging to my trees. I'll be a ghost here with all the others. Just before dawn I looked up and saw no roof at all but walls everywhere, all pink and black and orange, all open to the sky. At the top of the crumbling heights, little steps ended in nowhere. A great entrance opened up in front, then stairways, passages, ovens, fireplaces, garderobes, all rising and falling as if a wave of heat was passing over them, as if I was sick and in a fever dream. There was a courtyard, and small busy figures dressed in long clothes moving around in the background. There was a great height above my head, and voices coming to me from far away in the wood, but no words could be distinguished. They were for me, though. I knew that because my name ran through them like a refrain.

The moment peaked and reversed. Time weathered it all back down to stumps in a few seconds. It was early daylight and I was sitting with my back against a wall in among the ruins, smoking a cigarette. It had been raining.

Sometimes the rain in the woods makes me so happy it's more than I can stand, it's holy fucking joy.

There's Terry's knock on the door, *dum* da *dum* da dum dum *dum*. I was working away at some new leaf earrings with my diamond file and Harriet was playing with her hamster on the rug. Johnny was in the kitchen making tea.

'That's Terry,' I said, 'get the door, Harry.'

He ruffled her head as he came in.

'Hi, Terry,' I said, 'she's not in.'

'Oh.' He hulked by the door.

'Well, come on in,' I said after an awkward pause. 'I've no idea when she'll be back, she's off somewhere with Sage.'

'Yeah,' he said uncertainly.

'Wanna cup of tea?'

'Yes please.'

'Sit down.'

He sat leaning forward with his arms hanging over his big square knees. His eyes followed the scurryings of the fat golden hamster.

'Terry!' Johnny sounded positively friendly, coming in from the kitchen. 'Kettle's just boiled.'

That's nice, isn't it? Nice as pie. And he's been a right fucking pain all week, moody as hell even with Harriet, head down staring at the floor, grunting if he's spoken to.

Occasionally casting a thoughtfully reproachful glance at me but looking away as soon as I noticed. My diamond file slid smoothly along a leaf vein.

'So when are you off to Dorset?' Johnny asked, all hail fellow, well met.

'A week on Friday.'

'Huh.' He grinned. 'Driving Phoebe round the twist.' He went to get the tea and called back, 'Imagine being stuck in a car with *that* all the way to Dorset and back.'

Terry sniggered nervously. 'I've been chucked out,' he said.

'Chucked out?'

'Who's chucked you out?' I blew on the leaf.

'My uncle.'

'Why?'

'Dunno.'

A long pause.

'That's awful,' I said.

'Yeah.'

Can't you go to your mum and dad's? I nearly said that, then realised I knew nothing about them, had never even asked, and that as he'd been living at his uncle's ever since we'd known him there was probably some good reason why he never mentioned them. 'So what happened?' I asked instead.

His eyes moved slowly. His cheeks were square and flat like his knees. 'We don't really get on,' he said blankly, and after a moment, under his breath, 'We used to.'

'So where are you sleeping?'

'At me mate's.'

'Oh right. Is that OK?' Johnny brought the tea in. 'Sleeping on the couch, are you?'

'In the bath,' he said.

I made sympathetic noises.

'Kip here for a bit if you want,' Johnny said.

Oh no no no no. Terry here all the time, lolloping about and getting in the way. His open mouth.

'That's OK, isn't it?' Johnny turned to me.

'Oh yes,' I said cheerfully, 'till you get sorted.'

'Only be for a few days,' said Terry.

'That's OK,' I said.

'Sleep on this.' Johnny indicated our messy settee. It was not quite long enough but if he curled up or put his feet over the edge he'd be OK. 'You can park your car in the yard at the back of the co-op. I'll show you where.'

What had got into him?

Still, Terry would be working, wouldn't he? But then I remembered that a lot of his work came from his uncle, and now it would probably all dry up and we might just have him sitting around all day. And what about Lily? What if she wanted to bring Mark home? She'd go mad. I looked at the poor boy, bashfully smiling as he drank his tea, feeling mean and guilty for my ungenerous thoughts. 'I wish you hadn't done that,' I said, after he'd gone off to fetch his stuff. 'Don't you ever think about consulting other people?'

'Oh, it's all right,' said Johnny, grinning, energised, but when Lily came home and found out what he'd done she threw herself dramatically about the place: 'You haven't! No! You haven't! Oh, you idiot!'

'Who the fuck are you talking to?' he said, strumming his guitar. 'What's the big deal? He won't be here long.'

'This is awful. *Awful!*'

She actually screamed and flew into her bedroom.

'God sake,' he said.

'Well, you can't blame her. You could at least have—'

'Sorry sorry sorry,' he said, his eyes suddenly moistening. 'I only do what I think is best, and I don't always get it right.'

His good humour evaporated as if someone had pulled out a bung. He played his guitar doggedly and loudly, gazing fixedly at the hamster running between Harriet's constantly moving hands. After a while she put the hamster on her shoulder and sat on the rug listening, staring back at him. I was dreading the knock on the door. When it came it wasn't so bad. 'Bloody hell,' Lily said roughly, 'stuck with you, are we?' and bopped him on the nose with the hairband she'd just pulled out of her hair. He hardly spoke a word that first night. Whispered awkwardly a couple of times to Lily. Made up his bed on the sofa good as gold as soon as I told him to, and in the morning had it all neatly put away by nine o'clock, which, in our household, was pretty good.

28

So that's that then. Decided. No way was he getting lumbered with another miserable mad woman. Enough of all that with his stupid mother. Still, he thought, in a funny sort of way she's not a bad drinking companion.

It was the weather that made a difference. After that long spell of hot weather, back to cold nights, only this time there was more of a settled feel of winter in the air, and it was only September. A few days passed, he did nothing, the woman stayed hidden. Maybe she'd moved on. Can only hope. Or maybe she'd gone to another part of the woods, covering her tracks.

He took the scrap of paper out of the drawer in the kitchen table and read the name on it: Harriet Gilder. A number. Tried to think what he'd say. Hello, am I speaking to Harriet Gilder? Do you have a mother called Lorna Gilder? Well, I just thought I should let you know...

I mean really, what'll she do when it snows? What does she eat? Must be tough. Madeleine had allergies. *Allergies!* his mum said. *She's just a picky eater.* Couldn't eat tomatoes and potatoes and cheese. Pizza and chips was out. Madeleine. Let her handle it. Pass it all over. He put the piece of paper on the bedside table and lay in the dim room with the light from the landing slanting in by the far wall and the wind out there shrieking.

Moved on by now surely. Ring in the morning. Ring Madeleine.

So he did. He got her husband.

'Oh, hi, Dan!' he said enthusiastically, and Dan realised he'd forgotten his name again.

'Is Madeleine there?'

'I think she's around here somewhere – yes – yes – no. Oh! There she is. Maddy! Mads!'

And her talking in the background to someone.

He was being sensible. It stops here, he said to himself. It has to stop here.

'Dan!' She sounded warm and curious.

'That woman in the wood,' he said, 'I don't think she should stay there through winter.'

He told her everything, the exact location, gave her the name of the daughter and her number.

'Oh my goodness,' she said, 'and she's been in there *how* long? Oh, it must be desperately hard, that.'

'Well anyway,' he said, 'I'll leave it to you then, shall I?'

He could hear the husband talking in the background, or maybe it was the radio.

'Poor woman! Has she got mental health problems?'

It sounded so simple when she put it like that. Gary, that was his name.

'I don't know. Yes, I'm sure she has.'

'And how did you get the number? For the daughter? I'm writing this down.'

He sensed officialdom down the line, swinging into action.

'I took it out of her pocket.'

'You took it out of her pocket?' She laughed. 'How?'

'I gave her a cup of tea.'

There was a silence.

'She took her coat off. I went in her pocket when she wasn't looking.'

Another little pause, then she said quietly, as if she didn't want the people at her end to hear, 'You are such a nice man.'

'Anyway,' he said.

'Do you think you could show me where she lives?'

Oh fuck, he thought, what have I done?

'Might be good for you to introduce me.'

'No, wait a minute,' he said, and his words started stumbling. 'I'll go first,' he said, 'I'll go in first so as not to take her by surprise, then you can come in after.'

'Is she volatile?'

'Volatile?'

'Yes, do you think she's likely to get very upset, do you think we should bring somebody else along to…'

'Oh no, I don't think so,' he said, 'she's not dangerous or anything.'

He heard her tap her teeth. 'Can't do a thing today,' she said. 'Chocca. Just on my way out. Listen. If I come round your place tomorrow about nine, would that be OK?'

Oh Christ, he thought, it's not going away. I'm still involved.

'OK,' he said, then walked round and round the kitchen saying shit shit shit and thumping his head.

29

Terry was there for eight days. Lily and he didn't seem to take much notice of each other, and he was very polite and kept out of the way. He spent a lot of time in the yard at the back of the co-op polishing his beloved car. He ate everything I put in front of him gratefully, stuffing it away as if it was a mechanical process. Lily stayed out a lot at Sage's or Jude's or at Drama. Terry made a lot of mess very quietly. Once I said he could put some of his washing in with ours and after that he just shoved all his stuff in our laundry basket and left it there, and he had loads every day because he seemed to have a one-wear policy for everything. I kept finding myself draping his boxers over the radiator. 'This isn't fair,' I said to Lily, 'you've got to help more.'

'*I* didn't invite him in, did I?'

The rubbish bin filled up too quickly. I was taking it down to the bins one evening and some sharp-cornered thing cut through the plastic and split the bag and the rubbish went down the last flight of stairs, split teabags, coffee grounds and all. The thing that had split the bag was the sharp plastic corner of a discarded package that had contained a spanner. Who was buying spanners?

Damn Terry, can't be anyone else. It was from a place on the Uxbridge Road. I'd have to come back with a dustpan and cloth and clean all this up. Bloody Terry, I thought, you've moved in all right.

'You should see the amount of rubbish since Terry moved in,' I said to Johnny, getting the cloth and the dustpan and brush.

'Never mind,' he said, 'won't be for long.'

'And the washing.'

'I feel sorry for him,' Johnny said.

'You like Terry now, don't you?' I said.

'I quite like him,' he replied guardedly, 'but I don't respect him.'

One day Lily came into the kitchen and whispered to me, 'Mum, he's driving Phoebe Twist to her son's tomorrow. Johnny's at Hatchet all day, so I said Mark could come round with a video. Is that OK?'

Damn. My day off work. Never any peace.

'I suppose so,' I said. I'd like my own room. Just a little room where I could go. Johnny went out later, he took his guitar with him. He didn't come back. I went to bed at one, slept till four and thought he might have come in and be sitting up reading or something, but he was not in the flat. I worried then. It had happened once or twice before but it wasn't usual. About six the phone rang.

'It's me,' he said, 'sorry I didn't call earlier. It was an all-nighter. You know what it's like when there's a lot going on.'

'No I don't. You should have rung.'

'Sorry.'

'Sure,' I said.

'Don't be like that. I've got to go to work now.'

'Oh, you have, have you?'

'Yeah. It's OK. I'll have a good sleep later.'

'Fuck off, Johnny,' I said.

'Fuck off, you too.'

I rang off.

I slept again and when I woke I could hear Terry already up and making himself some toast, so I got up and put on my dressing gown and went in to make coffee.

'What time are you off?' I asked.

'Picking her up at half nine.'

He'll be gone soon, I thought, on his way to Dorset. Yawned. The phone rang. Terry was next to it. 'Bet you anything that's her,' he said, picking it up with his buttery hands.

His end of the conversation was all *oh, yeah, uh, OK, thanks.*

'She's got a cold,' he said when he hung up. 'She don't wanna go. I knew this would happen. I don't think she ever meant to. 'S'OK though. She's still paying me.'

'Well, that's good.' Christ, I thought, Mark's coming round with a video at one.

Harriet came out in her pyjamas with her hamster in her hands, sat down on the settee and turned on the telly. Lily was still in bed.

'So you've got a whole free day,' I said brightly.

'Yeah.' Terry grinned and sat down next to Harriet, another big kid.

I knocked on Lily's door, went in and closed it behind me. 'Lily!' I hissed. 'Terry's not going! She's cancelled.'

'What?' She was sitting up in bed reading *The Rats* by James Herbert and looked grumpy at my intrusion.

'Terry's not going. Phoebe Twist rang up and cancelled. She said she's got a cold.'

'U-u-urh!' she said, but she didn't look too bothered.

'Hadn't you better call him?'

'I'll sort it out,' she said.

By the time she'd got up and had a bowl of Fruit 'n Fibre, Terry was bobbing about restlessly between the window and the table. I went into our bedroom and pulled open the drawer where I kept all my jewellery stuff. I'll just stay in here, I thought. This should be my day off. The door was open. Terry said, 'I'd have been well on the way by now.'

'I know,' she said, 'it's a shame.'

'I've got this money,' he said.

'Have you? What money?'

'Well, I haven't got it yet, but if I go round she'll give it me. She's paying me anyway, she said.'

'Great!'

'I was all looking forward to a drive out in the country,' he said.

'Aw!'

'We could go somewhere anyway,' he said.

'Yeah? Where?'

'Dunno. Get out the map and just go.'

And she, the little bugger, the horrible thoughtless infuriating little bugger, called out casually, not hiding anything from anyone, 'Mum! Will you tell Mark I've had to go somewhere? Tell him I'll give him a call midweek.'

'You can't do that,' I said, rushing out of the bedroom. 'That's not fair, Lily, *you* tell him.'

They were half out the door. She looked back once and giggled then she just went, hair all a mess, sleep still in her eyes, in old jeans and a purple sweatshirt. I looked at the phone and thought about calling Mark. Terry had left it all slimy with butter. I didn't have Mark's number to call and let him know, make some excuse, save his feelings. Sorry, Mark, she's not feeling well. I threw everything in the bowl, all the mess they'd left from breakfast, cursing them all for the inconsiderate bastards they were, all of them, all of them. Harriet went downstairs to play with Eve and Steve's little boy, who was two now, and at last I had the place to myself. Oh blessed, blessed solitude. I was so tired, I went in and drew the curtains across, lay down on my bed and fell asleep very quickly.

The car went off the road in a very pretty part of Surrey, by a pond that swallowed up Lily and Terry and his wonderful car. There was no other traffic, no one else around, just one of those senseless things.

And after that, with breath-taking speed, everything else fell apart too.

When the news came, Mark was in our house, drinking a cup of tea, smiling at Harriet's hamster as it scurried round and round the table, big black beady eyes like berries. He didn't know where to look, what to say. The policewoman said, 'Shall I call your husband?' I looked over and saw this pale stranger boy looking at me with a face full of fear, as if instead of the deaths of two small people the great day of wrath had been announced, the chasm gaped, the veil of the heavens rent. I don't remember what was said, how he left. I remember going into the girls' room and seeing Lily's unmade bed, with a scrunched-up tissue sticking out from under the pillow and her James Herbert book, a quarter read, lying face down on the floor with its spine bent down the middle. I remember the policewoman. She was lovely. She held my hand. Then Johnny was there, and Harriet was on his knee, her arms around his neck, him with his eyes aflame, and I finally cried, in a weird way, politely, apologetically, a sad slow drip, because it was that or scream. Eve came in and made us all some tea. Steve looked in. Scared blank faces. The police had gone to tell Wilf. It was unbearable, it was endless. How time played, how it stretched and spun and contracted.

30

Dan went upstairs, into the bathroom. He felt awful. Can't believe this. You dig a hole, it just keeps getting bigger. In the mirror the skin round his neck was all scraggy. He should have felt relieved getting this thing off his hands at last, or at least starting to, but somehow he didn't.

And what exactly, he thought, was the point of it? What would they do? The great *they*. They can't put her away. Not a crime now to be sleeping rough, millions of them. Just get her out of the elements before winter. Some kind of hostel maybe? And if she won't, she won't. Least I tried. Least I know I tried, then if they find her one day frozen solid it's not my fault.

He felt terrible. She'll go mad. Thinks I'm a cunt already. Still, get her daughter in. She can sort it out. Fuck it. He went down and sat on the back step. It was some time after ten, he thought. A big starry frosty sky. The occasional swish of a tail, a cough, soft movement from the cows over by the hedge. He talking to the owls, a thing he did sometimes. They'd go: Woo-woo! And he'd reply, cupping his big knotty hands in front of his mouth and blowing. Whoo whoo! He'd been doing that for some time when he suddenly got scared so he went out into the middle of Gallinger's wide meadow and sat down and waited there to feel normal again. It was midnight by the time he felt like returning to the house, which lately had taken on what he could only describe as a crowded feeling. He felt it as he crossed the threshold, as if the rooms he could not see were occupied, as if the faces on the old photographs in the cats' room were moving, talking to one another. I'll get rid of them, he thought, once and for all. The room stank of cat pee. He yanked open the two top drawers on the sideboard and pulled stuff out, piled it up on top. Photographs, ancient yellowing documents that hadn't been important for decades. Just chuck the lot. When did he ever look at any of these pictures anyway? What did they mean? People made much out of these things. What's the point when things are gone? All they do is make you feel bad. A sheaf of pictures spread out on the filthy old table top. His dad he never knew. Died in an accident, something horrible involving steel and machines and negligence at work. She'd got money from the accident and came back here. There were no wedding photos of his mum and dad and none of them together. No pictures of the Brooms, his father's people, at all. Just these. It used to mean something but it didn't any more. His dad on a long flat grey and white beach with a bilious sky and the sea line in the distance. Just a bloke.

She used to say: your dad –
your dad used to say
your dad had one of those
your dad loved kippers
He pushed his dad aside. There was his mum all smiling

and blowsy in very bright sunshine, a girl. Then a couple of really ancient snaps of the back steps with him an unimaginable serious semi-baby, a monstrosity, he thought, almost afraid to think that that thing had been him. Fair hair (that didn't last), frowning brow and a silly little white collar. Gran. Never looked at these things. Couldn't say he enjoyed it when he did. They just mouldered away in these drawers occupying stale space and not affecting him in any way. He scooped the lot into a pile on the table and left them, thinking: there, I've made a good start.

Is she still up, I wonder? That woman?

What's the time? Past midnight.

He opened the back door and looked out. Dark as hell. Not going out in that.

Next morning, nine sharp, his phone blared out something that sounded like 'Where Did You Get That Hat?' played on a xylophone. It had been on the phone when he bought it off Eric and he hadn't got round to changing it yet.

It was Madeleine. 'I talked to the daughter,' she said. 'I think she's quite nice. The mother should be taking medication, that's what she's worried about. She said she's all right as long as she stays on that.'

He wished he'd never got involved.

'Actually,' she said, 'it was really interesting. I found out a lot. The poor woman's off her head. Awful story.'

What was he supposed to say?

'Dan?'

'Yeah.'

'So anyway she's coming up from Birmingham tomorrow,

237

and she's bringing some of her mother's medication with her.'

Oh God, he thought.

'So could you take us and show us where she is?'

'I've got a lot on,' he said.

He could hear her thinking on the other end of the line.

'It won't take a minute,' she said. 'Say, twenty minutes of your time.'

Cats. Fucking cats, scratching at the window, scratching at the door. Fuck off, he wanted to say. I've done my bit. No more.

'Well, you can't just go barging in,' he said. 'I'll have to go in first. She knows me.'

'Of course. If you think that's best.'

'Is it just you and her? The daughter? No one else?'

'Of course.'

Oh Christ oh Christ oh Christ. Confrontation. Scenes. People getting all het up. No.

'OK,' he said.

'Good. Look, I'll check back with her and give you a definite time later. Probably sometime late afternoon. Is that OK?'

'Yeah.'

Fuck.

A woman with heavy eye makeup, sitting on his sofa drinking a mug of tea. The heavy eye makeup out of place on her. She had a soft round face with a thin turned-up nose and a curved smile, long grey hair falling over her breasts. Her clothes were dark, plain and forgettable, her shoes sensible. She sat with her hands loosely linked and comfortably resting in the place beneath the roll of her waist.

'She's off her meds,' she said calmly.

Oh yes, this one would take charge now, he thought. Rain thrummed down outside, pinged up from the windowsill in bursts of silver.

'It's not that I mind people being able to do what they want,' she said, 'live any way they want. But what do you do when someone's a danger to themselves? And she is, or *may* be. There's the fire risk, for a start. It's a potential furnace in summer round here. And what if she fell or had an accident all alone out there, a woman of her age? I mean, think about it.'

They talked away, her and Madeleine. It seemed to be going on for ages and he just wanted them to go. Fuck off please, the pair of you, just go.

'Don't you get driven mad by all these cats?' said Madeleine.

'Yeah,' he said.

'You know, if you're going to have them all around, you really ought to get them seen to. If you ring Animal Rescue they'll come and check them out. They'll do it for free.'

'No, they won't,' he said.

'They will!'

'Oh, this rain!' said Harriet. 'I don't think it's letting up.'

'What does she do when the weather's like this?' asked Madeleine.

'No idea,' he said.

'I mean, what's she actually got out there? Do you know? What sort of a set-up?'

'I don't know. She's got a tent. Tarpaulin and stuff.'

'Yeah but...'

'It must be awful,' said Harriet.

'I know.'

'Give it another half hour,' Madeleine said. 'Then we'll make a decision.'

'They should never have closed that place,' said Harriet. 'Just put them out on the street and in these horrible places. I mean, what do they expect?'

Madeleine stood up. 'Can I use your loo, Dan?'

'First door you come to going up,' he said.

He'd scrubbed it, knowing they were coming.

When they were alone, Harriet looked straight at him and said sadly, still faintly smiling, 'I don't know what she's said to you. I don't know if you realise. My mother's a funny woman. You can't believe a word she says.'

'So I imagine,' he said.

'She'll say anything. It's all in her head. She can come across as fairly normal sometimes but scratch the surface...'

He offered her a cigarette but she shook her head. 'So she's scaring children and dog-walkers, is she?'

'I don't think so.'

'You know,' she leaned towards him in a confidential manner, 'she was never a real mother to me.'

'Wasn't she?'

'No.' She looked away then said, 'Oh yes, she was a funny woman, my mother,' as if she was dead.

After that they sat in silence, and he thought: they'll

never move. Never get them out of my house. And the rain went on and Madeleine returned and everything was awkward and they said it was getting late and they'd come back tomorrow. Harriet was staying in the Holiday Inn. She was wondering if there was any way she could get expenses from social services for all this but gave up the idea almost at once.

Anyway, she said, she couldn't really manage more than one more night. She had to get back to work.

'What do you do?' asked Madeleine.

'I'm a radiographer,' she said.

'What about the other sister?' said Dan, and they both looked at him.

'I didn't know there was another sister,' Madeleine said.

'My sister died in a car accident,' Harriet said.

'Oh, how awful!' cried Madeleine.

'Yes,' she said, 'it was. It was terrible.'

They left together but a couple of hours later Madeleine rang and told him all about it, what a sad case it was, the sister had been killed in a car crash and the mother had gone into some kind of weird state after that. Apparently she'd had a couple of peculiar episodes before. 'She's schizophrenic, you know. They get paranoid. You can't trust anything they say. And then the father pissed off, and it was just poor Harriet and her mad mum till she left home and went to live with a friend. Couldn't wait to get out. I mean, you have to sympathise. Some of the things I've seen. People's lives are just so messed up. Really, you just wouldn't believe. You wouldn't believe my files, some of the things I've got in my files. I could tell you—'

'Sorry, Madeleine,' he said. 'Got to go now.'

He looked out. The yard was growing muddy from the rain and the tyre tracks had made a mess. With a face of granite, he pulled on his boots once more, got on his yellow waterproof and plodded off. The afternoon was uncomfortably darkening. He didn't have to do this. Didn't have to do anything. I said I was going in first, that's what I'm doing, he told himself. As he got deeper in the wood, the sound of rain was like a constant waterfall. He stood still and looked around, rain dripping from his hairy overhanging brow in spite of the shiny yellow hood. You could hear water streaming away into the shiny clay beneath, a great thirst slaking. It was still light enough to see the quivering shine on the ivy.

He went on towards the big rock, then stood still again. Yes, this was it. And there, if he was not mistaken, was the faintest warming of the gloom in the thickets on the left-hand side. Lamplight.

So he just called. 'Hello-o-o-o-o...' sounding ridiculous to himself.

A moment.

'Hello-o-o-o-o-o...'.

The rain fell harder.

There was a rustling in the gloom. The foliage parted and her wan face looked out. 'You'd better come in,' she said.

The face withdrew, he stooped, shoved his weight through the gap in the leaves, shoved his face on through the gap towards the light, my God, she'd got it all pretty tight, and into this place. It was a little room. She could just about stand up in the middle of it but he felt like a giant. He crawled in and crouched like a troll. It was a tent inside a tarpaulin inside a cave of leaves accessed by a short but twisting tunnel. An old red and brown patterned rug decorated the floor. A Tilley lamp stood in a cracked yellow mixing bowl. The fire risk! he thought.

'Christ, I hope you're careful with that,' he said.

'Of course I am.'

The walls, if you could call them that, were hung with jewellery, long strands of beads and bangles and jangly things, all sparkly in the light from the Tilley. Spilt cards. Not normal ones, Tarot cards. All that shit.

'Your daughter's here,' he said.

Her face changed. She closed her eyes for a few seconds. Then she sighed. 'You have unleashed chaos,' she said, then gave a sudden unhinged laugh. 'My daughter! Which one?' and he froze, remembering that there was a dead one.

'Harriet hasn't bothered with me in years,' she said then. 'What's she after?'

'She's brought your medication.'

'You know, everything just gets too complicated.' She turned away. 'Why did you tell? You promised.'

'I'm sorry.'

He was now, though he didn't see any other way things could have worked out.

'How did you find Harriet?'

A long pause. 'When I looked in your pocket. That night – you know.'

'My pocket? My purse, you mean. You must have gone in my purse.'

'Yes, I did.'

A silence.

'Well, that was a shitty thing to do,' she said, then a bitter laugh. 'I like that. Don't go poking around in my house, you said. When *you* were the one who—'

'Sorry. It seemed necessary.'

'No, you're not sorry.' What else was in my pockets, she was thinking. What else does he think he knows? 'She can't make me move,' she said.

'Look, I'm sorry,' he said again. 'I'm just letting you know. They'll be here tomorrow.'

'They?'

'Yes, your daughter and...'

'That woman.'

'Yes.'

'A social worker.'

'Yes.'

'Oh well that's that then.' She sat up straight and started fumbling for a cigarette. He lit it for her.

'They never leave you alone, those people,' she said.

'She's only trying to help.'

'Of course.'

This place was much too small to smoke in. It was like being a kid in a den, doing something forbidden. 'Christ knows the state of your lungs,' he said.

'Christ knows the state of your liver,' she replied.

He smiled. 'Shouldn't think yours is too brilliant either.'

She smiled too, without humour. 'I wonder,' she said. 'I'm sure you're right about your woman whatsername, she's probably a lovely lovely woman and all that, but I do wonder – it's not for me, you know – all this *caring*'

– speaking the word with careful emphasis – 'I think it's just to make her feel good.'

'No, but—'

She laughed. 'She doesn't even know me. You know what will happen? They'll make me go back to that flat. I wish you could see it. It's OK. There's a BetFred and a carpet shop and a taxi place. If you go out of the door and start walking, it's just nothing every way you go. All just nothing. No one really wants to be there. No one loves it. It's just a place to be, it's just—'

She broke off.

'I won't stick it, you know. It's not *my* place.'

'It's the winter,' he said. 'That's the real problem. Oh sure, you're not doing any harm but when winter comes you can't be living in here. It's mad. You ever been up around here in the winter? It's crazy. You'd freeze to death. OK, maybe if this was the South of France or something—'

'You can live in cold temperatures,' she said, 'people do. Lots of people do. You've just got to be prepared.'

He snorted. He was smoking too now and a blue haze hung in the air.

'I wish I was clever,' she said. 'I was never clever. Then I'd know what to do.'

'Who told you that?' he asked.

'What?'

'That. That you're not clever.'

'No one. Me. I don't know. I don't think you realise,' she said. 'There'll be forms to fill in.'

He laughed at the way she said it, as if she'd said there'll be war and pestilence and famine.

'I can't do it. All this' – pointing into the air and swivelling her hand round and round – 'all this official stuff. All these people. Having to—'

It was just too awful. She broke off.

'Oh, someone'll help you with that,' he said.

'And Harriet. You don't know what she's like. She makes me feel about' – with her free hand indicating something less than tiny – '*this* high. She's like a steamroller.'

'Yeah, well,' he said. He could understand this. Families.

'What do you know about it? You don't know a thing about it.'

'OK then.'

He would have stood up if there'd been room enough.

'Best thing is if you come back now before it gets any darker. Sleep on the sofa like before. You can have a bath if you like. You'll want to clean up a bit before you see your daughter. They'll be round in the morning, first thing. Best if you look – you know. Best if you're there all ready. I don't want to have to traipse out here again.'

He didn't think she'd come, but she got a few things together wordlessly, slung a bag over her shoulder and reached for her torch.

'Lead on,' she said, and followed his wide back through the wood, the beam of his own torch lighting the tracks ahead. It had stopped raining but everything still sang. She didn't know why she was going. The idea of seeing Harriet again filled her with a harrowing mixture of wild excitement and terror. Little Harry with her gap tooth. What will I do? What say? She'll give me that look, as if the whole world is my fault.

He stopped.

'What?' she said.

He held up his arm to say hush.

The beam showed wrinkled bark and rampant ivy, weirdly detailed, nothing moving. Outside the beam everything was black.

He looked up.

Under and over the gentle dripping of leaves, there was a sound from above, quite far and seeming to overarch the forest like a lower sky. It was sharp and crisp and had the effect of being inside the ear as well as up there. To Dan it sounded like a big bird passing over, something wild and massive like a great auk or albatross or some other rare and difficult thing that should not be in the air above his wood. To Lorna it was a voice coming through countless layers of gauze, calling and wanting to be heard, incoherent and appealing, as if she was God and the voice some poor lost supplicant on a planet on the far side of several universes. That's the way things are for me now, she thought. That's what I hear.

'Going to be clear tomorrow,' he said.

'Dan,' she said, feeling suddenly as if he was a friend, a weird feeling.

'What?'

It was cold.

'Nothing.'

After a moment when there was no more sound than the rippling of the forest sucking in water, he walked on and she followed his broad lumbering shadow out of the wood.

31

He gave me a couple of blankets and a cup of tea. The fire was still burning.

His hair had grown free and tufted round his face, giving him a wild, sternly leonine look.

'Have you got a shower?' I asked.

'No. Just a bath.'

'Oh. I'll have a bath in the morning. What time are they coming?'

'I don't know. First thing.'

'Jesus Christ. Have I got to get up early?'

''Fraid so.'

'I don't know how I'm going to do this.'

'Oh, you'll be OK.'

Of course, he had no idea.

'So then,' he said, 'have you got everything?'

'Yes.' I started making up my bed on the settee. There was a little wooden dog on the table that wasn't there before.

'Did you make that?' I asked him.

'Yeah.'

'It's nice,' I said.

He said nothing.

'You're a good lad, Dan,' I said as he trudged up the stairs, but I don't think he heard me.

How could I sleep?

I went a-hunting. I'm good at silence. That room where everything you touch covers another, older thing. Excavation. I turned the light on. The photograph drawers were open and they were all shoved in a heap on top of the sideboard. I grabbed a big handful, took them back to the fireside with me and drank my tea, warming my feet on the fender as I looked at them, all these faded jaded greys, all the dead people smiling from the other side. And him young, a boy. You wouldn't know him. Same eyes though. Self-conscious. Oh what a shame, where all that goes to.

Thought I heard a sound upstairs, so I shoved everything under the sofa and went to the door and to look upstairs but it was nothing. Cats. Always cats. The house breathed out age. I like old houses. When I was fourteen we moved from our old house to a stucco semi-detached with a bow window. It had small square rooms and I had grey and yellow striped wallpaper in my bedroom. I had the room at the back and my brother Tommy was at the front. He used to come in in the middle of the night and say he was scared. 'It's all right,' I'd say, but I was scared too. We were never scared in the old house, dark and creaky as it was, but this new one was a strict, nasty house, humourless and mean. I went back to the fire and looked at the pictures some more. Look at him, look at him look at him, a poor boy too, just look. I kept hearing things, nondescript ticks and clicks, rustlings, some as close as the kitchen, as if someone was moving carefully so as not to be heard. It can't be him, I'd have heard him on the stairs with his heavy feet. The door to the hallway was open and the darkness stood beyond it like a curtain. If I'm going to put these back so he doesn't find out, I'd better do it now, I thought, now or never. It took all my resolution to get up and steal along to the cats' room in the dark and return the photographs to the top of the sideboard, foolishly trying to arrange them just as they were before, so he'd never know. Then I skittered back down the hall and got down on the settee under the blanket and stared at the fire that was clucking itself gently into peace for the night.

I thought about Harriet. Can't do it. Have to. Just no way of working it all out. Where can I go? The snow, would it be so bad? The woods in winter, the snow thick and heavy on the branches, falling and sifting down, and me there watching, warm with all my blankets wrapped round me, looking out. How could that harm me more than BetFred and a boarded-up hairdresser and dull yellow food containers made out of that peculiar thick brittle plasticky stuff, blown by the perishing wind along the street below? And who am I? Other people live with it, why can't I? What if that view from the window, BetFred, the grim, the dreary mediocrity – what if you looked at that and saw it like the wild wood, saw the beings there, those awful stupid boring people, as if they were wildlife in a wood? Try to make something of that. Where was the joy in BetFred and ketchup-smeared plastic?

So I went in the kitchen and got his whisky down off the shelf, and drank two or three and still couldn't put my mind away and get to sleep, so in the end I got up and went back to my den and saw my old Tarot cards hiding down there, and picked them up and gave them a good shuffle. Nice old things, a lovely Italian deck, very worn down, with gold on the Major Arcana cards. The people all look like Botticelli angels and maidens at the well. The lion is handsome, the moon sadly and serenely wise. It's embarrassing, says Johnny's voice, you and all this crap. It's pointless. It's really quite pernicious all that kind of thing. I just find it baffling how anyone can find things like that interesting. He was far far above all that shit. 'I just like the pictures,' I said, 'it's not as if I run my day on them, you know.' I never drew a spread and said aha the Devil and the ten of swords, I must not go out today. If he thought that was weird, God knows how he'd have coped with me now. Nothing strange happened to me in all the years I was with him.

When it was light I went up to the heights, I didn't know what else to do.

32

'She's gone,' Dan said. 'She was supposed to be here.'
It was raining again.

Harriet heaved a great exasperated sigh. 'Well,' she said, 'you'll have to show us where she lives.' She laughed without humour, rolled her eyes and repeated, 'Lives!' in a wry tone.

'Harriet's concerned,' said Madeleine.

Harriet looked away, bland-faced.

He went out to get his boots and Madeleine followed. 'I mentioned about that body,' she said. 'You know, it's worrying me, Dan. I mentioned about that body and I'm not kidding, she went white.' She leaned forward and whispered. '"My dad," she said. You should have seen her, "My dad." Cos he went off about then. It was awful! All sorts of things she was saying. She just kept saying, "What if it was her? What if she did him in? My dad. He just was there and then he wasn't." And she was a liar, she said, her mum was a liar. Told her he'd left them. But he wouldn't do that. He would never do that. That's what she said. Why would he? But then I thought –'

She was following him around irritatingly while he got his boots on, went into the kitchen, shooed out a cat.

'– I thought, come on now, let's get forensic here! And I said, Harriet, how tall was your dad? And she said he was tall. She wasn't sure but she thought at least five eleven, possibly more.'

'I see,' he said.

'Thank God. Because the man they found wasn't that big. Five foot six, they said. So I could confidently say, that was not your father, Harriet, that man was definitely no more than five foot six. Thank God for that. But do you know what she said after that? I think this is really sad. She said, "In a way I wish it was him, because at least then I wouldn't always have to wonder why he went away. At least then I'd know." Can you imagine that? How awful that must be?'

Harriet came out into the hall.

'I suppose we ought to get going,' Madeleine said brightly.

This is stupid, he thought, this is ridiculous, as they all trooped off through the trees with him in the lead. Last of the Mohicans, he thought. Pathfinders to Mars. How did I get into this? Nobody spoke. He went the wrong way and had to backtrack. At last he folded back the thick growth and revealed the canvas bedecked with strands of beads. He called out, then went in headfirst. She wasn't there.

'She's not there,' he said, backing out.

'Let me see.' Harriet bent down, lifted the flap and went in. Madeleine got down on her hands and knees and crawled in after. He could hear them mumbling together.

'I know,' he heard Madeleine say, 'I'm not sure that that's safe.'

Dan stood with rain dripping down from his eyebrows

into his eyes. He thought he might be coming down with a cold.

'Awful,' said Madeleine, coming out with a rueful smile. Her padded coat shone with rain. She pulled the cords on its hood sharply so that it tightened round her face and made her look suddenly old and plain without her hair.

'Awful,' echoed Harriet, crawling clumsily out and jerking to her feet. 'I don't know, just do not know, how anyone can live like that.'

'She's vulnerable,' said Madeleine. 'I'm not quite sure what to do next.'

Get rid of them, he thought, and said, 'Look. She's survived in these woods all this time, she'll stick it out a bit longer.' Can't argue with that.

There was nothing for it but to tramp back.

'It's really quite disgusting,' Harriet said as they walked along. 'I've kind of had enough of this. I mean, what is she becoming now? A horrible old vagrant. Did you see the bottles? And the sleeping bag?'

The rain eased up as they reached his house.

They shook the rain out of their coats. He put the kettle on, that's what he was supposed to do. Soon, he was thinking, they will be gone and it will all be over. A new cat, one he'd never seen before, eyed him from the windowsill outside. White sunken cat face, arched brown eyebrows. Why that urgency in the eyes? Where do they all come from? Madeleine and Harriet came into the kitchen after him, he hadn't wanted them to. They sat down at his kitchen table and started talking away as if they were in a café waiting to be served.

'I'm sorry about all this bother you've had,' Harriet said with a kind of defeated resilience, turning in her chair and watching as he rinsed a mug. 'It must have been awful.'

'Well no,' said Dan, 'she hasn't actually been that much bother.'

'How long has she had mental health problems for?' asked Madeleine.

Harriet thought for a moment. 'I don't know,' she said. 'I only became aware of it after my sister died. My half-sister. She went a bit funny then, but of course it was a very bad time, and my dad went as well.'

He put sugar on the table, milk.

'He went,' she said, 'he just went. Gone like that.'

She opened her bag.

'I remember my dad,' she said. 'I loved my dad. I always knew him really well, even without words or anything. My dad. I've got pictures, look.' She pulled a couple of small snapshots out of her bag. 'Look how handsome he was when he was young. Look at his hair. My dad. And I suppose it was all understandable, I mean that she should lose track a bit, a lot had happened, but really, she was never the same as far as I was concerned. She used to have jobs one time. You know, she did this and that, she had a waitress job and a thing in a print room and some other things, and the jewellery thing. But she just got worse. You know? And then it all sort of fell apart. After the crash. After my dad went. It was all bad news.'

'Tea,' he said.

'Actually, Dan.' Madeleine smiled. 'Do you mind if I make a coffee?'

'I'll do it.'

'It's ages ago,' Harriet said.

He put the kettle on again. The cat on the windowsill stared in with a look of outrage. You and me, cat, he thought.

'What I want to know is' – Harriet picked up her tea – 'what I don't think people realise is that I actually left home when I was seventeen. So I don't really know a lot about what went on after that, you know. We were never that close. It wasn't just me, it was her too, she was *weird*. She wouldn't ring you up like other mothers. She wouldn't be normal. She really just wasn't very good, you know, as a mother. She just wasn't. She had no fucking idea, if you'll excuse the language. Even with my sister. Much too soft with her. Ridiculous. Now, that's not good.'

'No,' said Madeleine.

'It's very difficult.'

'Yes.'

'So all those years when she doesn't get in touch and we just don't have anything in common, it's just like, I feel like, you know, as if we're just completely separate people. You know? They say you can't choose your family. Well, you can't.'

'Of course you can't.'

'And it's like there's this stranger out there who I don't really know, could be anyone, and then whenever something awful happens like this, it's me they get in touch with, and what am I supposed to do? I've brought her the meds. What can I do? What do they think? Am I expected to take her into my house? I have a partner. What am I supposed to do?'

'I do understand, of course,' Madeleine said, 'but we do at least have to keep you informed. No one's going to make you take her into your house or anything like that obviously, but you do see that your opinion counts in this.'

Harriet shook her head and held up her hands in a strange supplicating way. 'She had a place,' she said, 'she was OK. They closed it down. Care in the community! Hah, that's a joke.'

'I know,' said Madeleine. 'They put them in horrible B&Bs in grotty seaside towns and leave them to flounder and then wonder why they have problems.'

'Exactly. This is the problem. Whose responsibility is she? Whose *actual* responsibility?'

'Is there absolutely nobody else? No other relations?'

'She's got a brother,' said Harriet. 'He's in Australia. He's a solicitor.'

'Well, in the end,' said Madeleine, 'if she's not a danger to herself or anyone else...'

'*I've* got no other family to share this with,' said Harriet. 'It's not really fair to lumber my partner with all this.'

And on and on they went, discussing law and morality and the practicalities of the situation, and as he poured hot water onto instant coffee, he looked out of the window and saw Lorna lift the latch on the gate coming in from the wood.

'She's here,' he said.

Harriet put her head in her hands. 'Oh fu-u-uck!' she crooned.

Madeleine stood up.

'No no,' she said, 'this is good, this is what we came for.' She went to the door.

'Some ways,' said Harriet to Dan quietly when she'd gone out, 'I wish this stupid woman hadn't dug this whole thing up. They could have just left her buried out there, who fucking cares?'

Oh, this was all just such a nuisance to her. He knew how she felt.

'Can't do it though,' he said apologetically.

'I don't know,' she said, 'I don't know what to do about any of it. I need to know whether I can go home.'

33

U p on the heights, I kept thinking there was someone there with me, and if I could only hear, tune in like a radio, but when I did I wished I hadn't because it was just all the same old crap from the whisperers, about the fool I am and all the stupid things I've ever said or done when I make a fool of myself. But then it stopped raining and I saw the car and knew, just knew, that's Harriet. And I had to run down, didn't think, just did it, couldn't pass up the chance for another look at her.

The ginger-hair woman met me at the door.

'You must be Lorna,' she said. She was very nice, one of those sweet genuine smiles that illuminates the face and doesn't give a toss about the wrinkles. 'I'm Madeleine. Hello!' A funny greeting, as if we've met before perhaps by telephone or email or whatever, and already know each other. But we don't, not at all.

'Hello,' I said.

'Your daughter's inside,' she said.

'Harriet.' What could I say?

'Yes. She's in the kitchen. Are you cold?'

'No.'

'Anyway, come in and have some coffee. Are you hungry?'

'Not really,' I said.

'OK.' Smile smile. 'Well, come in.' As if it's her house.

Dan was leaning on the sink, glowering. Harriet standing, facing the door.

'Look now, why don't you sit down, Lorna,' the woman said. 'Would you like some coffee? Tea?'

You know the way they made me feel? Like I wanted to say, no, fuck it, give me whisky, give me dope, give me anything but you lot. Let me go.

'Tea,' I said.

'Tea.' She moved towards the kettle but Dan gestured her away and set to with cups and spoons and things. I sat down, and Harriet sat down on the other side of the table, and we looked at each other in hopeless stalemate. I looked and looked, she was so fundamentally of my life, so rooted. Couldn't see that child, the gap tooth, the anxious little face. Looked in her brown eyes for a sign. God knows what she saw, I hate to think. And before anyone had a chance to breathe she said, 'Well, Mother, here we go again.'

'Hello, Harry.'

Looking at me like I'm trash.

'It's me,' I said.

'I know,' she said and almost smiled. 'That's the trouble.'

A mug of tea appeared on the table and the ginger woman said pleasantly, 'Now, you two just have a talk. We'll leave you to catch up for a bit, then we can all...' She had a deep tote bag into which she delved and brought out a packet of Hobnobs. 'Have you got a plate, Dan?'

He opened doors, clanked about. A plate appeared on

the table and Madeleine offloaded a mound of biscuits from the packet. 'There,' she said. I looked at Dan. His eyes were bleak and old and angry. They left us somehow, closed the door softly.

'They called me,' she said eventually. 'It was kind of a relief. I knew you were off the grid, of course. I got a call from Marion.'

Which one was Marion? Those people. Always calling. Strangers, sizing me up, part of their working day. Kindly, unwanted, troublesome. All on first name terms with me though I could never remember theirs.

'Have I broken the law?' I asked.

'Well, you tell me, Mother.'

'I don't think I have.'

'You know,' she said, 'this is just trouble for an awful lot of people.'

I'd forgotten how pointless it always was to talk to her.

'All these good people having to run round after you.'

'They don't have to,' I said.

'Oh, come on! You know they do. This is the real world, Mother.'

I couldn't look at her enough but it would never work, she and I just couldn't cope with one another. There was a time she wouldn't bring her friends home because of me. Before she left. And she blamed me, she always blamed me for what happened. It must have been horrible for her.

'I don't know what to do about you any more,' she said, 'you're getting older now, you can't just carry on...'

'You don't have to do anything.'

'I do. They ring me up. They hassle.'

'Well, I don't ask them to.'

'But they do.'

'Fuck 'em,' I said.

That didn't help at all. She took a long drink of her tea and put her mug down with a bang. 'Well,' she said, 'now's the time to get sensible.'

I picked up a biscuit and thought about taking a bite. I can't eat. I keep trying but everything tastes bad. I put it back on the plate. I didn't know what to do and my throat felt as if it was going to cry. So I stood up without drinking any of my tea, and went round the table because all I wanted to do was give her a hug, I just wanted to touch her and get an echo of the way it used to be, years and years and years ago when I'd put her to bed and give her a cuddle. But she wasn't having any of it.

'No!' she said. 'Mum, you can't just do that!'

'OK,' I said, 'OK, but don't worry. I'm going now. I'm OK. Don't you worry,' and I walked out.

Her voice followed me, angry and hard: 'Don't just walk off like that! That's just typical!'

The back door was open. Through the sitting room door I saw Madeleine sitting by the ashy fireplace, turning the pages of a notebook. I'm notes. I'm words. On a page. My head's light. I used to feel like that before I fainted. I fainted a lot when I was a child. That's just another of the things written down. Quite a little story. That's funny, I haven't fainted for years, and it was once so common. Where did that go? All those funny head things. I'd say to someone, some friend at school, 'Do you ever get that thing like when your head feels as if it's...' and then I'd try to explain the ineffable, and they'd say, 'No. I've never had anything like that.'

Out the back door. Dan was standing smoking in the yard in the after-rain, two cats at his feet, looking up at him as if expecting something. No one followed me.

'I'm going,' I said.

He took the cigarette out of his mouth and nodded.

No one followed.

34

He thought they'd never leave. Sat there yakking away at his table for at least another hour and decided nothing.

'Basically,' said Madeleine in the end, 'we can't drag her kicking and screaming out of there as long as she doesn't cause trouble. I'm inclined to just send a report to her last social worker or whoever, tell them where she is and leave them to it for now. We can keep in touch. Keep an eye on things. You'll let us know, won't you, Dan, if you notice anything...'

'Sure.' Oh great, he thought, dump it all back on me then. 'So what about winter?' he asked.

Madeleine looked at her watch as if that would tell her how long they had before it got really cold. 'I think we have a little leeway,' she said.

'One thing I have to make clear.' Harriet was up, buttoning her jacket over her large breasts and faffing about with her scarf. 'She can't come and live with me. It just isn't viable. This is about the worst possible time for this—'

'Fuck sake,' he said, suddenly sick of it all, 'I wish I'd

never said anything at all. Just leave her there, for God's sake. Tough old bat, just leave her.'

They both looked at him, surprised. He started picking up the half-empty mugs from the table and sticking them in the sink. Fuck off, his back said.

'OK, so...'

Madeleine said they'd be in touch but it didn't look like there was really very much they could do for the moment. 'Let's wait and see,' she said. 'She may move on, or go back. Anything could happen.'

So they mumbled themselves out of the back door and into their separate cars and thank God were gone.

It was late afternoon. He was hungry and the cupboard was bare. He went down to the pub and had a ham sandwich with crisps and a couple of pints, then went home and tried to feel normal again, but it was all just a mess in his head. He put on music in the kitchen, bang bang bang sadness and pining. Turned it off. TV. Whisky. Smoke. Light a fire, though it's not really cold. Nice evening. Stood at the back door, the night bright with a moon coming up over the trees. The owls were beginning to call. One deep in the wood, one closer. Fuck it, he thought, leaving the back door open and heading off through the little side gate into the wood, the bottle swinging from his hand. He swigged from the neck as he walked. He'd forgotten the torch but it was light enough to see and he wasn't thinking ahead.

She was in but she was packing up her things. The canvas

was up, and the Tilley lamp hung from a branch just outside the doorway. She'd rolled up the old red and brown rug and was stuffing a scruffy old backpack with clothes.

'What'll you do?' he asked, crouching awkwardly.

'I don't know. Pack up first. Set off.' She looked at the bottle and laughed. 'Look,' she said, 'I got one too.'

He held his up, settling on the floor. 'I've got more.'

'I know what I'm not going to do,' she said.

'What's that?'

'I'm not going back to that place in Crawley.' She laughed, and told him again all about that road and said, wouldn't it be nice to be able to do that, to live with BetFred and squashed food and a triple-layered concrete car park where pale youths drove cars too fast round and round and round. And to find there, I don't know, content or fulfilment or one of those things, and not always be wondering why the hell it all was, and realising nobody else felt like that.

'Oh, everyone feels like that,' he said knowledgeably.

'I don't think they do.'

'Of course they do. That's just what it's like for everyone.'

She went on packing for a while and he grew stiff sitting on his haunches in this little space. 'Christ's sake,' he said, 'you know you'll get arthritis and rheumatism and sciatica and everything else too living like this.'

'I know,' she said.

She pumped the Tilley lamp and it glowed a bit brighter. The drink slid down and down, warm and freeing. And the night grew dark outside, and the ghost of a possibility failed to manifest. It wasn't on. No no no. Come off it, I couldn't let anyone see my stomach now. Sod all that pride in what you are crap, no one's ever getting a look at my stomach from now on, not unless it's a doctor and absolutely necessary. Not for me. Not for you. Not even in the dark. Men don't care as much. Maybe in the dark. And the well is dry. I've reached some place, she thought, where I can see things whole, the young boy in the gross old man, the baby in the waste-of-space, the bullied in the brute. This man in his awful bathos, this morphed clay thing blooped out of soft-eyed youth. My flabby belly, his paunch. Never going to happen.

'So what happened with you?' he asked. 'She said. You lost a daughter. I'm very sorry for that.'

She smiled.

'She told you.'

'Yes.'

'She left some meds, didn't she?'

'She did.'

'Got them here?'

How stupid. They were sitting on the kitchen table.

'No.'

She laughed, and she looked funny, her eyes shining strangely, and he got that fear again, him out here in the dark wood with a mad woman. Oh Allison Gross who lives in yon tower, the ugliest witch in the north countr-ee...

'Shall I tell you,' she said, 'shall I tell you about it? Do you really want to know?'

35

We couldn't go on much longer, me and Johnny. Through everything we'd maintained a surface normality, though words had been pointless for a long time. We had this string tied around us both, we were everyday's reality, always there together, him and me. And there was so much to do! So much to do! And these strangenesses in his eyes, and no doubt he saw that in me too – I don't know how many times he looked searchingly at me and said, 'You've changed.' And me thinking it's him. I didn't want to touch him. Couldn't. It was absolute.

'Lorna,' he said, 'Lorna, what's happening, what's happening?'

'I don't know.'

Harriet's big red eyes had stopped weeping, she looked almost normal, though really all of us were running on empty. Finally, when she was in bed and asleep, he said, 'Why was she there?'

His face was dark and strange, all the blood in him rushing to the surface.

'Why did you let her go?' he said.

There was no way we could have touched. An invisible field separated us. It had been forming for years.

'I didn't.' My throat was sore.

'You're the parent, Lor, you're supposed to be in charge.'

She just went. Fast. A moment, and gone.

'She'd be alive now if she hadn't gone,' he said.

I looked at him. Stone.

We got through it. Here's the funny thing. Phoebe Twist turned up to the funerals. That hideous woman. Sat at the back looking like death. And Johnny, he couldn't go. Just couldn't. He said: *Let the dead bury the dead and who is to be fed be fed.* He was angry. Furious. He didn't want Harriet to go, thought she was too young. Don't upset her. She was all pale and quiet. 'I'll come if you want me to,' she said. Of course you should come! Your sister! She came. The crematorium was full. Her school friends. Teachers. Wilf, who never worried, his face streaked with tears. If the bomb was dropping he wouldn't worry till it hit him on the head. Oh Chicken Licken, the sky has really fallen. Mark was there. Hard for him, I suppose, he didn't know anything about Terry till the crash.

'I saw another side of Lily,' he said to me after it was all over.

And I thought, yes, who am I to think I was the only one who knew her? What if this weird pale boy, so strange to me, what if he was the one who got the real deal? Sweet boys really, Terry and Mark. She didn't do too bad, my Lily, sweet sixteen and two of them so fixed on her. In love? Well, by the standards of sixteen, oh certainly, though so few years had rolled under the bridge that all of them were untested.

★ ★ ★

We lasted another few weeks. The atmosphere around us got sick.

One day Johnny said to me, 'You don't love me any more.'

And I didn't and I did.

'You are dead,' he said, 'I will mourn you.'

The next day he was gone.

I will never forgive him for what that did to Harriet.

Someone can just vanish. It's less rare than you think. I knew a young guy who went to India and got out of his head far too much on Goa Beach and ended up hospitalised, and all his friends had by this time moved on and he'd fallen out with his girlfriend, and hadn't had any contact with his parents, if they were even alive, for years. He just never came back. Amazing how someone can just never come back. And every now and then one of his old friends might say, 'I wonder whatever happened to poor old Simon? Did anybody ever hear anything?' And nobody ever had.

Sometimes I think *I'll* never come back.

I did drink a lot after Lily died. I really did try not to let any of this affect Harry. But she was so hard. So hard to me always, after he'd gone. We were alone together now, and she wouldn't take a hug or anything from me. She didn't have to be like that. She missed him fiercely and everything was my fault, she always thought there was something I wasn't telling her about where he'd gone, but there was nothing at all. No one knew anything, certainly not the Hatchet lot, who, when the whole thing was over, just faded away. Never came near. Shallow people, shallow friendships. I must have been a fool. I'm having nothing more to do with these people, I said. I made up my mind. I'm not chasing after them if they can't be bothered. I never went back to Hatchet, never saw any of them. Not that they'd done anything but I just couldn't take any more of that place. It's where the hate began. And though I hated the hate, I couldn't stop my own hate growing inside, for what he'd done not just to Lily and Terry but to me, and to Harry, who had loved him completely. I couldn't forgive him for any of it. A little while later, don't ask me how long, time was funny around then, I walked past Hatchet, and it was all closed up with a mountain of mail on the mat.

One day when he'd been gone about four or five weeks, I decided to clear up a bit. I'd get rid of some of his things. It was a terrible thing to have to do but I had to do something, cut something out, and I couldn't afford to feel anything. It was brutal survival. I cleared his drawers of the socks that were left, the old ones with holes, a lone pair of holey underpants, a couple of t-shirts he'd never worn. It was like dying. For Harriet too, her beloved Dad, it didn't bear thinking about, and I couldn't stand that he'd done this to her. To me, yes, I could cope. But not to her. It killed us, you know. She just drifted further and further from me till she was sixteen and buggered off to live at a friend's, and never wanted to keep in touch with me.

So there I was, putting his things in bags, and I got to his books on that shelf and I hated them. I hated their smugness and their cleverness. I hated that they thought they knew so much and looked down on me, and I shoved them into a holdall from the back of the wardrobe, as many as I thought I could carry. He hardly ever read fiction. Most of it was battered old Marx and Anarchism and all this Gramsci, Bakunin, Bataille and Foyerback or whatever he was called, and a lot of postmodern stuff. And there was a manual for a Ford Cortina car. Terry's car. It looked new. What was it doing on Johnny's shelf with Johnny's books?

I kept thinking about it all the way down to the Oxfam shop where I handed the books in, and all the way back. Harriet came home from school and said nothing to me.

'Come on, sweet,' I said, 'let's be friends.'

I made her tea while she watched kids' TV.

A papercut under my wrist.

This niggling thing, under every second of every moment, as I walk around town, cook dinner, take Harry to her piano lesson, hear her cry, think about Lily.

I think about how Johnny never much cared about Terry till he heard about the Dorset job. How after that he was all friendly to the lad, and invited him in against all previous odds and told him to park his car in that little yard at the back of the co-op. I think about how he was out all night the night before she went away with Terry, about the spanner someone bought just around the corner from Hatchet, and the reason why there was a brand new manual for Terry's car on Johnny's shelf with Johnny's books. I think that I don't know why I'm thinking about these things so incessantly, why they will not, *will* not leave my mind. After all, I don't know anything about these things. Johnny was no mechanic. I think about the car on that pretty country lane with no other traffic around, veering off the road and over the verge and into the deep pond, and as always the things beyond that that are unimaginable, though still they come. There's no stopping them.

And I think of how angry he was at Phoebe Twist for not going to Dorset that morning, at Lily for going instead for a country ride, and at me for letting her go.

They grow deeper and deeper, the blood-red papercuts, sharper and sharper. He hurt me so bad. Cut me down. Might as well have taken a knife and stuck it straight in my chest.

36

This man is still in my den. Go. Go now.

I kept saying it, go, go now, please go. Like the werewolf imploring a friend to leave before the moon is full. First he just sat there staring at me, as if he was trying to work something out.

'I'm going to sleep now,' I said. 'Please go.'

Very slowly, with a slight groan, he got himself up and hauled himself out through the flap. When all sounds of him blundering in the undergrowth had faded, I lifted up the rug from where it lay rolled up next to my backpack and took it with me. I would need it. An idea was forming in my mind. My throat felt very dry, I had to lick and lick my lips to get them working. I was out in the wood and I could see everything far more clearly than I should have been able to. I walked and wandered, stopping every now and then to listen to the sounds of the wood, the little creatures, the birds ruffling in sleep, falling into harmony around me. Everything moved. Far above through the trees was a deep starless blue sky. I gave a long low whistle, and the ghostly sound lingered. If anyone else was here in these woods it would put fear in them. My heart was a pounding mill and

I'm lonely for them, Lily and Harry and Johnny and the times that wring your stupid heart in the early hours like a terrible old song. How many times has she appeared in the night? Where are you? I say. Are you here? Is it really you? *Of course*, she replies, smiling. Her teeth. Her eyes. I knew she was only in my mind. It's different when the real thing happens. You just know. Lily never gets out of my head into the real world, to walk and talk and touch me. In a sense, neither does Harriet. I don't know that woman. I know Harry in the garden with her tortoise, how we searched and searched for poor old Toby, how he still haunts these woods now, only he's turned into a prehistoric monster. How many times did I wish and wish that if anyone would come to me out of the fog, it would be Lily, but it never was. Still, you could say, what's the difference? The whole thing is just in your head, not just them old dreams, the lot.

I had a weird taste in my mouth. It's one of those signs. Yes and there goes the shake and thrill of it up and down me. Teeth like castanets. Poor trees, poor blasted trees. They've been murmuring for a while now, I can no longer deny it. Could be dragons, elementals, the cold boy, mad King Goll – *they will not hush, the leaves a-flutter round me, the beech leaves old* – What a game. At first I pretended it was just the sounds the world made, saying my name. But it's not, it's the old thing, like they've never been gone, murmuring voices rippling softly, a constant stream, heard behind a distance, from a distance inside. They're always there, they just lie dormant, sometimes for years, like a volcano. Whispering, chuckling, the odd one rising now and then, the odd phrase emerging:

it was another time
she was on the bus and never
but if you did know
what would you do about it?
not you
now you know
They also laugh.

I hear voices that have been inaudible for ages. Still distant. Sometimes I thought they were there as I was going off to sleep, only they could have been the heating, or something outside, or stuff moving through a pipe. Just the world. They're coming in over the waves in the air, from high in the sky, still quite far away, so many all murmuring together like the civilised hum of a great room full of polite people making conversation. My heart thudding got in the way of the voices, irritating me. I walked until I came to the ruin. It had changed. At first I thought it was a dark castle, blocking out the trees over a long area, but when I turned to look around at the woods folding over the path behind me and then looked back, there were lights on inside, and colours, as bright as if a strong light source lay behind them, running down in the windows like pouring water. I wondered if I walked towards it, would it all vanish, because it was too perfect to be real, and I didn't want it to stop. It soared up and up, a thing of mythical proportions, away and above the trees, with those pouring waters rushing down behind the windows.

How lucky I am! There's no approaching a sight like that, not if you don't want to get burned. I sat with my back to the wood and my face towards where fog came from the heights, slipping down the long slopes like grey suds, thickening as it came. I haven't got a home anywhere. I'd love to light a fire. I have matches in my pocket, and a tiny bottle of vodka. I drink my vodka. Anything goes. I can play and misremember because it's all misremembered anyway, and the hours fly by. The stones and leaves dance, sweetly, sedately. Rivers run in the leaves' black veins. The things out there, whispering, are real, that much is obvious. I know what they should be but I don't think they are. They should be all those people I know who've gone, but they never are, or if they are, they're still so far away that I can't get them. They're just people I don't know, their endless meanderings wandering by. Still, every so often I feel as if they fill me with themselves, all of their weird and groping selves, sometimes I almost feel as if I *am* them. We are legion. Here in me they never stop their bickering. I remember one day laughing at it all, I said: What point? What point trying to unmix this ball of worms, let them writhe. Then was consumed with horror at what I was.

I looked down and saw on the stones in some ancient path that ran from where I sat to where the great doors had stood, a worm, a thin long thing trying to get somewhere. I hate worms, can hardly look at them. I watched in fascination as it slumped itself feebly a little way along. These too, I thought. Me and thee, worm. You make every fibre of my being curdle. And I thought about the body that came down, and felt sorry for it. Are you here still? All the time you were up there in that terrible lonely place did your clay meet them, the worms? The horrors, the horrors. Death by worms, the boats. What have I done? Oh God, what have I done, what have I done? Did you walk? Oh but you're long gone now. It's all long gone in the end.

I forget the stages, if stages there were, by which the ineffable again corralled me, but I wasn't even in the woods any more. It felt as if considerable time had passed, or as if I'd just come to in a dream. A wild sea spread out beneath me, small grey sea horses dashing themselves to delightful death against the cliffs. I was on a lip of rock very high above the sea. I put both my feet right on the edge and swayed forward, looking out across the deep black-blue ocean, the needle rocks below, and everything said, do it, do it, let go. One step. Now. Jump.

But I stepped back, and when I sat up I was in the wood and the night had gone into some impossible place deep in my grinning skull. I'd been biting this nail for three hours now and still never never never getting to what I was biting for. My head was too full. They'd turned the noise up.

Babbling fools. 'Shut up,' I tried to say, but I couldn't get the words out. Hundreds and hundreds all splurging their stupid thoughts. Will they just shut up. Shut the fuck up. One of the walls crumbled greyly, off to the side. It made a sound like an iceberg breaking off. A few small stones shot out and rolled across in front of me in the moss and vetch. I picked one up but it was hot so I dropped it. I wanted to stop my head and all these voices so I walked out of the wood and it was like pushing through seaweed under the sea, drifting to the outer edge where the trees meet the big fields and the big slopes rising up towards the Long Wights.

I walked up to a high ridge and lay down in the grass with my hands behind my head, watching meteorites streak across the sky. One high above, then another a few minutes later, lower down over Copcollar. All the people grew quiet. I waited ages, half an hour, I don't know, willing another one, and at last it came, busting out of nowhere and dashing itself out in a long lonely streak across the west.

They started whispering again, in a soft inviting way, making me know that something was coming. Not like the things in my head, Lily's teeth, her eyes; this was something to be seen perhaps, something slowly bursting from the cocoon between there and here. I turned on some high ridge and looked back, scared in a way I'd never yet known.

Someone was walking up the hill. I couldn't tell who. My eyes closed. Handless Jenny. No. She doesn't come around here.

I opened my eyes. It was still walking up the hill. It seemed to carry with it some element of the fog that had now settled and lay low in the hollows. The darkness obscured its face. For a long time it seemed that it walked but never came any closer. After a while it walked on by below me and disappeared around a protruding shelf of land at the highest point of Gallinger's field.

I've ripped a great strip of skin off my thumb and it hurts. The rim where the end of the nail meets my cuticle is bloody.

I was alone on a hillside somewhere under a picture-book sky with a gorgeous crescent of a moon, God's sickle, and a refined scattering of perfect stars, and I was in a moment of pure naked terror. There was a watcher in the woods; I felt its eyes and I didn't know that it might not be some evil thing. So I ran further up till I reached the Stones and got right in the middle, thinking this would either be safe as a ring of salt or very dangerous. There I sat down and waited for my breathing to steady and my heart to die down. It made my ears pound. Someone passed between two stones on the outside of the circle, right on the edge of my vision. The fear shock was like electricity, the dentist's drill on the spasm of a raw nerve. This was not a safe place. My feet, as if directed by some other will, walked across the empty moonlit ring, but there was nothing there, nothing there.

When I turned back, something too white was crawling into the ring from the other side. A cold hand nipped the scruff of my neck. It came not quickly but steadily. One shoulder pointed forward. Low to the ground one arm, one leg, reaching together. It came at a crooked slant across the grass towards me, right up like a slow dog, face to the ground so that all I could see was the top of a cold bald head, sickeningly round like the head of a worm. Three feet away it stopped then turned up its head to look at me. Its neck grew disgustingly thin, stretched up and up towards me like a snake standing on its tail, with a round blank head on the end of it, white and faceless.

I screamed till I was mad and hoarse and woke up at the high point of nightmare, alone somewhere on the hillside below the stones, facing towards the woods and shivering like a dog.

37

All the cats came inside that night, all together, even the
ones that never came in, even the ones that didn't like
each other.

That disturbed him. It seemed to mean something. What
was out there freaking them out? He tried turfing some of
them out the door but they just ran round the front and got
in again through the old pipe.

He stood at his back door looking out towards the trees,
couldn't sleep. He didn't want to know that stuff she'd
told him, about her daughter. It had nothing to do with
him. Now he felt awful. And the other daughter (you can't
believe a word she says) and Madeleine, back tomorrow
they said. He felt like closing and locking all the doors and
just pretending he wasn't in when anyone knocked. He
hadn't asked for any of this. Honestly, you do your best and
keep on and all this gets thrown at you. What the fuck was
up with those cats? Skittering about like loonies.

'Shut up!' he yelled. His own voice was an affront to
the darkness and silence of night. And anyway it had no
effect, the whispering skittering went on, up and down the
stairs, along the landing, in the kitchen. He closed the door,

locked it, went upstairs and went to bed, leaving the landing light on.

So what?

He closed his eyes and tried to sleep, turning away from the door so that the light didn't disturb him too much, but half an hour later he was still wide awake, still listening to the whispering and skittering of the cats, their tiny paws never still. What time was it? Reached for his watch on the bedside table. Christ, only eleven. Surely not. Felt like three in the morning. What had happened? Had he lost some time? No, gained some time. No, didn't know, just – this wasn't right. Shouldn't only be eleven. No wonder he couldn't sleep. Too much was happening.

Might as well get up as lie here.

The fire was still glowing. Three cats on the sofa, all looking at him with their wide haunted eyes.

Two more in the armchair.

'OK,' he said, 'so where am *I* supposed to sit?'

He threw some coals on the fire and shoved one of the cats off, the big orange one, making room for himself. Going deaf, that cat. It went and sat on the chair, looking like a grumpy old man. Like me, he thought.

'Don't look at me like that,' he said.

But the cat went on looking anyway, green eyes full of reproach.

'So what you gonna do about it? Eh?'

The cat made a strange movement with its head as if it was about to charge but then thought better of it and settled down.

Everything was wrong. He sat there, just sat and sat

and everything was wrong, and the night was hissing. No, that was just the fire. And all the hairs on his neck were on end.

Oh stop.

Stop.

And he thought of that woman still out there and was angry at her for making him feel bad. Packing her things. Where would she go? Fuck, what a life, eh? Horrible. Losing a child like that. And then the bloke buggering off. No wonder she was bonkers. Still. If she was normal, probably the daughter would take her. But then. No. Couldn't see her and that daughter living happily together, wasn't going to happen, was it? And I mean really, you had to see the daughter's point of view.

'What do you think?' he asked the orange cat.

Fucked if I know, said the cat. Nothing to do with me.

Whatever, he thought. The poor daft thing's probably harmless. Out there alone, mad. Could see her point. What's it to them if she dies of cold? You just want to be alone in your head sometimes and they never leave you alone. He drew in a long stoical breath through his nostrils and stood up. Like it is sometimes, you don't actually make a decision or think anything through, your body just does it for you, gets up and puts the guard on the fire, finds itself unlocking the back door, stands in the awful darkness at the top of the back steps, calls out: *Are you OK?*

And of course no one answers.

Because it's all nonsense, life is nonsense.

He looked up at the incredible starry sky. Fuck, that's amazing. His head spun. That's real. What the fuck more do you want? Oh Christ, just go out. See what happens. He was shivering. Take it as it comes.

He walked to her den. The wood chuckled and rustled, the shadows pulsed, the whole place breathed at him. She wasn't there. He went on to the old ruin. Every step recoiled. She wasn't there but she was on the hill beyond. Bloody woman was mad, what was any normal person supposed to do? There went a shooting star. Make a wish. Can never think of one at the time. She was sitting with her back against one of the great stones, cuddling her rug.

'Hello,' she said.

'Come down now,' he said. 'You're not well.'

She stood up, very quickly it seemed to him, not in a natural way. Big man that he was, survivor of sea voyages, he was scared. He heard his teeth chatter, fast like a woodpecker, and that made him more scared.

'Does the wood hate me?' she asked. Her voice sounded funny, lower. 'I can't get my words out,' she said and giggled.

She's lost it, he thought. The thing, he thought, is to get her to take some of those pills. I should have brought them out with me.

'Of course the wood doesn't hate you,' he said.

'Are you sure?'

'Of course I'm fucking sure.'

She took hold of his arm, her fingers urgent on his sleeve. 'Why are you always so angry?' she said.

'I'm only angry when there's something to be angry about.' He shook her off. 'Come down now, you're not well.'

'Listen,' she said, as if she was hearing something.

'No.'

'Oh please,' she said, 'don't be scared.'

This was all too embarrassingly intimate.

'Come on now,' he said, rough, 'come on, you're not well.'

'Listen,' she said more urgently, 'I want to show you something. It's not nice. Please.' With her face crumpling.

'Stop it!' He took her arm above the elbow. 'Pull yourself together! You come down to the house and have some tea and a lie down.' He started pulling her, but she held back, surprisingly strong, crying out, 'Wait!'

But he was stronger. He started walking her down the hill, pulling her along.

'Please,' she said, stopping short and digging in her heels, dragging him back by the arm. This moment of intimacy on the side of the hill was horrible and strange for him.

'Oh, to hell with you,' he suddenly shouted. 'Just fuck off then, you're nothing but a nuisance. A fucking nuisance, you fucking hear me, that's all you fucking are, just a fucking useless human being, now fuck off and stop hanging round.'

And he walked off.

'Well, if you won't come,' she whispered, and ran the other way, down and back into the wood, down to the edge of the great forest, full of shapes that wroil and coil in its black border.

The trees grew faces and fingers, arms. These I knew for pareidolia; you're nothing, I said, mind-games, and ran out again near that cottage where we used to stay – and it was of course now just a sad old ruin, and no one seemed to have lived there for a long time. The windows were boarded up or invisible with dust, the door locked with a padlock, all its old red paint hanging off in strips, and the garden was high with long-established weeds.

You can, of course, love and hate at the same time. I know it. It's the darnedest thing. That's an Americanism. Harry used to hate it when I said things like that. 'For God's sake, Mother,' she'd say, 'if you could hear how ridiculous you sound.'

Four years later Johnny came back.

I was alone in that old cottage where we'd watched the swarm. Harry hadn't wanted to come. She stayed more and more at her friend Holly's house these days, and when she was at home she hardly talked. It was all my fault, all. Losing her dad, losing her sister. Who else could she blame? I was sitting on the old bench in the garden, a strange sultry summer evening of silent intermittent lightning, working away with my diamond file, the one I'd saved up for, the one that slid against the silver like a knife on butter, on the leaves for a necklace, and I heard the creak of the gate, and there he suddenly was, the Demon Lover, beautiful as ever with his big brown eyes.

'Hello, Lorna,' he said.

He had blood on his face. A visiting ghost.

I said, 'What do you want?'

'What do you mean?' He laughed softly. 'It's me.'

And like a ghost he scared me into a state where every passing moment that followed was swollen and too full.

'How are you, Lor?'

'You can't do this,' I said, and the voice coming out of my

mouth arrived from far away, the other side of the heights. 'Can't just come back like this.'

'Lorna – Lorna,' he said. 'Can I come in?'

The bench beside me was strewn with bits of jewellery and little sharp tools, beads, string, tiny pliers. I picked up my diamond file and smoothed away. 'What for?' I said, testing my voice, and yes, it still came from afar, further still, from up there somewhere in space.

'What for? Oh Lorna! What for? Please, don't be like this.'

He spoke as if everything was normal, as if he'd just returned from getting a pint of milk and some bits and pieces from the shop. And I, *I* was being so unreasonable.

'What do you want?' I said.

'I want to come in.' He sat down on a garden chair with his bag between his feet and stared at me, wild-eyed, as if I was some strange beast he'd never seen before. 'Can't I even come in, Lorna?'

In the *Bhagavad Gita*, before the great Battle of Kurukshetra, the warrior Arjuna, seeing in both armies the faces of his dearest friends and closest relations, is overcome with horror. In his anguish he turns to Krishna, and between the two hosts, god and warrior debate. Surely, surely, to kill all these people, friends and kin, would be a great sin. Better I should die. Why so? the god replies. Every soul has already lived and died more times than can be numbered. Strike or stay your hand – no matter. The one who kills believes that he is killing. The one who has been killed believes that he dies. They are both wrong, for one doesn't die and the other doesn't kill. The soul endures and will be born again. Please let morning come, the cock crow, and all dead people run back to their deep beds.

I knew what he'd done.

He smiled at me, deep in my eyes. 'It's *so* good to see you again, Lor,' he said.

'How did you get here?' My voice was faint. 'How did you know where I was?'

'Rang Steve. Said you were here. I was up in Liverpool with Maurice.'

'Maurice?'

All of these people were never supposed to come back. I was finished with all that.

'Maurice. We came down from Liverpool together.'

'What are you talking about?'

'I came down from Liverpool with Maurice,' he said again.

Didn't make sense.

'Is that where you've been all this time?' Behind him I could see the stars coming out above the woods. 'In Liverpool?'

'No no no.' And he waffled on and on. Half of it just went right through my head without trace. From time to time lightning flickered in the sky, eerily silent. He said he'd been in Ireland these past years. Always stayed in touch with Maurice – Maurice, the pride, the wonder – guess where *he's* been. Guess! Istanbul! Fucking Istanbul!

Oh God, give him a medal.

'Anyway, he's back now,' he said, 'and he's going to Paris. I don't know what it is, it's something important by the looks of things.'

'Something important,' I repeated like a machine.

'Was up north, you know. That's where he went. Met me in Liverpool and we came down together.'

I laid down my tools and my unfinished leaf.

'Guess what?' he said. 'He was talking about God. *Maurice*. Can you imagine? I don't mean in a naff sort of way but like deep, all these concepts.'

'Did you do it?' I said. 'Did you do something to the car?'

'Of course I didn't!'

I knew at once he had.

Because he knew at once exactly what I meant. And his face, a wrongness in it, a guilty consciousness. He pressed on with a wild look in his eyes, and all that hardness I'd seen before was gone and there was just this shitscared little weasel who'd caused it all, though God knows what the poor weasel had done to earn its reputation for sneaky weakness. London, they were driving down, drop you here. Then Paris, ultimate destination, gosh how exciting, but the car wouldn't start, horrible old banger, so we got on the train and you know he's always wanted to see the Long Wights, so he got off in Gully and got that little bus but it only went as far as that other little village, what's it called, so we walked up to the Wights and we were going to walk down the other side and round the edge of the wood to here, but then... and we've been up on the heights. And I said that he could maybe stay in the other bedroom or if you weren't keen, cos like I said, we may have one or two things to sort out, he could find a B&B in the village...

'He's not here?'

'Not any more.'

'You can't stay here,' I said, 'you can't stay here and he can't stay here.'

'He was asking about you, Lor. How's Lorna? he said.'

'He's not staying here.'

'I know, Lor.'

'Where's he gone?'

'Back to the station, I suppose.'

While he spoke his eyes had filled up, and now tears began pouring down his cheeks and his voice thickened.

'There's blood on your face,' I said.

He wiped his face with his fingers and smiled.

He looked just like before.

'I got in a fight,' he said.

'You? A fight?'

'Yeah. With Maurice.'

38

The stars whispering above in that story-book sky. His face appeared again, still angry. It was between the moon and me. 'For Christ's sake,' it said, 'you make things impossible.'

I started to laugh.

Dan raised his eyes to the heavens.

I closed my eyes.

He jerked my arm and shook me.

I don't know how it was that I found myself in his house again. I don't remember getting there and I didn't want to go in.

'No, no,' I said.

He said, 'Stop it! Stop all this!'

'I was going somewhere,' I cried.

'No you're not.' He pulled me and made me go in. I was on the sofa, he brought me some pills and a glass of water and stood there till I'd taken them.

'Pills to purge melancholy,' I said, and laughed.

The fire was out and it was cold so I put the rug I brought from my den over my knees. I tried to talk but he wouldn't hear a word, he was furious, he lit a fire roughly but with tender skill, and I watched his stupid wide capable back and it made me cry.

'Don't do that,' he said, 'it doesn't help.'

'It's only water,' I said, 'just water that comes out of the eyes.' The fire was blazing up and the cat on the end of the settee purred in content, folding its paws underneath its dirty white chest. I hid my face in the cushion and tried to be asleep in the hope that on some other morning I might wake and find that I knew what to do. He drank from the bottle. 'Tomorrow,' he said, 'I'll call your daughter. She can deal with this.'

I was sleepy. 'I'll move on tomorrow,' I said from the cushion, 'don't you worry your pretty little head.'

He almost smiled. 'You should get some sleep,' he said.

'It's no good.' I opened my eyes and lifted my head. 'I won't sleep. I'm wide awake. I don't ever sleep.'

'Yes, you do.'

'I don't. I haven't slept for days.'

'You probably do sleep, you just don't notice.'

I reached out and picked up the little wooden dog from the table and turned it round in my hands. It had a face and detailed little paws. 'You're quite talented, aren't you?' I said.

But when I looked up he'd gone. I slid away. Sometimes I woke, sometimes he was there, sometimes not. He kept the fire fed. I kept sliding away and coming back again. 'Dan,' I said one time, finding him there, reaching out and holding his calloused hand, 'can I tell you?'

'What?' he said unwillingly.

My strange confessor.

★ ★ ★

I'm the evil baron. I did that thing. It'll never ever go away. Lock it away in a haunted house, up in the attic, down in a deep dark wood. Done is eternal and so is the proof, eternal though buried. All that remains is the boiling oil.

'Lor, can I have a cup of tea? I'm parched.'

'You should go.'

'Go? It's me! What are you talking about?'

'You can't do this,' I said.

'Oh God, I know it might seem weird,' he said, 'but settle down. Life's like that.' He smiled. He actually laughed. 'Things get weird.'

Sometimes things look as if they're there but they're not. Careful now. Soon he'll be gone. The dark falling on the garden made his face dim, it changed and wavered in front of me. Look away. But when I looked back he was still there, and there was nothing I could say to him. I just looked at him and he looked back at me with his darkening face and dried blood on his face and there were no words for a long time, though his mouth was moving as if it was speaking. If he moved towards me, I thought, I'll die screaming. Just fall down and my heart will stop. Begone, demon.

Over the trees the sky was that beautiful blue, so deep it hurt. An owl called hollow and low and another answered from further in the woods. My eyes were hot. 'Go away,' I said feebly.

'Don't be like that,' he said.

I looked down at my diamond file, scraping softly at the silver I was working on, the little lines coming out from the central vein of the leaf. I love working silver. I hated him. I thought of Lily, her face in my mind just as she was, the way her upper lip curled. I felt her moment of pure terror in that instant when the car left the road and she saw the water through the windscreen coming up to meet her. Her and that poor daft stupid lad. 'I know it was you,' I said, 'you did something to the car.'

He stepped forward into the light from the window and the back door, into *my* light so that I had to stop my scraping. Oh how naked, the petrified leer, the whimpering laugh that came out of his mouth. His eyes were bright and mad and scared, never leaving me, stuck on me, open wide and never blinking. I was sure then. He couldn't deny the fact of it.

'I know I can't explain it in any way you'd understand,' he said. 'Don't even try, Lorna, this is just you and me now.'

Nothing to say then, another long nothing time in which that thing I term my soul curled inward and I felt as if something inside me was rocking itself.

'There was always much more to it than just you, or me, or anyone else,' he said. 'It happened so it had to happen.'

He wanted to come near but I kept him away with my eyes. He looked at me hungrily, as if amazed, kept shaking his head, saying, 'Wow. Too much. Too much,' and laughing that well-remembered laugh. 'Talk about strange days.'

Lightning flashed.

Whenever, wherever, whatever, he'd always been fundamentally, profoundly incapable of admitting fault or guilt. Neither was permitted. 'You need to see the whole picture,' he said.

And when I still didn't speak he said, 'You were supposed to be with me, Lorna.'

Reproach even.

'You stopped being with me.'

Tears ran down his cheeks. 'I didn't do what you think I did. I did do something but it was never intended to turn out that way. You know that. But what if I did? I didn't, but what if I did?'

It wasn't real, the garden, the moon, the ghost of Johnny.

'Look,' he said, 'I've had a horrible day. I had a fight with Maurice.'

'I know.' I was very frightened. I stood up. 'You said.'

Then he told me. Something terrible had happened. No, don't get upset, it's not *that* bad. They'd walked all around the stones, in and out of them, Maurice had taken pictures and now they were above, looking down.

'How soon are you leaving for Paris?' asked Johnny.

'Probably Wednesday.' Maurice was fiddling with the camera, and Johnny said he wouldn't mind having a go with it. 'Aren't you coming? I said. Aren't you coming to see Lorna? But it was all Paris and secrets and something big and he was acting like he was too important, you know, and I'm thinking well you're a right cunt now, aren't you, you twat, and I said I might go as far as Paris with him, I know some folks in Avignon, but he wasn't having any of it, you know, trying to put me off, like, who the hell does he think he is? I said, oh fuck, you think I want to trail after you? Just we're both going in the same direction. He's quite bald at the back now you know.'

'Does he know?'

'What?'

'Does he know what you did?'

'Yes, he does. I wish I'd never told him.'

'Why?'

He wiped his face and rubbed the back of his hand under his nose. 'Said he didn't want to know. Said he wished I'd shut up and kept it to myself, said he thought the others suspected, it was pure madness, it sits like a lump inside, he said, that horrible knowledge. He just went on and on as if none of it was anything to do with him, and he asked me why I'd gone off like that and I said my head was all messed up and I just had to get right away, and then he said...'

His throat seized up.

'Harriet,' I said.

He looked at me as if I'd hurt his feelings.

'You think I didn't think about her? You think I didn't think about both of you every single day?'

'What good was that?'

'I didn't want to make things worse. I had to sort my head out.'

'Fuck off, Johnny.'

'I don't believe this,' said Johnny, 'how could I have known what would happen? You're like him. I wouldn't have done it if it wasn't for him. I was the only one who actually *did* anything. Like you said, the rest of them, they were all just wanking off. So now I have to take the blame, well no, no, I won't take it all, and if you think it hasn't killed me every day, and he said, you know what he said, he said don't blame your misjudgement on me, I won't accept that responsibility. Fake. All fakes. Just mouths spouting words. I told him. And there was me like an idiot taking it seriously, and he says, serious? Serious? You think knocking off some silly old bag was serious? And you couldn't even do that right. Oh well, I've seen through him now. Talking like he's throwing pearls at swine, the woman was meaningless, he says, even if you'd put her at the bottom of the sea with a bullet in her head, who'd have cared? Who'd even have noticed? Like treading on a bug, that's all. And you, thinking you've done some splendid thing! No you didn't. You killed two irrelevant people and no one cared, no one noticed. How did that change the world? And he went on and on and on, she was everything we're up against, everything, she's nothing, he said, and he starts walking on and I was having a go with his camera, I was taking a picture of the stones from above, and he was going the wrong way but he wouldn't listen, like when did he ever listen to anyone? I told him, if you go that way, you'll end up at the edge and have to backtrack about a million times and climb down rocks and things and go round boggy bits and holes in the ground, the map's deceptive, and he started going on and on, trying to make everything normal, on and on about this Paris thing, like it's some big thing, all top secret, and he said he couldn't tell me about it because other people were involved and it's all like yeah yeah, who the fuck do you think you are? Going on like it's huge, like it's the glorious fucking revolution, and he's no idea, no idea at all of the significance of what I did.'

'What you did,' I said.

I was losing time. It's melting. I think I did understand him. I think I saw his mind move, the way it turned irresistibly to the presented opportunity, too apt and perfect not to be grasped, God-given he might have said if he'd believed in God, which he did after a fashion though he'd never have said so. Came a point when all reality ran to that point, and people turned into ciphers.

'I feel sick,' he said.

'Do you?'

'Horrible taste in my mouth.' He took a great gurgling swallow. 'I hit him,' he said. 'It was awful, Lor. I hit him with the camera.'

Why should she be gone? Why did he not grieve? What was he? Not that lovely man I met in the record shop, that sweet man who walked beside me in his big coat.

'It's not like I thought about it. I was holding it by the strap and I just swung it. You know, Lor, when something just seems to happen by itself. I just swung it and it cracked on the side of his head, right on the ear. And his glasses flew off.' He laughed. 'Sailed through the air.'

The lightning flashed.

'Bastard,' said Johnny, to a place on the ground in front of the back door. 'Bastard bastard bastard. All *he* did was sit with his fucking feet in his Doc Martens up on his desk. Phoney. Fake. All the time lying and lying and lying, don't ever again try to tell me you were ever a friend of mine. It was *me*. Me! *I* was the only one who dared, who actually did it, put myself out there on that ledge.'

'You didn't leave him there?' I said.

'Christ,' said Johnny, 'I think I'm going to be sick.'

'Where is he?'

'Gone back to the station, I suppose, like he said.'

'He was OK?'

'Oh yeah. Bit groggy.'

'You said a fight. That doesn't sound like a fight.'

'Well, it was. Honest, he got up. He went down but he got up again. Absolute cunt. You should have seen him grovelling about for his glasses, feeling around, like this...' and he patted the air in front of him feebly with a gormless look on his face. 'Oh God, Lor, you know me. I hate violence. It's not me. He got up and he hit me, look, here' – pushing the hair back from his forehead – 'What could I do? I don't fight. I don't know how to. It was ridiculous, he's got this backpack with a stupid logo and he's trying to fight with it on his back, he looked so stupid flailing away. I kicked him. I had the camera, I was going to keep it, I think, but I just threw it down, and he went after it, crawling around without his glasses.'

I picked up my file and slid it into the groove in the centre of the leaf.

'You and your jewellery,' he said.

'So he's gone?'

'I assume so. Lor, please, I need to rest.'

I shook my head.

'Lorna!'

'You can't do this,' I said.

'If you knew what a horrible day I've had. I lost my way. Went all over the place before I found the path, falling over things, I was sick, caught my foot in a hole, went flying, right into this rock, it's all fucking booby-trapped up there, crazy. Fucking hurt. Bastard! Hope he missed his train. Told him he was going the wrong way. All his own fault. Honest, the blood was just pouring down, can't I at least come in and clean myself up? You wouldn't turn a dog out, would you, Lorna? And I was just going down and down and looking for the path and thinking all the time I'd come to you because you'd know what to do and because, I don't know, and got to the path in the end and then I reached the road and some woman gave me a lift, only I didn't know where I was going, it all looked different somehow, I was trying to think of the name of this cottage and all I could think of was when me and you were here and everything was OK and it made me want to cry, I think I actually might have done and this woman kept saying, are you OK? Are you OK? And then I recognised the T-junction and I said, drop me here, and I knew it then – that way to the village, that way to the woods, and I walked and walked and it was suddenly *there*, the cottage, God, it was like seeing an oasis, I thought I'd never get here and I'm walking down the lane looking at the roof and remembering the chimneys and there's no smoke and I thought, if she's not there I'll kill myself, I'll just sit down in the garden and that'll be it for me. I'll just sit there and stare into nothing and give up.'

The file slipped and made a mark that spoiled the whole thing.

'This is *me*, Lor,' he said.

It was him.

'What about Harriet?' I said.

'Harry.' His eyes closed. 'Oh God, if you knew – I can hardly bear – she's what now? Twelve? Thirteen? Harry.'

'Give up, Johnny,' I said, 'you can't make anything right now. It's all gone.'

'No.'

'No! It's gone. It's all gone.'

'No. It's me, Lorna. *Me*. Don't you understand? How can it be gone? It can never be over. Think! All that time, all those... No! It's not possible. Things don't end like that. Don't you see? Nothing was intended! Don't you remember? Surely, you see. Surely. Through everything, go back, Lor, how it was, please, Lor, go back, before...'

These cobweb layers, this madness.

'Oh Lor,' he said, 'I've had a terrible day.'

Her death meant less to him than a falling-out with Maurice.

I stuck the diamond file in the side of his neck and he stood for a moment with a small wooden handle sticking out of the right side of his throat. When I pulled it out a jet of blood followed, spurting out in a horizontal arc. I looked in his eyes and he looked right back in mine: love, hate, horrible bewilderment. He opened his mouth as if to speak and his eyes never left mine.

He went over in the grass on his side, wound to the earth, kicking with his feet. I never saw such amazement as I saw on his face. Blood came shooting out, fast and dark, and his shoulders jerked, and his knees tried to bend and pull up towards the foetal position but they couldn't make it.

The top of my brain flew off. Next thing I knew I was on the ground outside the open back door and I'd wet myself. It was warm.

Johnny lay still.

He was looking into the grass in front of his eyes. I think I might have lain there a long time. And everything was important again and there was meaning in life and things that must be done. OK, I'm done. That's it, the lot.

There was a flash of lightning, an instant.

39

What a night that was indeed.

I sat up. He lay in that small low-walled garden with blood on the grass all around his head and shoulders, blood dripping from the stalks and blades, sucked into the earth.

I knew he was dead and I'd done it and it didn't mean a thing. My mind was clear. The first stars were softly ghosting in the blue light. Soon be full dark but the moon will keep it bright. The gate was open.

I changed my clothes, got my torch, put it round my neck. I would not be without it on this kind of a night. My chest was heaving inside. I didn't waste much time. I dragged him out to the car, a terrible job. You know what they say. These strengths you don't know you have. Trust me, they're true. But they wreck you. That's how I fucked my back and it's been fucked to this day.

It took me about an hour to get him through the gate to the car. No one came by. If anyone had, the whole game would have been up.

The worst thing was getting him *in* the car, that really was a nightmare. I cried. I ran round the car. Then saw the inevitable, he is to be got in. You can do it, you know. Call your dark angel. Everyone prays, you pray, of course you do, you just do. I laid him with his back and head against the side of the car, the door wide open, his neck uncomfortable over the ridge. I climbed in sideways, backwards, my skirt rucking up exposing my socks and hairy legs, no time to lose, arms under his armpits, now growing cold, my back cracked as I hauled him in, the weight of the whole world.

That took another good hour.

Then I had to get his legs in.

Then I had to stop after closing the door, stop and do nothing, just stare down the lane where dusk gathered, getting my breath, licking my lips, hot against the cooling night air, and weeping steady pointless tears, mechanical as time.

I drove him through Andwiston and up over the heights, part way down the other side. It's wild round there, very beautiful with twilight and a big moon. The lightning had stopped and no storm had come.

We had a night of it. I talked to you in the van. 'Sorry, love,' I said.

I put him in the storm drain up beyond Beggar's Ercol. No one goes up there. By the time I reached the track, the long ride between high hedges, the first light was beginning in the east. I stopped at the gate, got out and opened it, drove in and slowly across the field. The car was not made for this terrain and it bumped and rocked. I pulled up near the hedge and got out and looked around at the empty field, and it was cold and sad and terrible, and I knew it was ridiculous and impossible, it damn near killed me getting him up here and what now? But I'd seen it once a long time ago while walking, side of the field, the hole where the water goes down, a black mouth lurking under the hedge. I walked the perimeter, looking for it, walked twice around and was beginning to whisper to myself as the sun began, just yawning, not even stretching, maybe beginning to think of the possibility of getting up, and the night turned into birdsong. I found it on the third circuit, returned to the car and drove as close as I could get, then pulled him out. It was easier than getting him in but my arms and shoulders were so tired that I groaned and tears ran from my eyes. 'I'm so sorry, sweetheart,' I said. The back of his head hit the earth, which made me feel sick, made my stomach jump, but nothing could hurt him now, it didn't matter. I set to again as before, arms under his armpits, like ice now, all of him hardening, dragged. Not far this time. To the storm drain, an opening some three feet high and six wide, curtained by wet trails of filth and deep green slime, and then I rested, not for long because the light grew and grew. No one came up here. I remember when I first saw this thing, I thought, creepy, you could imagine goblins sneaking out after you passed, following silently on behind. I scared my brother. Something's crawling up, I said, and we ran.

First I tried to push him in but that just didn't work, so there was nothing else for it but to get down on my hands and knees and crawl in head-first through the muck then turn around. My murdering arms reached out from the drain, caught him tight, put my arms under his warm armpits. His head with its black curls fell against me backwards All calm, I pulled. Slowly, slowly, I edged him in. Six inches. Pull. Scraped my knees. Pull. Crawling belly-down backwards in the wet, thinking nothing beyond the next few seconds, back, pull, breathing loud and hard, pull. He stuck. I rested, put up my hands to feel how high above me the roof was, no more than a foot I thought. It was not quiet, the earth made sounds, water ran, small things in the walls ticked and slid.

I have no idea how long this part took. It seemed very long, hours. Looking back, I think it was probably no more than an hour and a half. I got him past the sticking point and then the tunnel sloped suddenly downwards and it got easier. We went in and further in, till I could lift my head and see that gape of early morning light with its ragged fringe, and it seemed far away. Oh my God. I should just stay in here. Just lie down and sleep, I'm so tired. But still back and further back, until my head hit the roof and I switched on my torch and saw a wall with tiny black insects crawling all over it, and the slope still descending into nothing, and could go no further.

'Here you are, love,' I said.

I rolled him into the side. Both of us were soaked. I stayed with him for a while, maybe ten minutes, maybe twenty. It was so hard to leave. For a while I just looked at his face in the torchlight and remembered how much I loved him even though I hated him too, how he was infused in every part of me. It had been quick. I don't think he suffered long but he must have experienced the knowledge and terror of what was happening. He didn't deserve it. And yet still, even now, I think he deserved it. He didn't know that though. He was the wronged one always. Sometimes I think they both deserved it, he and Maurice, and I thought of them together forever in some seedy little side alley of hell. What sin? For turning people into symbols, Lily, Terry, Phoebe Twist, all the same. Because that's what he did when it was all over, I believe, he changed her for his own peace of mind from a girl to a thing. Give it any name you want. It was not nice. If he could have avoided it he would. The tears in my eyes were boiling hot. His lower lip hung full and childlike.

Why are we here? he asked me. *Where have you brought me?*

It's OK.

So sorry, my love. So sorry we ever met because I couldn't not have not loved you, even though it meant I had to hate you in the end.

But not this. Lor, Lor, Lor, not this. Not this.

Then again, who could kill the soul?

Still bewildered, love?

Still.

When I crawled out, the sun was up. I got in the car and drove out of the field, closing the gate, went home like any other normal person, parked in the lane outside the cottage and went inside. No one would come. I'd clean up later. For now I must sleep. I looked at the clock, it said ten past seven. Is that all?

I threw my filthy wet clothes on the bathroom floor, showered, closed the curtains and got into bed, and oh my bed was lovely and warm and cool and clean. But there was no sleep. I couldn't stop shivering. The water was dark black, long streams and trails forming stickinesses of green algae. Below the ground I heard it, water sloshing, a voice in the ground. Silver as moonlight.

40

He built up the fire. Something to do. What time is it? Feels very late. But look! it's only midnight. How is that? he thought. Time's gone mad.

Can't trust a word she says, the daughter said.

He picked up the bottle of pills from the table and set about reading the label.

'How many of these are you supposed to have?' he asked.

'Can't remember.' She lay back and closed her eyes.

He got up, got his reading glasses.

'Hm,' he said, 'looks like no more till tomorrow,' then something struck him.

'Should you be drinking with these?'

She laughed. 'You make me laugh,' she said.

'I don't know,' he said, 'drink might stop them working.'

'Doesn't work like that,' she said. 'Takes weeks anyway. Doesn't just kick in overnight.'

She jumped up and stood staring down into the fire.

His head was all mussed up. Not long now, he thought, till morning. Her daughter's coming. Or is she calling? Or was that Madeleine? Anyway, whatever, one or both will turn up soon and take her away. He wouldn't say a word. It was all just stuff in her head. *They* could sort it out. A dead man came down when the hillside slipped. She heard it. She made a story. That's what they do. People who confess to things they haven't done. It's all in the mind. Not her fault.

'You go to sleep,' he said, 'drink that and go to sleep.'

The big black and white cat, mother of many, was up there next to her, looking into her face intently as if with sympathy, but she hadn't seen it.

'Look at that,' he said, 'I never seen that cat take to anyone before.'

She looked at it and it darted its face forward with a rough growl.

'Hello,' she said.

The cat took a step or two and lay on its stomach with one paw on her leg.

'Never before seen,' he said.

She smiled.

'All that,' he said, 'what you said – I don't think you know what's true. We think things, we remember things differently.'

'Yes. And some things are just so real but they're not. I know, I know, I know.'

'It's just the past,' he said. 'It's gone, caput, over.'

'Just like that.'

He shifted awkwardly, narrowing his eyes as he spoke. His clumsy hands splayed out on the air. 'I don't know,' he said, 'I don't know if anything you say is true. I know you have problems. You've got to go somewhere else, where people know what to do with you. I don't know what to do.'

'What to do with me?' She laughed. 'What to do. Indeed, indeed, the big question.'

He shook his head. 'There *was* a body,' he said. 'We know that.'

'These cats,' she said, 'you really have got to stop pretending they don't live here. Give up. This is a cat palace.'

'That wasn't him,' he said, 'the body.'

'Too short.'

He laughed though none of it was funny. His eyes creased. 'How many more up there, you reckon?'

'God knows. The earth teems.'

'Come on,' he said, 'I'm not having this.'

She blanked and looked down. 'So that's it anyway,' she said, 'it's all up. Now I've told you.'

'Yes.'

She said nothing but looked at him as if waiting for him to say something, but he couldn't get his thoughts in order and the room was too hot, and he was beginning to think he'd pushed a bit too far with the booze, even for him.

She said nothing.

'You—'

'I've told you,' she said, 'I'm not telling you again.'

'The thing,' he said, 'the file.'

'The diamond file.'

He shook his head. 'Never heard of a diamond file before.'

'No reason to,' she said. 'You'd never need one.'

'So,' he said, pulling sense back around him like a blanket round his shoulders, 'so' – someone like that, he thought, you'd never know what was real and what wasn't – 'so let's

just say, let's say' – he flipped a cigarette out of the packet
– 'let's just say...'

She looked harmless. The witch in his garden. She'd been
scary, but he hadn't been afraid of her now for a long time.
He pitied the mess of her. Made him feel like a normal
person.

'Let's say,' he said, 'for the sake of argument—'

'I've told you the truth,' she said.

They sat a while.

'So what now?' he said.

She looked at him. 'Can I have one of your cigarettes?'

He opened the pack, took one out, tossed it. She caught it
deftly and put it in her mouth, and when he tossed his lighter
she caught that too. 'Thanks.' Her hands shook visibly.

'Stop trembling,' he said roughly.

'Can't.'

'Try!' Sternly. If she went to pieces, he hadn't a clue how to
deal with it. Slug from the bottle, meaningless, just another
little smear of courage, another little trick on the mind, let it
go, let it happen, nothing can be stopped anyway, not when
it's gone this far.

'So what now?' he said again.

'I don't want these to start working,' she said.

'What?'

'It's like, looking at this cat now—'

But she was muddling words – so she just looked at him
because she didn't know how to say, and he was looking
back and she thought, it's these I'll miss when the meds kick
in, these moments when you catch something from another
person but you don't know what it is but it's more than

real and too much to take, when you see yourself rippling away under someone's eyelids, when a cat's paw comes into focus, a complication you see in someone's eye stops you in your tracks. These I'll miss. But not to feel! Oh God, let me not feel!

'Stop this,' he said, horrified.

Because she'd started to cry and it was embarrassing. She stood up. 'I did it,' she said, 'I really did.'

'Stop this!'

The fire blazed on her face.

'Sit down,' he said, standing and pulling her arm.

She was all over the place, electrified. She drew in smoke as if it was life-giving air. 'I know I'm evil. I want him down from there.' She jerked away from him and started for the back door, trailing the old rug from her ridiculous hovel behind her. 'Everyone will know,' she said, 'everyone will know.'

'Wait!'

She turned.

'Where are you going?'

'You gave me two pills,' she said. 'God knows what they were. I'm wide awake.'

'It's half past twelve.'

She gathered the rug into a roll and put it under her arm. 'It's all right,' she said, 'everything's under control.'

'The fuck it is.'

He followed her to the door. The moon was high and bright, nearly full.

'Look at the stars,' she said, then pushed him back lightly and walked out into the yard.

'What you doing?'

But she ignored him and walked away round the side of the house. He went to the corner and called after her, 'You cause so much trouble for people. You think you can just do what you want.'

He saw the dark shape of her for a few moments against the light coming out of the side door window, then she was swallowed up in the night. For a while he heard the sound of her footsteps, then not even that. He walked back to the house, slammed the door, went back to the fire and chucked on another log.

'Idiot!'

He sat down, grabbed the bottle, threw back his head. 'I can't stand all this,' he muttered. 'None of it's even true.' Let her. Do what she wants. He'd had all he could take. He sat for half an hour gazing into the fire. He thought about going out and getting in the car, drunk as he was, and driving down the lane to see if she was OK. Nah. Much too drunk to drive. Ridiculous. Fuck her and her madness. She'd be somewhere along the steep track leading up to the Wights. God, he was tired. None of it was his problem. Nothing of this would change, his house, his garden, the cats, his grandma's old car, the back step with the gouge where his mother had hit it with an axe. That was a terrible thing. That old pickaxe, still around somewhere. No use for it. In the shed somewhere. The way she swung it, right up over her head and whack! He'd screamed. Four or five. It was like it was coming down out of the sky. Nothing more terrifying than when your mum turns into a demon and her eyes turn black. But they don't really. Stop all this, just morbid imagination, things that pop into your head, and she lets them get the better of her. He could have fallen asleep then, but the booze in his head and gut was wide awake and swirling, and shivers were running up and down his chest. Wonder how a heart attack feels. He opened his eyes and raised his head and for a moment the world was blurred and his eyes were running, and his nose. He yawned mightily but it turned into a kind of sob, pointless and inexplicable. Why this terrible watery feeling, as if his chest was turning to mush? He was going to be sick, that's what it was. He rushed to the back door, yanked it open and just got to the bottom of the steps before he spewed out a gallon or so of bilious alcohol that splashed dramatically across the yard. The cold air made his teeth chatter. He staggered a couple of steps, raised up his face and contemplated the night sky, the sprinkling of stars and the eerily glowing moon, and for a long moment gave up all expectation of ever reaching normality again.

After a while he went back in, and watched the fire till it sank down into its cradle, then he put the guard up, locked the back door and went to bed.

41

I walked along beside the wall, to the gate, but the old gate was no longer there, just those rusted posts that somehow were still familiar. Hello, walls. I thought time was playing tricks. Down along the lane I stopped and listened. I wanted him to have followed me, my only friend, that clumsy silly man who was all wrong. Damn, still there! The sound of water running down under the road, under the house, down and away under the woods and meadows, its channels splitting and diverging all over the place and somewhere no doubt in that mythical mystical mine under the ground, where all the little streams combine into one great subterranean lake. Six hundred years I was a stone, six hundred a drop of water, six hundred, the sunlight that passed once a day on that one spot on a wall no longer in existence. Six hundred more I was the ditch in the lane a few hundred feet down that curly leafy lane from our holiday house, I was the black strings of slimy dirt hanging like thin teeth over a gap more than a foot wide, I suppose, don't ask me, shaped indeed like a mouth. And gurgle gurgle shine shine went the water over long green strands of hair. That's where I'm going.

Clear as day, all that time. Walking down the lane with the limp roll of the rug gathered up and hugged close: this is why I came here. I should have done this years ago. I see my way, nothing's changed. I like that. Nothing changes round here. If they ever touch my wood I'll kill them. I remember the exact turning with the thorn tree, up above the Long Wights, the tracks never driven. I remember the car rocking and bouncing on the rutted track, creeping forward, the bushes on either side closing in and scraping the windows, and everything so dark that I couldn't even see the place ahead where the midden darkness of an empty space where once there was a gate waited like a fall into unconsciousness.

Not that it makes any sense or any difference. I know it's not him any more, but I'm getting him out of that place. Over the years it has lain inside me, foul and wet, black and freezing, rank, green and stinky. I walk. It's a climb, I breathe hard, never thinking how much further there is to go, one foot in front of the other, stars and moon above, on and on, up and up, till at last here it is, the approach, my feet slipping in the grass that's covered it all. The gate-place, fully dark between the faint leafy tremblings on either side. Still advancing, my side hurting, I find myself laughing. Such fools. Life's wasted on the living. In the gateway I stand still. When you reach the darkest place, if you stand long enough you begin to see things. The old lost field stretches before me. Don't move. Listen. Water running underground. Big sky. Because this is impossible and not to be borne, I have emptied myself, there's only my walking feet, my breath, the smudged and blurry picture my eyes see, moving as I move. Go on, slightly towards the left.

It takes a while. I have to get down on hands and knees and feel my way beneath the hedge, pushing under, not here, not there, stopping, listening, as if you might give me a sign, as if a voice might call me, this way, this way!

Not that I can see but I know that this is it, this void. Suddenly my hands feel nothing but space and damp air. Cold. I've been saving the torch for this. Now I switch it on, get down and turn myself into a mole. I've done this before. Head first I go, flattened, crawling. In here there's no sky, no world, no life. The light jerks and swerves over low walls of ridged mud, curtains of mould that hang like cobwebs, dripping serenely. There's no time. Whatever's left of me is gone to ground, watching, wondering at the strange dream. Perhaps I can never come back. Perhaps this is my end.

Oh.

There you are.

You've been washed many many times. You have no face. Oh my boy, you're flat. And what are they? Secretions. You are nothing but secretions. You're not even skin and bones, just empty rags. Your brown boots, rotted. Your ripped green t-shirt, filthy dirty, what's left of it. Hello, face. No face, only skull, a little skin, dark and pinched on top, and a few wisps, non-colour, nothing, and in my mind your curly black hair, so rich and thick. Poor Yorick. Poor little bones. I don't even know how to pick you up.

There are ridges under the cloth.

Here's real. Cold trickling walls, your flat rags.

He always loved touch. Hands. Lips. Hair. His face now is anybody's, all skulls are the same. Where've you gone?

You great fool, the greatest fool that ever lived. How could you? Now, idiot, look, just look at you.

I couldn't bear it so I turned off the torch light.

I think I've been here a long time. In the dark there's nothing. Time's gone. Maybe I'm not even here. Floating off on nothing, dipping and falling and rising again. Not even thinking. Maybe I slept. Anyway, there I was sitting upright, and he was still there with me because he was breathing, sussussussuroo in the dark. The light. The button you push up. Click. There you are! We have to go. I won't leave you here any more. It's not fair. You'll fall to pieces if I'm not careful. So, crawling like a worm I brought you out, slow inch by inch, rolling the rug along, the light before me showing that this is hell indeed, this wet slime of a place, crawling on my belly through the earth, and all the years fell away till I was there again, hauling and hauling, deep in the earth where I was no one and he, in death, was more alive than I ever knew him. I saw his face when it was lovely, his dark eyes and hair. God, he was gorgeous. I used to look at him and think, Lord have mercy, all my dreams came true. And what did he do? Turned it all to shit. Mud on the road. I remember I wrote at my lowest point, with a pen that broke the paper, stabbed it: Make my body mud on the road, let the wheels roll over it till I'm crushed in the ruts. My lowest point. All that sweetness came to that in the end. But I got you back. Didn't see that coming, did you? That's what I said to him. Do you know the nights I lay awake hour after hour in the long dark, and every instant was impossible, every second hurt. What happened, it served you right, oh God it served you right. You made that happen. Lily and that poor boy, thick as a plank, should have been the old bag, the cow, the evil cunt, ugly evil cunt, ugly evil withered vile old bag of a cunt. She's dead now, you'll be glad to know. Such a miserable existence the sour old creature had. In the end she took pills and ended it. Well, no wonder. What did she have? Money. But that's all.

The light shows strange walls, complex, striated. Above, a smotheringly close roof of dirty strings that threatens death. Is this what it comes to? This pinpoint of a moment in the middle of eternity, me in this place?

But you know, one thing I've found out. Nothing goes away, not one little thing. Takes a slight thing sometimes to press that button, click on that link and suddenly, hey, there it all is replaying like an old film you saw years ago on the TV when you shouldn't have been up and watching. And the way it curdled your blood and shrunk your bones then when you were a child, it all comes back.

42

He was out by the beehives, late on in the next afternoon, when his phone rang. Jesus Christ, he was going to have to do something about that stupid ring tone. Driving him mad. His back was aching and the late sun streamed down through the tree trunks and fell on a lacy thickness of undergrowth.

'Hello?'

'Dan, it's Madeleine. Just thought I'd better update you on the Lorna Gilder situation.'

'Yeah.'

'Well, basically it's all sorted.'

'Good.'

'Basically...'

'Yeah.'

'You weren't in this morning, were you? We knocked on your door.'

'Yeah.'

Banging and ringing for ages, what did they think? That he was suddenly going to materialise after ignoring them for the past twenty minutes? Lying with the pillow on his head. Cats. Still in. The place was beginning to smell, he'd have to do something. Whoever you are you can fuck off. I don't want to know.

'No, so we thought she might be there but obviously not, so we went into the woods and there she was at her little place just sitting there waiting for us basically. It was really unliveable, you know. Soaking wet. Really horrible old rags that had got wet and not dried properly because you couldn't, could you? So most of it was so awful we had to leave it behind. She was OK with it. And she was absolutely filthy. I mean, not just a little bit but like, you know, as if she'd fallen in mud and just let it dry on her. We couldn't leave her like that. I mean. Can you imagine? If it was *your* mother' – a slight miss there as the awkward presence of his mother arose between them – 'but she didn't seem to mind anyway. Came quiet as a lamb.'

'Her pills are here,' he said.

'Oh. Well, she's got some more now, so it's OK. Do you want me to pick them up and get them back to a pharmacist for you?'

'No, I'll do it.'

'OK.'

'So – where's she gone then?'

'Same place she was before. Her daughter was on the phone all afternoon to them. It was some sort of semi-sheltered thing, they know her there and she'll be fine. They've been very good. And she knows people there.'

So that was that.

Over, thank God.

'Her daughter took her back in the car. Down south. Nice woman but a bit brisk and detached I thought. If that was *my* mother. Still, she *can* be awkward, I did see that. Poor woman. And how can you judge, the history they must have between them. I feel quite emotional. I tried to give her my nice little blue case on wheels for her stuff, I would have let her keep it, but she wouldn't have it, hanging on to this hideous old plastic holdall with a broken zip. All she had in there, from what I could see, was a dirty old rug. It was awful. Couldn't take it off her though. Think her daughter's had a lot to put up with. Anyway, we took her back to my house and she got cleaned up and had something to eat and I fixed her up with some clean clothes. I had to chuck her old stuff out, it was past all hope.'

'Gone back to the same place then,' he said.

'I think so.'

BetFred. Bus stop.

'I felt sorry for her actually,' Madeleine said, 'Lorna, I mean. The way her daughter was bossing her about. Sit there, Mother. Do this, do that. And she was so quiet, as if she'd just given up, just doing what she was told and holding onto this old holdall as if it was a baby.'

One of those telephone silences.

'OK then,' he said, 'thanks for letting me know.'

'I'm sure she must have been relieved though. I mean Lorna. To be going back. She *must* have been. By far the best thing.'

'Probably,' he said, and yawned.

'So anyway, I thought I'd just keep you posted.'

'Thanks.'

'I've got a backlog now. It was actually all quite stressful.'

'Uhuh.'

She sighed.

'OK then,' he said. 'Thanks for helping.'

'Bye then.'

'Bye.'

He was still worn out from last night's booze. The bees were getting quiet for winter. It was really coming now, a harsh one. He went in and the house was cold. What was the coal and wood situation? Shitty. Cut wood tomorrow. He lit a fire and fell asleep on his back on the sofa in front of it, woke to heavy rain. Torrential. Christ, that's hail. He thought about the woman's little silly house in the woods made of sticks and canvas and plastic sheets, all getting hammered into the forest floor. Tomorrow he'd go there and take a look at it and it would be all broken up and fallen in with some of her jewellery still hanging on it.

Oh well. Down to the village in the rain, to the pub. Got Marlon to sell him a bottle of Talisker. The telly was on. They were supposed to be making improvements to the place but it just looked more ordinary, more like everywhere else. If they took the old dragon from the wall, that was it. He wouldn't come in any more.

He got talking to Pete about people he didn't know. Pete's daughter was going on a cruise. The Baltic states.

'You been round that part of the world?' Pete asked.

'I did once.'

'You've been everywhere.'

'No. Furthest I've been is Iceland.'

'When you didn't see the Northern Lights.'

'When I didn't see the Northern Lights.'

'I never have either.'

Dan's back was sore. It was sore every day now. And one of his knees was cranky. Fuck old age. He wondered if he should tell Pete about the woman and all that stuff she'd told him. But then. If he was going to tell anyone, I suppose it should be the police, but then again, like the daughter said, after all, you couldn't believe a word she said. What do you do? A crime? So, if it really was a crime, what? Murder? But then, what then? What would happen? Arrest. Trial? He didn't know about the law. She'd go on trial. Obviously. But then again, mental health issues. Yeah but still have to go on trial, no way round that. But then. Prison? No no no, some kind of institution, what do you do with people like that? And anyway what if it's not true, or true some other way, or her daughter who's OK now is going to have to go through some horrible trauma knowing what happened, what's the point of that? But she deserves to know. The truth. What is the truth? Truth.

'So,' said Pete, 'yeah, I'd better be off.'

Dan hadn't got a clue what he'd been talking about for the last ten minutes. Still, he knew he'd been chucking in the odd word.

'Yeah,' he said, 'seeya.'

The TV over the bar showed people in an airport. Stuck. Bad weather. Snow wherever that is. More forecast.

I don't know how you work these things out, how the hell, he thought. It's wrong whichever way you look at it. The thought of her locked up seemed wrong. Oh fuck it, another drink.

It was snowing when he left an hour later. Delightful. The big flakes falling grey against the dark sky. Pissed. Lovely, going down the old lane with his arms out catching snow. She made his heart hurt, she was such a lost cause, that woman. Nothing to be done. Ah God, the old days, him and the fat boy, Frankie, and Eric Munsy and whatsisname throwing snowballs on the way home from school. One hit Mrs Turley on the back. Mrs Turley taught history. They all ran behind the hedge and killed themselves laughing. Didn't hurt her. And where were *they* gone now? Just playing. Getting home he went through the blue snow garden, the flakes swirling and skirling, through the gates to the hives so he could look down beyond the slope and the hedge and see the open sky over the long field. There he scooped up a fair-sized snowball in his bare hands and hurled it way over the hedge. Good one! Play! Play! Play on. Another. There was a sound from the dark under the hedge at the bottom of the slope.

What was that under the whisper of snow?

Oh nothing. Mew mew. Cat. Can get in when it wants to.

His hands were wet and burning.

'Hey, pussy cats!' he yelled, going in. 'Come on in now. Gather round.'

The fire was just about still going. He put on some music. A log on the fire.

Once there was a ghost on the stairs.

Nah! It was nothing! Nothing else happened after that, did it?

He wouldn't think of it.

'Where are you, you fuckers?'

They came after a while, slowly, one by one, the big orange one, the matron, the black and white dandy. Who could ever keep track?

43

Winter passed.

The old orange cat died. Usually they went away to die, but this one died in the armchair by the fireplace in its sleep, and he found it dead there one morning. He buried it out back, by the bees, put a stone on top of the spot and found himself looking at it now and then when he was out there seeing to the hives.

Two or three weeks later a new cat turned up, also orange. It just walked in the back door one morning as he was drinking his tea, came into the living room and sat on the end of the sofa staring at him. Its eyes were orange like its fur, and it reminded him of the old cat except that this one was half grown and thin and skittish.

'Well,' he said, 'you're a one, aren't you?'

After a few days it seemed to be following him around. Once it sniffed his feet as he sat on the back step, but if ever he tried to touch it, it flinched and ran. He began to think perhaps it was an offspring of the old one's, and started calling it Ginger 2 (though the old one had never actually had a name) then Gin 2, which ended up as Jintoo. He'd come home stupid and drunk and lie on his back on the sofa and shout, 'Hey Jintoo! Jintoo! Come on, you fucking cat!'

Sometimes the cat came, sometimes it didn't.

When work was slow, sometimes he slept the day away. But always at night he was wide awake and the dark crowded his windows. He found himself listening to nothing, a sudden realisation that he'd been doing it for much too long. He broke eggs into a pan and thought about chickens but then the idea of chickens and cats together, no, couldn't be, unless, such a lot of hassle. His hair grew longer. He drank from the same old chipped cowboy mug every day. One day, down by the hedge at the bottom of the slope where the bees were, he saw something, a difference, he thought, a re-arrangement of something, and when he went down he saw a stick cross tied up with knotty brown twine, six inches high like something a child would make. A few heads of Michaelmas daisies and dog rose scattered the disturbed earth in which it stood. Peculiar.

He didn't want to touch it. Could have been anything. Kids. Still, he didn't want to touch it. But who'd been mucking around down here? Kids. Leave it. Instead he sat down under the hedge and prodded at the earth, then went and got a trowel and dug and piled and delved until at a depth of about two feet something was revealed, a corner of a rug, red and brown, so rotten and dirty it was impossible to tell if this really was the rug he'd last seen being lugged about by that woman, and when he knew by the way it stuck and snagged when he tried to pull it out that something was wrapped inside, he gave up. Small like a baby gathered into the last swaddling, there with the bees hovering above in the white and purple clover, whatever it was could stay there.

The cats were taking over the house. That room, the cats' room, was a disaster. He'd gone in and just grabbed a load of stuff and shoved it all in some big plastic bin bags and taken them to the dump without even looking through anything. Could've been anything, but what was all that, anyway, just the past. Now was this only – what existed. He'd put down litter in ridiculous things like old drawers, anything he had, and they were using it, and now he had to go round emptying it all the time or it stank out into the hall and he wasn't having that. So he cut a hole in the bottom of the door and just kept that door closed all the time so as not to have to think about it all the time. So fucking stiff he was, he groaned when he stood up.

April showers.

The April showers, he sang to whichever cat happened to be in the vicinity, *may come your way –*

The windows streamed, thick ropes of water. It was like a hissing in his head.

They bring the flowers that bloom in May –

They scampered down the hall.

Oh, fuck off, you miserable sods, no taste.

So when it starts to thunder don't run under a tree –

No, that's a different song.

He stood at the open back door and watched the rain. The sound of it was all-obliterating, it ran away in all directions like water flowing underneath the ground. There was a funny light in the sky. Maybe a storm brewing. Electricity. It was lovely. He waited for the first rumble of thunder in the distance. The stones, they say. They draw electricity, thunder and lightning. He felt like a walk, down the lane with his mac on and his hood up, all fresh and nice. All glistening, and the long puddle down the centre of the lane shining silver. He didn't go too far. The outline of a barn on the skyline was rimmed with black. Smelt the cowshit, and the herbs in the hedges. Oh come on, let's have a big big storm. He jumped the stile into Gallinger's field. Round the gate was all trampled mud from the cows, though the field was empty, they were all in the upper field. Squelching through the mud he looked to the skyline and thought of Pepper and Lady and Little Sid, coming with their lurching shoulders across the field to him to eat from his flattened palm, to snort upon his face and blink their patient soulful eyes at him.

Funny how the memory of three horses could cut right through. God, the quick pain.

In the end he walked and walked till the darkness came down, and still walked. He went home, sighing, ah God, another night, how long could this go on, and where was it all leading, same as ever, and now he was wet and achy so out with the old companion, the bottle, onwards, music, to the head, by the fire, like to be one of those old geezers you see with a fiddle or something, that must be nice even alone, making music by a fireside. Things aren't like that nowadays. You wouldn't really need anything else. The fire burned his eyes. He fell asleep and woke and drank and slept and woke and it was deep in the night, got into that good old state, drinking and sentimental, but close to panic, talking to the rambling cats. Sometimes he wondered whether they were on his territory or he was on theirs.

'C'm'ere, you old fucker,' he said to Jintoo.

Poor Jintoo.

'How did your ears get like that so soon,' he asked, 'all notched and snaggled? What have you been up to, eh?'

Stuck music on a random play. Didn't even know what this was. Jazz. Thought of his old dog, good old Billy, bounding through the wood with a look of joy on his silly face. Tears streamed down. He chased the orange cat down the hall, caught it and scooped it up into a big strong hug next to his chest. It tensed and a low snarl came from its throat.

'*What*, you fucker?'

He crooned to it.

The autumn leaves

Dancing, the poor thing struggling.

drift by my window

Though these were April showers that come your way, they bring the flowers that bloom in May and the cat lunged out of his arms, he grabbed at it. Next thing he knew it was hanging from the end of his arm, its teeth and front claws fixed in his hand while its mighty hind legs kicked away at him over and over again.

He roared, shaking his arm, but it clung on tighter, more furious.

'Get off, you cunt! Fucking bastard cunting fucking...'

Hurt like fuck.

With his good hand he grabbed and pulled. Every

claw and fang sank deeper till it let go suddenly and flew through the air with a screech, landing on all its feet and streaking away through the open door into the hall. Ungrateful bastard. He grabbed a log from the wood basket and hurled it after. Oh fuck! That hurt. The log hit the edge of the door and fell to the floor. Jesus, look at that. Holes oozing blood. Everything throbbing. He cursed his way into the kitchen to the sink, ran the cold tap and stuck his hand under it. Blood dripped into the sink. Worst of all, though, was the feeling of betrayal in his chest, ridiculously out of proportion to anything that had actually happened. That cat. That cat was my friend. Why? Why? His palm hurt, a sharp whining pain worse than the punctures the cat had made. There was a dark line under the skin. When he touched it it screamed. The tap ran, rain trickled down the black window.

That's a splinter. He got a tea towel and wiped his hand, knocked his cowboy mug on the floor as he turned. It smashed, the bits flew everywhere, great jagged bits and hundreds of tiny deadly shards. Blotting away at the blood. Need a needle. God, how he hated that! Poking down under your skin. From that log. He got down on his knee and picked up the main bits of his mug and put them on the draining board. He felt sorry for it lying there shattered. He should wrap them in newspaper or something and put them in the bin in case one of the cats walked on the draining board and cut its paws. They weren't supposed to, but who knows what they did when he wasn't there? Why am I thinking about the cats? Bastards. Look at my arm.

The music schmoozed along beside him, a nice gentle plonking piano and a languorous vocal: *but that was long ago and now my consolation is in the stardust of a song.*

You could never find a needle of course when you wanted one. Good God, this was no life. Probably go septic and they'll find me eaten by cats. Fucking cats.

The nightingale tells his fairytale

He just wanted to go and sit down and have another drink, didn't want all this hassle of opening drawers and looking on shelves and not being able to find the damn thing, whatever it was, this just didn't feel right or fair, he'd been good to those bloody animals. Tweezers, some of those tiny tweezers. A pin. Whistling, who was this, lazy whistle to the piano.

My stardust melody

The music rippled away into silence and someone walked along the landing.

He couldn't move, just froze there with his mouth bone-dry.

No mistaking it.

The creak of a stair.

His arm, his hand burned. The thumping of his heart made him sick.

'Who's there?' he shouted.

No sound.

He stood with his raging hand held up foolishly, listening intently to nothing but the rain. A minute passed. A sound once it's gone is gone, there's nothing left so it never existed. You doubt your own sense, and rightly. If he was ever to move again he had to go and look upstairs, so he walked to the door. Nothing there of course. Nothing on the stairs, nothing in the hall. The dark at the top of the stairs was thick. He turned on the landing light before going up. Nearing the top his mind forced vivid impressions upon him, hideous faces that suddenly appear, voices, things that aren't there but don't know it. But there was nothing: only the sound of rain steadily dripping into a bucket at the end of the landing. All the doors were shut. He had to try the rooms, open the doors and check each one. Nothing in here, nothing in there, nothing in the bathroom. Outside his grandmother's old room, he hesitated with his hand on the door knob.

He hated this room. A pointless, dead area smelling of mould and the remembered smell of the commode, a horrible place to have in your house. Was he mad? Why was it there? Whose fault was it if not his? He could have got rid of it whenever he wanted.

He turned the knob and the door whined open. The first thing he noticed was the flickering light that had no right to be there. A small flame shivered on the mantelpiece above the black hole of the grate. The air was icy. Something was on the chaise longue, indistinct, stretched out. Still steeling himself for the ghosts and ghouls of imagination, he turned on the light, saw the crappy old backpack slumped on the floor, and was washed by a wave of relief so huge it swept him back towards the mellow wistfulness of before.

'Get up,' he said.

She had taken the heavy brocade curtains from under the window and completely buried herself, head and all.

'Get up,' he said, but she didn't move.

'Oh, come on.' He sat down on the end of the chaise longue, squashing her feet and making her move them. 'I know you're in there,' and even now when he knew who it was he still flinched a little when she sat up and put her head out, as if she might have been a corpse thing, the woman in room 237.

'What the fuck,' he said softly. He couldn't be angry. He tried but it wasn't working. She looked the same. A red scarf had been tied round her hair but it had come adrift and hung down. She hadn't been asleep, her eyes were wide awake. No way she could have slept through the racket downstairs, the music, him bawling at the cats, singing, for Christ's sake.

'I was sheltering from the rain,' she said.

He shook his head and almost laughed, then looked away. 'So,' he said, 'back to the poor old fucker with the open door.'

'Your door was unlocked.' She pulled the curtains round her. 'I knocked but there was no one in. I have a new camp now. Not in the old place. The rain got in and it's all flooded.'

She'd waited for spring. It made sense. The bluebells coming out, the smell of grass, wild garlic. What must he have sounded like, roaring away? What stupid things had he said, what stupid songs, stupid everything. His palm was on fire. Poisoned. Amputation.

'I was going to go when the rain stopped,' she said, 'you'd never even have known.'

'Fucking cheek. I thought you were a ghost.'

'It's all ghosts round here,' she said.

He walked to the mantelpiece. 'Still talking shite,' he said and blew out the tea light. 'So it's OK is it for you to come in lighting candles and setting the place on fire?'

'It's true,' she said. 'I set up camp in a hurry. My fault. The rain came in, a river, I had to, anyway, so, I wondered how you were.'

'Well, I'm OK,' he said.

'What's the matter with your hand?' she said. 'You're holding it funny.'

'Cat.'

'Let's see.'

He turned his back, stood up. 'Downstairs,' he said. 'Now. Freezing. Turn the light off.'

He went down and waited in the pigsty mess of a place that he'd not cleaned since, oh Christ, poked about in the woodbox, put a log and a few lumps of coal on the fire. Someone in his house again; always strange, but this time stranger still, and for no reason he could explain. Thank God he was pissed. How anyone coped with anything otherwise he had no idea. He sat down and glared at the fire as if it was an oracle. She appeared a moment later in the same long coat she'd worn before, only this time it looked as if it had been cleaned, and there was a lily of the valley brooch on the lapel. The red scarf was round her neck. He didn't want to speak, all too weird, just sat and watched her holding her hands out to the now blazing fire.

'If you start with all that weird stuff again you're out on your ear,' he heard himself say, 'right? Rain or no rain.'

'What's wrong with your hand?'

It was lying on his knee, palm up, with a dark line surrounded by red in the middle of it.

'What did you do?'

'Fucking cat attacked me.'

'What were you doing to it?'

'Dancing with it.'

She smiled. 'I can see you,' she said, 'dancing with your cat in the middle of the night.'

He drew back when she approached, but she came on relentless and dropped down onto one knee in front of his chair, and he didn't want her nearness at all, it was all too much now, too late, too fat, too smelly, too gross. 'Give me your paw,' she said and grabbed his hand. It hurt like hell and she felt him stiffen. 'Hurts?' she said. He nodded. She spread it out with both of hers. 'Got to come out,' she said, 'sorry, just got to,' and removed the brooch from her lapel.

'Oh God Christ,' he said, 'not that.'

'You'll be fine,' she said, like all those kindly ladies in the far-off infant clinics who gave him stickers for being a brave boy. It was excruciating. The silver clack as it opened, the sliding of the pin swiftly under his skin. Air hissing through his teeth. She was strong. With one hand she held him firm, with the other she plied her needle. '*Wo-oe's me, wo-e's me –*' she said, sing-song.

The pain was vile and made him want to puke. They always said that, doesn't hurt, course it fucking hurts.

'*the acorn's not yet fallen from the tree –*' quick and ruthless as she needed to be.

He was cold in spite of the fire. What creepiness is she trying on now? This thing, reciting, whatever it is she's doing.

Why?

'*that's to grow the wood –*' she said, delving deep.

Couldn't trust a word she said. Trying to scare him.

'Nearly there.'

Abashed, he looked down.

'God love you,' she said, 'like a big stupid kid, aren't you.'

She drew out the splinter with the pin, flicked the spiteful shard of wood, long as a sewing needle, towards the fire, pinned the brooch back onto her lapel and pulled the scarf from round her neck.

'*that's to grow to the man –*'

It was coming onto morning. The rain had started again, a lively downpour, sparking silver at the windows. The older he got, the more it seemed that simple moments like these could sprout a hundred – no, more, many more, and still more filaments of memory, all of them laden as myth.

'*that's to make the cradle –*'

She wet the corner of the scarf with her spit.

'*that's to rock the bairn –*'

and applying it to his palm

'*that's to lay –*'

and pressing hard with her thumb.

He shivered.

For a long time they sat without speaking. He didn't know what to say or do, so he did and said nothing, while she pressed her thumb into the dark place in his palm, rubbing at the pain. His stupid eyes welled up and he felt idiotic. Those words, those words, he thought, what do they mean? Just her, being clever. Always someone being clever.

'I'll go when it eases off,' she said.

He nodded, looking at the window.

Slowly, the room filled up with cats. Jintoo was there, acting the innocent.

'Got any Savlon or anything like that?' she said.

'Somewhere. In there.'

'Stick it under the tap,' she said, so he went into the kitchen and turned the tap on and held his hand under it and looked out of the dark gaping windows, and she was behind him in the window and it was no good, no good, he was useless in these situations.

'You'll have to get it seen to,' she said, 'just in case.'

A door opened upstairs. They looked up.

It might or might not have been.

'Think so?' he said.

'Yeah. I would.'

'God's sake,' he said, 'it's just one thing after another.'

Bare feet on the landing, softly hurrying to the top of the stairs. She heard it too.

They looked at each other. Is it? You hear it?

Or is it just me?

'I'll come with you if you like,' she said, 'but you really should get an injection or something, just in case.'

'OK.'

No more footsteps, nothing at all. Order in the house.

'It's happened before,' he said. 'It'll go quiet now. I think.'

'Yes.'

She smiled as if she knew what he was thinking.

'Come,' he said.

Back to the fire.

'You should call a cab,' she said. 'Are you OK for money?'

'You,' he said, 'asking me that?' He laughed.

'Just asking,' she said.

He called a cab.

It didn't stop hurting. She held his hand in the back of the cab all the way.

'Don't be scared,' she said, 'honestly, it's all going to be fine, I promise you,' and though he felt fear in his scruff and marrow, there was something else, a pang, an uprising through all his senses, not new but unplaceable; and he realised it was the exact feeling he'd had all those years ago when he'd got up on the big horse Pepper and ridden the beautiful thing round Gallinger's field, and the sun and the sky and the air and the whole world had fallen perfectly into place around him.